THE FAIRHAVEN
CHRONICLES
BOOK 2

MERCIES &
MIRACLES

THE FAIRHAVEN
CHRONICLES
BOOK 2

MERCIES & MIRACLES

SHARON DOWNING JARVIS

DESERET
BOOK

Library of Congress Cataloging-in-Publication Data

Jarvis, Sharon Downing, 1940-
   Mercies and miracles / Sharon Downing Jarvis.
      p.   cm. — (The Fairhaven chronicles ; bk. 2)
   ISBN 1-59038-218-8 (pbk.)
   1. Mormons—Fiction. 2. Bishops—Fiction. 3. Southern States—Fiction.
I. Title.
   PS3560.A64M47   2004
   813'.54—dc22   2003023884

Printed in the United States of America   54459-7164
Malloy Lithographing Incorporated, Ann Arbor, MI

10   9   8   7   6   5   4   3   2   1

For Andy, Farrah, Camille,
Sierra, and Brady—with much
love and gratitude for each

CHAPTER ONE

"WHEN DARK CLOUDS OF TROUBLE HANG O'ER US"

Morning, Miz Hestelle."

"Mornin', Mr. Shepherd, how're y'all today?"

"Oh, we're doing fine, thanks," replied Bishop James Shepherd of the Fairhaven Alabama Ward, stooping to pick up the rake his son Jamie had left out in the backyard. His nextdoor neighbor, Hestelle Pierce, leaned her bulk against the fence, apparently hoping for a chat. He sighed. He was already running later than he'd intended.

"I believe I feel a mite better, now the weather's cooled off," remarked Hestelle. "My, that was one hot summer, wadn't it?"

"It surely was," he agreed, with feeling. There was a definite change in this morning's air—a coolness wafting down from the hills that was welcome. He felt like putting on new sneakers, gathering up his books, and heading for school. Funny, he thought, how childhood colors the rest of our days.

"Sometimes I envy my kids when I see them heading off to school with their book bags. They'd think I was crazy if I told them that, wouldn't they?" He chuckled.

"Oh, I used to love school," Hestelle said. "'Specially the beginning of each year. I purely loved going school shopping with my Mama down to Birmingham, getting my new saddle shoes or penny loafers, and new skirts and blouses. Us girls couldn't wear pants to school then, way they do now, you know. And I was always excited to get my new books, and pencils and notebooks and crayons! Tell the truth, the excitement didn't last much past the first couple of homework assignments, but I still remember the feelin'. Makes me plumb homesick for those times." She sighed. "Way things are going in the world, now, makes me long for the old days, too."

He nodded. "Isn't that the truth? But you know, about school—my kids make a big fuss, and act like they hate for it to start, but I think I can detect some excitement underneath it all. Tiffani's a junior this year, Jamie's in fifth grade, and Mallory's just starting kindergarten. At least she's openly thrilled with it all. I hope it lasts."

"Land, I can't believe Tiffani's that old," Hestelle commented. "Seems like only last week she was runnin' around the yard with her jump rope, about little Mallory's size."

"Time passes, Miz Hestelle. I'm just starting to realize it passes too fast."

"Ain't that the pure-n-tee truth? And I'll tell you what else, Mr. Shepherd—the older you get, the faster it goes by."

He glanced at his watch. "That's what I hear. And you know, it's passing too fast right now—I'm getting late for a meeting. I'd best run. You take care, now—have a nice day."

"Yessir, I'll try to do that," she agreed, moving toward her house.

He set the rake in the garage and climbed into his truck. His meeting was with the social worker assigned to Melody

Padgett's case, and he wasn't looking forward to it. It had been four months since the family protection services had removed little Andrea Padgett from her home, and the police had taken her father, Jack, in for questioning about a complaint that he had abused his wife and might possibly be a danger to his daughter. Jack Padgett had been ordered by a judge to live separately from his wife for at least six months while undergoing evaluation and counseling. Melody, left alone in her beautiful new house, had been devastated—especially by the mistaken notion that it had been her bishop who'd made the call about the abuse. Bishop Shepherd had finally been able to convince her that he hadn't been the one, and he had been working with the authorities to see that Jack was able to receive counseling through LDS Social Services. Now he was trying to persuade the caseworker that it was in no one's best interest, nor had it ever been, to keep little Andi from her mother and her home.

He drove the twelve miles to the county seat and the building that housed the county social services offices. He circled the block until he found a parking place for his truck. Riding up to the third floor in the elevator, he tried to marshal his thoughts and think how to present them to Melody's best advantage. It shouldn't be hard; Melody wasn't the abuser. Jack, after a few minor violations of the restraining order that had been placed on Melody's behalf, had agreed to obey the court and stay away for the duration.

"Good morning. I'm James Shepherd," he told the girl at the reception desk. "I have an appointment with Mrs. Parkman."

"Oh, right—have a seat, Mr. Shepherd. The others aren't all here, yet."

"Others?"

"Yes, sir. There'll be several people at the evaluation meeting."

"I see." *Great*, he thought. *I'd hoped it would just be the two of us.* "Who'll be there?" he asked.

"Sir? Oh—um, usually the caseworker and her supervisor, the family counselor, the psychologist, maybe a clergyman, a representative from the police—sometimes a lawyer—people like that."

"And how many of them will be on Melody's side?" he mused in a low voice as he turned away. Apparently his voice wasn't quite low enough, however, because the receptionist bristled.

"Sir, these meetings are not a matter of taking sides," she told him with an air of controlled patience. "They're about sharing various professional opinions about what's best for a family—especially the children."

"Oh, right. Sorry, just thinking out loud."

She gave him a suspicious look and went back to her work. Obviously, she was more than a receptionist—probably a social-work intern. Already, he felt at a disadvantage. He sat on an uncomfortable plastic chair in the waiting area and watched on the wall-mounted television silent images of exhausted workers trying to clear the debris of the twin towers and the Pentagon.

Once the meeting was underway, he listened carefully to the professional evaluations of the situation. Melody's caseworker, Mrs. Parkman, presented Melody's request to have Andi restored to her custody and home, and stated her opinion that, with some reservations, she felt that action would probably be appropriate.

"What reservations do you have, Mrs. Parkman?" inquired her supervisor, a man of some sixty or so years.

"Well, Mrs. Padgett is still quite emotional. She seems to cry very easily, and I'm not entirely certain that her emotional state is such that she could create a positive tone in the home for her little girl."

Bishop Shepherd cleared his throat. "Pardon me?" he asked. "May I comment?"

"Let's see—you're the family's clergyman, is that correct?" asked the supervisor.

"That's correct. Her bishop, which is something like a pastor. I just wanted to make an observation, if I might? Melody Padgett is quite understandably emotionally fragile right now, it seems to me. It was a tremendous shock to her to have her little girl snatched from her home with no warning, at six o'clock in the morning, by strangers . . ."

"I don't care for your terminology, sir," stated the supervisor. "We do not 'snatch' children, we *remove* them, temporarily, for their own safety and well-being."

The bishop felt his neck growing warm. "I'm sure that's true, but *snatched* is how it looked and felt to Melody, and no doubt to little Andi, as well, no matter how well-intentioned you folks may be. Melody is the victim in this case, not only of her admittedly abusive husband, but of the very folks who claim to have her best interests at heart. She's the one being punished, by being forcibly separated from the little daughter that she loves very dearly. And how is Andi's emotional state? Does she cry herself to sleep at night, wondering why Mommy doesn't ever come to get her? What was she supposed to think, when she was—um—*removed*—from her home and family and all that was familiar to her, and not even allowed to take along her own teddy bear? My firm opinion is that it's high time to return Andi to her mother. Why punish the two of them for Jack's behavior?

And frankly, folks, if someone came to my home and removed my little girl, for her own good, I believe I'd be in a pretty rough emotional state myself, and I know for a fact that my wife would be!"

"Yes, well, thank you, Mr. Shepherd. We'll take your opinion under consideration. Of course, as you may or may not realize, this is just a preliminary fact-finding meeting. It is the judge who will determine whether the child will be returned to her mother. We merely offer him—or her—the benefit of our opinions. You may be asked to be present at that hearing."

Bishop Shepherd nodded and subsided, trying to listen calmly and evaluate each speaker's attitude. The policeman also felt that Andi should be returned, as long as Jack was kept well away from the home by a restraining order. He had his reservations about the possibility of complete rehabilitation of abusive husbands or parents. He'd seen too many repeat offenders, and Jack Padgett struck him as the type.

The psychologist begged to differ and offered statistics showing that abusive behavior could be modified, and gave his opinion that Jack seemed to have sufficient motivation to make the desired changes. He was, however, concerned about whether Melody had received sufficient counseling to strengthen her to perform successfully as a single parent for the time being. She hadn't, after all, been able to protect Andrea from seeing her father's inappropriate treatment of her mother.

The counselor from LDS Social Services felt that the family could be saved and rehabilitated. She thought that it would be in Melody's and Andrea's best interests to be reunited as soon as possible, to prevent the child from forming even stronger attachments to her foster parents. She suggested parenting classes for Melody and continued counseling for mother and child. The bishop sent her a look of appreciation. There were then a few brief discussions about timing and procedure, and the meeting ended.

Bishop Shepherd walked outside into the sunlight with the LDS Social Services representative, a Sister Hallmark.

"Thanks for your input," he told her. "You were more convincing than I was. I'm probably a little too personally involved with the family, but I hate to see Melody suffering so from loneliness and frustration—it makes it seem like Jack's found a new way to hurt her, although I know that's not a fair assessment."

Sister Hallmark smiled. "You're a good bishop to have in her corner," she complimented. "I'd like to think my bishop would go to bat for me, that way."

"What's your take on the consensus—will they recommend reuniting them?" he asked.

"I hope so. I think the main concern is that Melody didn't report the abuse she was receiving to the authorities, and so she wasn't able to protect the little girl from the effects of it."

"I realize that was a mistake on her part," the bishop said, "but I don't see it exactly as weakness. I think, from her point of view, she was trying to be strong and endure whatever it took, to keep her family intact. She absorbed an awful lot, and went along with a lot of unrealistic and unjust demands on Jack's part—all the time just thinking that if she could somehow be a better wife, the problems would stop."

Sister Hallmark nodded. "You know, it's quite common for an abused wife to blame herself. She has to learn not to do that."

"Right, and I think she realizes that, at least intellectually. With time, I hope she'll really believe it on all levels."

"She'll need to, for the family to succeed. She can't afford to let things fall back into old patterns."

When the bishop got back to town it was lunchtime, and he fought a losing battle with himself over where and what to eat. He parked at the Dairy Kreme and ordered a cheeseburger and a strawberry-banana milkshake. As a sop to his screaming conscience, he left off the fries. It had been a difficult morning; he needed comfort food.

Once back in his office at Shepherd's Quality Food Mart, he put in a call to Melody Padgett. She was at work herself, having taken a job in a classy little boutique in the new shopping area south of town, but she answered her cell phone.

"Hey, Melody, it's Bishop—thought I'd let you know how things went at the meeting," he said. "I'm somewhat optimistic. The lady from LDS Family Services put in a good word for reuniting you and Andi, and so did I."

"Oh, thanks, Bishop! I appreciate it so much. Um—who was against it? What did they say?"

"I'm not sure anybody was flat-out against it, but some of them were kind of cautious, and felt you were still sort of stressed out, emotionally."

"Well, you know what? I'd like to see how any of them would feel, having their child just taken away like that! I worry about Andi all the time, Bishop. How's she getting along without me? Who reads her stories at night? They don't know her favorites! Who does her hair and dresses her, and who knows how she likes her oatmeal with strawberry jam swirled in it? And with all the awful news about nine-eleven on the TV, which just adds to it, I reckon I am stressed out—and I figure I've got a right to be!"

He swallowed. "I know. Just—whenever you have to meet with someone, try to seem calm, but concerned."

"It's that Parkman woman, isn't it? She's always going on about, 'How come you're so upset, Mrs. Padgett? Andrea's being well cared for.' Like any old body could take my place! It just makes me furious."

"Frankly, it does me, too. But let's just try to cooperate with the powers that be, in hopes of speeding things up for you. I reckon they mean well—I just happen to disagree with them about your situation. But we'll keep plugging away, Melody, and do all we can, okay? Now, how's your job going?"

She sighed. "It's the only thing that keeps me sane, Bishop. I dread going home to that big, empty house, but I've got to keep it all up in good shape, or for sure somebody'll say I'm not competent or something. Honestly, I don't feel like I live in America anymore."

"You know we all pray for you—as a bishopric, as well as Trish and I at home—and we pray for Andi and Jack, too. Listen, let me know if you need another blessing, okay? Anytime."

She thanked him, and he turned away from the phone with a sigh of his own. His secretary, Mary Lynn Connors, had returned from lunch and seated herself behind the computer. She looked up curiously, twirling a lock of long brown hair around one finger.

"So I overheard what you just said," she began, "and I gotta ask you. These here blessings you give folks—how exactly does that work?"

He sat down, surprised. "Um—well, the person who asks for

the blessing sits in a chair, usually, unless they're sick in bed, and two or three men who hold the priesthood place their hands on the person's head and bless him with health, or comfort, or whatever's needed."

"How's that different from just prayin' for 'em?"

"It's like a prayer, except in a blessing, the person speaking talks to the person being blessed, instead of directly to the Lord. It's like, 'we bless you with health and strength to overcome the infection that's troubling your body . . .' or, 'we bless you with confidence and courage to undergo the treatments prescribed by your doctors.' That sort of thing. And, of course we mention the priesthood we hold, and close in the name of the Savior. That's pretty much how it goes."

Mary Lynn was silent for a moment, considering. "And it works?"

He nodded. "I've seen it work, numerous times. Seen people healed, comforted, strengthened. Of course, it works on faith in Christ, and it also depends on the Lord's will in our lives. It's not always His will that everybody be healed of everything. Sometimes we just need to learn to endure, or to allow other people to help us. And sometimes, naturally, folks just plain need to die. Can't have everybody livin' forever—at least not in this mortal life!" He smiled.

She regarded him for a long moment. "Huh," she said, and bent her head so that her long hair fell forward to hide her face. He knew he was dismissed.

It was Tuesday night, the bishop's customary night in his office at church for interviews and other business. His counselor

Robert Patrenko was there, as well as ward clerk Joseph Perkins and executive secretary Dan McMillan. Sister Rhonda Castleberry had brought over a Crockpot full of chili and a pan of cornbread, and the four men took a break to enjoy it, using the counter in the clerk's office for a dining table.

"Brethren, how're your families doing, with all that's happening in the world?" the bishop asked, as he ladled a second serving of chili into his plastic bowl.

"Kind of nervous," Bob Patrenko replied. "My wife's still glued to the TV. Seems like that's how she deals with tragedies and wars and such—has to keep facing it and learning all she can about what happened. I can't take any more, after a while. It brings me down."

The bishop nodded. "I think Trish watches a good bit of the coverage during the day, but she doesn't want the kids seeing those images over and over, so we've been doing other things in the evenings. Normal things. It helps that school has started, so Jamie and Tiff at least have homework to keep them occupied. I'm pretty sure Mal's too young to know what's going on. How about your family, Dan?"

"We try to just watch the news, maybe once a day. It's too intense to follow all the time, especially with Joanie expecting. Sure sad, though. Kinda puts a pall over everything, you know? Hard to get excited about sports, or much of anything."

"That's pretty much how I've felt, too," the bishop agreed. "It's almost like that big gray cloud from the towers has found its way into all our lives and sort of sapped the color out. I reckon with time, we'll feel better. I just keep thinking about all those folks whose lives are forever changed. My heart goes out to them."

"And mine," agreed Joseph Perkins. "What we oughta do,

maybe, is organize some kind of humanitarian aid project for the ward—I mean, they say there isn't a whole lot we can do, but if nothing else, it might make our folks feel a little better to try to do something."

The bishop nodded. "Ladies are way ahead of us on that," he said. "They sent off a big packet of quilts for the Ground Zero workers to wrap up in while they're on break. And our contributions to humanitarian aid through the Church have increased dramatically, haven't they, Joseph?"

"Yes sir, they sure have. Been amazing to me how much some folks have come up with. You know who I'm worried about, though, is the Jernigans. Have you seen them yet, Bishop?"

The bishop shook his head. "I haven't. They're still in their high-security, lockdown mode. I've talked to Ralph a few times, but he doesn't feel secure enough yet to venture out of his place. It's hard to talk him out of his fears, because all this has done is reinforce his worst ones, bless his heart. He's not at all sure there won't be terror attacks here in Fairhaven—or right out there on his own land, for that matter."

"Well, nobody's real sure of anything yet, you know? I can see how people like Ralph could get really scared," remarked Dan. "You think about it—if terrorists can hijack a plane and fly it into the Pentagon, and two more into the Twin Towers, it does give you the feeling that just about anything could happen, just about anywhere, like the fourth plane that those good folks diverted into that field in Pennsylvania. Whole thing makes me nervous too, to tell you the truth."

"Sure it does. Makes us all uneasy," the bishop agreed. "But you and I keep coming to church and going to work and doing things with our families, in spite of it all. Ralph isn't near strong enough to do that, and I don't know if Linda's much better. I feel like we need to pray for them especially—and anybody else in our ward who might be traumatized by what happened last month—as well as for our president and the country in general. Of course, I'm sure we've all been praying along those lines ever since it happened, but let's make it a part of our purpose for fasting next Sunday, all right? Bob, will you pass that along to Sam?"

Jamie was in the kitchen, making himself a piece of toast and a glass of chocolate milk, when his father came home that night.

"Mmm, that looks good—maybe a tall glass of that will quench the fire of Sister Castleberry's chili," the bishop remarked, reaching for a glass of his own. "How you doin', Jamie, my man?"

"Fine. Hey, Dad, some guy's coming over to see you in a few minutes."

"Tonight?" He glanced at the kitchen clock. "Somebody from the ward?"

Jamie shook his head. "I don' 'hink so," he mumbled around a mouthful of buttered toast, which he finally swallowed. "It sounded like that Big Mac guy—your friend you went to school with."

"Oh, is that right? Wonder what he's doing in Fairhaven." The bishop stirred his milk and drained the cool beverage in one long series of swallows. He exhaled. The fire did seem to have abated. He carried his briefcase to the rolltop desk in one end of the dining room that served as his home office, then wandered back toward the kitchen. "What're the girls doing?"

"Mal's in bed, I reckon, and maybe Tiff is, too. Mom was trying to help her cut out somethin' to sew for her homemaking class, and Tiff kept pitchin' fits about how hard it was."

The bishop smiled. "How's your homework situation—under control?"

"Yeah, I reckon. I had to write a—what d'you call it—an essay. Yuck."

"What about?"

"Well, see, that's the thing! It's s'posed to be about how nine-eleven affected me personally—and I don't reckon I really know. I mean, I don't get exactly who those people are, and why they did what they did. How come they hate us? And how'm I s'posed to feel about it? It didn't happen to me, but I feel like it did! It keeps bein' on TV and in the paper, and when I try to go to sleep at night I keep seein' the explosions and the people running like crazy. I'm plain sick of it."

The bishop went to his son and wrapped his arms around him, kissing the top of his light brown buzzed head. "I think you just expressed to me exactly how the things that happened on September eleventh affect you, Jamie. If you can say those things in your paper, about how you're confused, and tired of it, and feel like it happened to you, then I reckon you'll have written an honest and good essay."

"Yeah? Huh. Maybe I oughta change it some. Thanks, Dad."

"Thank you, son, for sharing with me. Remind me to try to explain more about it to you, sometime, okay?" He patted his son's shoulder as the boy headed toward the stairs. "Not that I understand a whole lot more than you do," he added softly.

CHAPTER TWO

"OUR MUTUAL FRIENDSHIP RENEW"

Peter MacDonald didn't ring the doorbell. He didn't have to. The bishop saw him coming and went out on the front porch to greet him with a hearty handshake that turned into a hug.

"Mac! What brings you to town, man?"

"Finding us a house to rent. I'm moving the family home."

"Serious? Here, come inside, I'll get you something to drink. Are you hungry?"

"No, no, I'm stuffed. Had dinner with Aunt Mat, and she laid it on like Thanksgiving."

Mac, who topped his friend Jim Shepherd by three inches in height and a good sixty pounds in weight, followed him into the living room and sank gratefully into a comfortable chair. The bishop turned on a table lamp and took a matching chair just beyond its pool of light.

"I remember Aunt Mat," he said. "She probably thinks it is an early Thanksgiving, if you're moving your family back here, within feeding distance." Mac's mother's younger sister, Martha

Slidell, known as Aunt Mat, was famous for her bounteous table and her love of cooking for people.

Mac chuckled. "That's about right. Well, you may recall, Jimbo, I threatened to do this several months ago."

"I do recall. You were getting a little anxious about life in the big city and its impact on your family. So—does September eleventh have anything to do with this?"

"It just capped the decision. I don't know, Jim—I really like Atlanta. We've all enjoyed living there. But the kids just haven't been thriving the way I want them to. Petey's getting ideas I'd rather he didn't have, and Ruthie's a shy little gal who gets overlooked and pushed aside too easily. The one I feel bad for is Ruthanne—I'm really uprooting her from a garden she was blooming very happily in, and I'm sorry. But everybody's so jumpy, now. There've been so many warnings that terrorists could target the larger cities in the east, and even CNN's had some threats. You know they're based in Atlanta. This anthrax thing has everybody spooked, too. Taken all together, I figured I had reasons enough to go ahead and do what my heart had been telling me for some time—come home."

"Well, I, for one, am delighted," the bishop assured him. "We're kind of spooked around here, too, of course—but probably not to the extent that folks in the bigger cities are." *With a couple of notable exceptions*, he admitted to himself, thinking of the Jernigans. "Have you found a place to live? And what about your church?"

"My assistant pastor is a fine and capable fellow. He'll be able to take care of things until they can issue a call to a new senior pastor. In fact, they may even petition to have him promoted. He's quite popular. I have enough saved to live on for a while, and I'm sure I can get something to do until a church opens up in this area. I know Pastor Hollowell at Friendship Christian is due to retire before too long, and maybe his congregation would be happy to have a hometown boy minister to them. And yes, I think I've found a house that Ruthanne will be able to live with, at least on a temporary basis. It's a new section of town—at least to me, I hadn't seen it before. Over on the northwest, just beyond Indian Creek Park."

The bishop nodded. He knew the area. It was where the Padgett home was located.

"Actually, there are quite a few places up for sale and for rent," Mac continued. "That's because of the pull-outs, I assume?"

"Yep," his friend confirmed. "It hit the local economy pretty hard, having ChemSoft leave and the base close in the same year. We still have unemployed folks in our congregation who haven't worked since one or the other facility closed."

"I suppose that would be quite a blow, in a town the size of Fairhaven. Do you know of anything else on the horizon—any businesses looking to locate here?"

The bishop nodded. "I attended a Chamber of Commerce meeting last week, and they mentioned some interest on the part of an electronic parts plant—I can't recall the name of the company, but they said the facility would create at least four hundred jobs in the area, and they'd sure be welcome. Wal-Mart's showing some interest, too. I don't know—I think we'll pull out of the slump okay—it just takes some time. We already have a couple of new restaurants in town, in spite of everything, and they seem to be prospering."

"Your store still doing a healthy business?"

"Pretty good, so far, although there's more competition from the big guys all the time. We keep trying to find ways to compete.

My secretary thinks we ought to put in a deli bar, and sell salads and sandwiches at lunchtime. I'm considering it."

"Would that take a big outlay of money?"

Jim nodded. "Considerable. But it may be worth it. We remodeled a couple of years ago, and we've sure been glad we did that. Have you seen the store, since then?"

"I don't believe I have. I still have memories of wavy old hardwood floors, dim lighting, and ceiling fans."

The bishop laughed. "Oh, man—all those features are gone with the wind. We're real uptown, now. You'll have to stop in and check us out." He smiled. "Of course, Ruthanne may prefer one of the chain stores, so I won't hold you to anything."

"Ruthanne shops sales, so I expect she'll get to know every market in town. How's your family doing, Jim?"

The bishop nodded. "We're blessed to be doing very well, right now. All busy, of course, going in five different directions at once."

"And how's your church calling—bishop, is it?"

"Bishop it is. It's about a challenge and a half, I'd say. But it's good. I'm sure you know what I mean when I say it's good to be able to get to know the people really well, and try to help wherever there's need. And somehow, since I became bishop, there seems to be a little different sort of line of communication with the Lord, if that makes sense. I'm sure it's because He's mindful of everyone's needs, and He wants to be sure I'm mindful of them, too. Sometimes I can look out over the congregation and just know who's having difficulty, or who I should make an effort to talk with. That's been quite an eye-opener for me."

Peter MacDonald nodded thoughtfully. "It's amazing to me,

how your church is able to meet the needs of its members as effectively as it does, without a full-time, trained clergy."

The bishop laughed. "I don't know about trained, but it feels pretty much like full-time, most weeks," he said. "But the secret has been to surround myself with good men and women, and delegate like crazy. We also have our home and visiting teaching programs, and they're a major help to a bishop. I certainly couldn't get around to visiting everyone once a month, so I'm grateful to have other eyes and ears on the job."

Big Mac's eyes narrowed, "And the members—do they follow through? Actually make these visits, and become that involved with the families assigned to them?"

"For the most part, they do pretty well."

"Don't the people being visited feel like Big Brother is watching them, just ready to report any irregularities?"

The bishop considered. "Some may feel that way, but I hope not—it should all be done in a spirit of love and helpfulness, not in an effort to be informants or some kind of standards-police!" He grinned. "In fact, if I see that a home teacher is getting critical of someone he visits, he can expect a change of assignment."

"Pretty ingenious system you guys have going," responded Mac with an answering grin. "I may have to adopt some of your ideas in my next church."

"Who were you talking to?" Trish asked sleepily, as Jim crept into bed a short time later.

"Peter MacDonald. He's moving his family back to Fairhaven."

"Mac and Ruthanne are moving back here? Why?"

"I think he feels this is a better place for his kids than the big city, especially after nine-eleven."

"Oh. Well, I agree with him, there. It'll be nice to have them back."

"It will," he murmured, raising himself on one elbow to bend over and kiss his wife's cheek.

Though what he had told his friend Peter MacDonald was true, about the members doing a fairly good job in visiting and home teaching, the bishop of the Fairhaven Ward had already decided to institute a new and more ambitious home teaching program than had been implemented in recent years. Ward clerk Joseph Perkins had culled from the membership records a list of those who were less-active or part-member families, or who had just gradually lost contact, or whose whereabouts were unknown, but were believed to still be in the area. It was the bishop's sincere opinion that of the people who had once been involved with the Church, or believed in its precepts, most would still have some vestige of interest or belief, even if they had become estranged for one reason or another. He and his counselors and clerks had prayed about the individuals or families whose names appeared on that list, and had divided it into home teaching lists for themselves—this in addition to the families they already were assigned to visit.

On the bishop's list was Hazel Buzbee, an elderly woman who had been baptized along with her grandson some twenty-eight years earlier, and who had drifted into inactivity after the grandson moved away. The bishop barely remembered her, and he found his way with some difficulty to her modest home, located east of town, at the end of a red clay road that dissected some corn and soybean fields. Hazel apparently didn't have a telephone—at least, not one that had a listed number. Maybe she had a cell phone, he reflected—but, looking at her greenish-gray, weathered little house, he somehow doubted that. There was a small garden patch on the sunniest side of the yard, where a few late tomatoes still hung heavy and red on their lush plants. A row of collard greens stood stiffly silver-green beyond them—their color reminding him of the house itself.

A long-legged dog of some hunting variety mix lay stretched out on the covered front porch, and a gray cat hunched in the porch swing, barely deigning to open its eyes at his approach.

"Hey, boy," he said softly to the dog, who sat up and thumped its long tail against the board floor. "Hey, fella—is your missy home?"

He climbed the rather shaky steps to the porch and called out. "Hello! Sister Buzbee?"

He knocked on the door, and heard the knocks reverberate throughout the rooms inside. "Hello?" he called again.

"I don't want none," a cracked, elderly, but very loud voice shouted behind him. He turned to see a bent old woman carrying a shotgun tucked comfortably across her hip with one ropy arm. "I don't read magazines nor papers, I don't want a phone, and I don't need no insurance. I don't want to put sidin' nor paint on my house, and I'm not gonna live long enough to need a new roof. So, whatever you're a-sellin', I don't want it."

The bishop swallowed, and made himself smile. "I'm not selling anything, Sister Buzbee. I'm Bishop Jim Shepherd from the LDS Church in Fairhaven. How are you today?"

"You're who?" Sister Buzbee shouted, and the bishop realized the extent of her deafness.

He shouted back, feeling foolish, but neither the dog nor the cat seemed to mind, and apparently there wasn't anyone else about.

"Bishop Shepherd, from the LDS Church. I've come to see you, Sister Buzbee!"

"Mormon?" she inquired, and he nodded vigorously.

"Wal, so'm I. Land! Ain't none of y'all been around for a long spell. What do you want?"

"Just to visit—to see how you're doing."

"As you can see, I'm still stumpin' around!"

Was there a glimmer of humor in her eyes? A slight upward twist of her cracked, sunburnt lips? He wasn't sure.

"I'm glad to see that. You know, I remember when you used to come to church with Sammy."

"You ain't old enough to remember that!"

"Yes, I am! It was right after my mom and I joined the Church," he shouted. "Do you remember Sister Velma Shepherd?"

Sister Buzbee narrowed her eyes, squinting up at him. "Thelma Shepherd? Nice lady, kinda tall, light hair? When we used to meet atop of the lodge hall?"

He nodded, not bothering to correct her on the name. Close enough.

"That's your Mama? How's she doin'?"

He shook his head. "Not too good. She had a stroke. Lives with my sister now, in Anniston."

"Well, I swanny. Thelma Shepherd. Hatn't thought about her in years! And who else did I know, back then? Lemme see . . ."

"Hilda Bainbridge, and Roscoe?" he shouted.

She nodded deeply. "Hildy was real sweet to me. She still with us?"

"She is, but Roscoe died last spring. She's real lonely without him."

"Tell me about lonesome," she yelled back, gesturing around her with the muzzle of the shotgun, which the bishop wished she would put down. "I been on my own out here for longer'n I care to recall."

"Do you have anybody to help you?"

"Oh, the little couple at the next place look in on me, and ever now'n agin Mr. Johnson from the store down the highway brings me some canned goods. He knows what I eat."

"What happened to Sammy? Where is he, now?"

"Vietnam happened to Sammy. He never recovered from that agent-whatever stuff. Died, back in seventy-five. Never was well, after that war."

"I'm so sorry. So you've lived all alone, all this time?"

"Wouldn't have it any other way. I like my privacy."

The bishop nodded, but he had a thousand questions. What if she fell ill? What if she fell, period? A broken hip or arm, and she could die where she fell, but not until she had suffered untold misery.

"Do you ever go to the doctor?" he asked.

"What for? I ain't sick! I'm jest old—and too mean'n ignorant to die. How come you're askin' all these questions? You ain't thinkin' of movin' me outta here, are you? 'Cause I'm not goin', and that's a fact. Iffen I die out here, that'll be the Lord's will and mine, too. This here place ain't much, but it's my home."

"I understand. I just wanted to be sure you were safe, and being looked after."

"I'm safer here than most places I can think of."

"Is there anything we can do for you?"

"Why should you? I ain't been to church fer years."

"Doesn't matter—you're still a member, and you're one of the Lord's children!"

"You say you're bishop, now?"

"Yes, ma'am, I am. Plus, I'm your home teacher. I'm planning to come see you at least once a month, if you'll let me."

"I drink coffee."

"Okay. Can I still come see you?"

"Others have said they'd come, but I'm too far out. Nobody has time."

The bishop privately agreed that she was pretty far out, all right, in more ways than one, but in a peculiar way, he was charmed by her. "I promise I'll come," he told her. "My mama raised me to keep my word."

"I won't come to church," she warned him. "I don't go anywheres."

He nodded. "All right. I'll try to bring a little church to you, if that's okay."

She squinted at him. "How do you mean?"

"Just a little message from the prophet, or the scriptures. Maybe the sacrament, if you'd care to take it."

She stared at him for a long moment. "You can do that? The sacrament?"

"Yes, ma'am, we sure can."

"I reckon I'd like that. But not just yet. I got to get myself prepared."

"All right. Is there anything else I can bring you, next time

I come? Something good to eat, maybe? My wife's a good cook, and I own a grocery store."

She frowned. "Reckon I don't think of anything. I eat pretty simple. When will you come again?"

"Um—how about three weeks from today? That'll be— um—November first. Will that be okay?"

"Days're all the same to me—it don't make no never mind."

"Thank you, Sister Buzbee—and it's real good to see you again."

Her laugh was a dry cackle. "Now, I know your mama didn't teach you to lie!"

"No lie," he insisted. "It's been a pleasure. Next time, you won't need your shotgun. Just watch for my truck."

"Oh, this ain't loaded. I ain't had no shells for years, now. I jes' carry it around like a lapdog, to keep me comp'ny."

"Ah, I see. All right, now, Sister Buzbee. You have yourself a good evening."

"Bishop? Could you leave me a prayer?"

He was embarrassed he hadn't offered. He stood close to her, bowed his head, and offered a prayer in as loud a voice as he dared, praying for her well-being and calling down the protection of the Lord and an assurance of His love for this dear, widowed sister. Her amen was resounding. He shook her callused hand and turned to leave.

"Bishop?" she called after him. "Can your wife make sweet potato pie?"

He turned back, with a smile. "I'm sure she can. Would you like one?"

"Been thinkin' on one for a long while, but I don't have an oven that works."

"I'm sure she'd be glad to make one for you. I'll ask her."

"Onliest thang is—tell her she cain't put too much nutmeg in it."

"Nutmeg," he repeated. "I'll be sure to tell her."

"I thank you, Bishop. It's good of you to come."

CHAPTER THREE

"AMID THE CONFLICT, WHETHER GREAT OR SMALL"

His wife gazed at him in consternation. "Sweet potato pie?" she questioned. "I've never even tasted a sweet potato pie, let alone made one!"

The bishop considered. "Mama used to make one every now and then. I expect Paula or Ann Marie'd have her recipe."

"Most likely Paula. You think Ann Marie has a recipe for anything that isn't printed on the side of a frozen-food carton?"

He chuckled. His younger sister, Ann Marie, was the least domestic woman he knew. Paula, his elder sister, was an excellent homemaker and cook who at least occasionally made delicious things from scratch, but Ann Marie considered her freezer and her microwave her best friends in the kitchen, if not in the world. Her husband tended to treat himself to large lunches at good restaurants.

"If Paula doesn't have the recipe, I'll ask Ida Lou."

"Good idea. Anyway, it isn't needed for a few weeks, so don't stress, babe."

"I'm not stressing. I just like to plan ahead."

He nodded. He knew she did that, all right. Practically all of their Christmas was already bought and most of it wrapped and hidden. He was sure she had her menus prepared for Christmas and New Year's, and probably a guest list of people to invite. Three weeks, he realized, was not a very long time in the day-planner of Trish Shepherd. She loved to plan, loved to anticipate, and wasn't too fond of unexpected guests for dinner or spontaneous changes of plan. She liked things to proceed according to her notion of propriety, and her favorite surprises were those she instigated herself.

Friday evening, the bishop and his son, Jamie, hopped into the truck and drove across town to pick up Buddy Osborne, whom the bishop had persuaded to go with them to the Fairhaven High School football game. He wanted to see Thomas Rexford, affectionately and appropriately known as T-Rex to most of his acquaintances and fans, play against Redstone High, their arch-rivals. T-Rex was a linebacker with a promising future in football if he could stay healthy and out of trouble with girls and grades. His bishop wasn't sure which were the most troublesome.

Buddy's mother came to the door of her mobile home, wiping her hands on a towel and frowning out into the fading evening light.

"Hi, Sister Osborne," the bishop said. "How are you, tonight?"

"Oh, okay, it's y'all," she said by way of greeting, and turned to call her son. "Buddy! Your ride is here."

Not "your friends are here," or "the bishop's here," the

bishop noted. Just "your ride." She turned and headed back toward her kitchen, leaving him standing on the small porch. Country music played from a radio across the small living area, which was decorated—cluttered, he suspected Trish would say—with what appeared to be souvenir-type trinkets: ashtrays, figurines of Disney characters, and small Elizabethan lords and ladies. Of more interest to him were several miniature Nascar models on a table near the door. He supposed they were Buddy's. He would have to ask.

At the stadium, as it was grandly called—it was really just a playing field and a couple of stands of wooden bleachers—he experienced a sort of déjà vu moment, or a memory, he wasn't sure which. He was seventeen again, and thrilling to the bright lights and the band and the enticing smells of hot dogs and popcorn in the cool night air. He was feeling free and unusually sociable, strolling into the area with Big Mac and a couple of other guys, calling greetings to people he knew, and all the time looking for Trish, hoping to maneuver his group into sitting where he could see her, without letting her—or the guys—know what he was up to. He had managed it, sitting two rows behind and a little to the north of her group of giggling, bright-eyed friends. He didn't remember the game—who the opposing team had been or how it had turned out—but he remembered the sheen of Trish's dark hair in the lights, and the sound of her laughter and cheers.

On this evening, it wasn't Trish he looked for; it was their elder daughter, Tiffani, who had given him strict instructions not to attempt to sit with or talk to her and her group of friends.

"And don't *spy* on me," she had concluded, fixing him and Jamie alternately with a determined glare.

Her father pretended a wounded innocence. "Would we do that?" he asked.

"Dad, you know what that makes me want to do?" asked Jamie conspiratorially.

"Spy on her?"

"Yep. And throw paper airplanes at her, and try to toss popcorn into her mouth when she yells."

"Uh-huh, that does sound like fun."

Tiffani looked exasperated. "Dad, I'm serious. I'm old enough to go to a football game with my friends, without my dad and my brother *and* Buddy Osborne, of all people, hanging over our shoulders and watching every move we make."

"What moves are you gonna make?" asked Jamie slyly.

"Dad!"

"Okay, okay, princess. We promise to be good. Don't we, James?"

"I don't know. Reckon I'll try. But a football game won't be near as much fun if we can't *spy.* I mean, what else will there be to watch, besides my sister and her dumb friends?" Jamie grinned at Tiffani, who gave him a wide-eyed, warning look reminiscent of those her mother was capable of giving.

The bishop spotted the girls in the stand almost immediately, pretended not to, and herded the boys out of teasing distance—but not so far that he couldn't keep an unobtrusive, fatherly, spying eye on Tiffani. She sat with Lisa Lou Pope and Claire Patrenko, two girls from the ward. He hoped that Tiff and Claire would be a somewhat calming influence on Lisa Lou, who was so boy-crazy and flirtatious that, as her bishop, he worried about her probably far more than the situation warranted. He watched the play of light on Claire's dark hair, remembering Trish at sixteen. Tiffani's hair also reflected the light, but with a glow of antique gold, much like the color his own had been at that age.

The game proved to be a pretty interesting one. Having been soundly trounced by Fairhaven in their last match, Redstone was hungry for a victory, and the score bounced back and forth with regularity, making him wonder about the effectiveness of either team's defense.

At halftime, watching the bands and flag twirlers go through their intricate maneuvers on the field, he enjoyed a chili-onion-and-slaw dog he knew he would live to regret in a couple of hours. Returning to their seats for the second half, they passed behind Tiff and her friends, and he couldn't resist saying in a loud whisper, "Pretend you don't see them!"

"Oh, hi, Bishop!" said Lisa Lou, twinkling up at him, and Claire turned to smile and wave. Tiffani's head stayed firmly face forward, and the bishop grabbed Jamie just as he craned his head over her shoulder to peer at her in a typical brotherly, bug-eyed fashion. "Come on, guys, we're an embarrassment," he said, chuckling. That set Tiffani's head nodding emphatically.

Buddy Osborne smiled a little, watching the interplay. He was a solemn kid, and, the bishop had long suspected, clinically depressed. It was hard to elicit any enthusiasm out of Buddy, although the boy was gifted artistically and quick with mechanical things. His family situation was not the best, the bishop knew. Buddy spent summers and holidays with his dad, which meant mostly alone, as his dad worked long hours and spent others playing pool and drinking beer with his friends. At his mother's, Buddy was without the computer that kept him company at his dad's place, and he had the added problem of not being especially liked by his mother's new boyfriend. The bishop suspected that Buddy just tried to make himself as small and inconspicuous as possible, wherever he was. He wasn't the type to want to bother anyone.

He was several years older than Jamie, but Jamie's natural friendliness and pleasure at being included with his dad and an older boy seemed to bridge the gap. Jamie chattered to Buddy, apparently not troubled that Buddy seldom replied. It was enough that he listened and paid attention.

The bishop watched the two boys when Fairhaven scored a touchdown in the second half.

"Ya-hoo!" yelled Jamie, jumping up and waving a pom-pom someone had dropped. "Way to go, Mariners!"

Buddy just nodded and smiled, watching Jamie and other enthusiasts. "Cool," the boy said softly.

Toward the end of the fourth quarter, the Redstone Rockets were moving the ball steadily down the field. "Defense! Defense!" roared the Fairhaven crowd, in unison. Most, including the bishop, were on their feet. He didn't like the situation. Redstone was making it look too easy, and in this game, it appeared to be a matter of which team happened to be ahead when time ran out. There were seven seconds left. The score was forty-one to thirty-five in Fairhaven's favor. Six and it would go into overtime; seven and Redstone would win.

"Okay, defense, time to come alive," he yelled. "Hold 'em back! Go, Mariners!"

Thomas Rexford was in at middle linebacker. On third and goal, the Redstone quarterback faked a handoff to his fullback but kept the ball, sprinting to his right, looking for a hole in the blue and white of the Fairhaven defenders. Seeing a gap, he cut sharply toward the goal, and it looked for a moment as though he had a clear path to the end zone. But suddenly, there was number forty-seven, the fabled T-Rex, who met him head-on in a bone-jarring tackle that knocked the ball loose. With two seconds on the clock, three Mariners fell on the fumble, ending Redstone's chances for a score.

The crowd erupted in cheers and whistles, and the bishop wondered for a moment if the bleachers would hold under the stampede of pounding feet. Jamie was dancing up and down, grabbing Buddy's arm and hauling him up to celebrate, whether he felt so inclined or not. He apparently did. For the first time, Buddy yelled, too. "Yay, T-Rex! Way to go!" The bishop's enthusiasm doubled, and he squeezed Buddy's shoulder and rubbed Jamie's buzzed hair.

"T-Rex! T-Rex!" the crowd chanted, and Thomas Rexford pulled off his helmet and raised both arms in a salute to the crowd. Just as things began to quiet down, one of the Fairhaven cheerleaders, in an excess of enthusiasm, raised her arms in an answering salute, shook her lithe body in a sort of shimmy and yelled, "Hey, T-Rex! I wanna have your bay-bee!"

T-Rex looked startled, but he grinned and blew her a kiss. His coach whirled and pointed a finger at the girl, motioning her to sit down. Then he did the same to T-Rex, who subsided to the bench amid a wave of laughter and a few catcalls. The Fairhaven quarterback took the snap and went down on one knee, and the Mariners chalked up another victory against the Redstone Rockets.

For the bishop, much of the joy had gone out of the moment. He was embarrassed for T-Rex, embarrassed for Jamie and Buddy and Tiff and her friends, and disgusted with the cheerleader, whoever she was, for her unseemly display of immodesty. Apparently the cheer coach was unhappy with her, too, as she gripped the girl's arm and whispered angrily to her on their way to the girls' locker room. The girl's expression was mutinous.

"How come she said that?" Jamie was questioning. "That was dumb. She shouldn't talk like that to T-Rex."

The bishop shook his head. "You're absolutely right, Jamie. She shouldn't have said that, at all."

He repeated that thought later, at home, in Tiffani's presence, and she frowned.

"Dad, she was just kidding," she said in the patient voice teenagers often use to explain the obvious to slow adults.

"I actually assumed that, Tiff," her father said, in the patient voice adults often use to let their teenagers know they're not entirely out of the loop. "I just object to the impropriety—the immodesty—of her remark. And it looked to me like the cheer coach and Coach Snyder agreed with me."

Tiffani shrugged. "Angie's got a big mouth. She didn't mean anything by it."

"Angie who? What's her last name?"

"Why, Dad? Are you going to complain about her, or write a letter to the editor or something? I mean, it's not like she's LDS, or anything. You don't need to worry about her."

"Does she ever date T-Rex?"

"Who knows? I don't know who-all he goes out with. I don't follow him around and check up on him. And in case you haven't noticed, I don't exactly hang out with the cheerleading crowd."

He studied his eldest child. Why was she being so defensive about all this? Did she think he was going to embarrass her somehow by complaining about Angie-whoever's behavior? Or did she secretly wish that she did hang out with the cheerleading crowd?

"Well, Tiff—what did you think about what Angie did?" he asked.

Tiffani pursed her lips and moved impatiently in her chair at the kitchen table. "It was stupid," she said. "Kinda funny, but stupid. I don't know. I don't think it was such a big deal."

"What about Claire and Lisa Lou? What did they say?"

"We all just laughed at first, and then we were like, 'Oh my gosh, I can't believe she really yelled that, in front of everybody!' That's all." She frowned up at him. "Why do you keep asking me about it? I didn't do anything!"

"I know, I know, sugar. I'm not getting after you. I'm just a little bit—well, ticked off. Embarrassed, actually, on your account and Jamie's and Buddy's and all the decent people there. And I worry about Thomas, having to deal with that kind of stuff from girls. It's disgusting."

"Oh, Dad—don't you know we all hear way worse than that, every day at school?"

He sighed. "Well, I wish you didn't have to. When I was in high school, there was plenty of talk, all right, but—I don't know—not the level of ugliness there seems to be now."

"Well, things have changed since then." Her inflection made "then" sound like the Dark Ages.

Her father nodded. "One thing you'll learn, Tiff, as you go through life, is that not all change is for the better."

"I didn't say it was better! I just said things have changed since you were in school."

He regarded his daughter with concern. Why was she being

so prickly? Obviously, he wasn't approaching this the right way. Maybe there wasn't a right way.

"I reckon they have," he agreed mildly, and dropped the subject.

He began his fast after lunch on Saturday, kneeling in prayer in the room he shared with Trish. He had closed the door; all family members knew not to knock or come in when it was closed. Moms and dads needed private time, either together or apart, and he and Trish had insisted on this rule. Not unless there was a dire emergency was it to be broken. At Mallory's age, of course, an emergency might be the fact that the graham crackers were out of her reach, but she was learning, as had her brother and sister, and he felt pretty well-assured of his privacy on this golden fall afternoon, especially since everyone seemed occupied with some activity or other.

He poured out his heart in thanksgiving to God for his blessings—his family, his freedom, the gospel of Christ and His atoning sacrifice, his calling as bishop, the relative peace of their community, his source of income—all the things that came readily to mind as he reflected on his life. Then he mentioned his concerns to the Lord, beseeching His comfort to be with Ralph and Linda Jernigan in their state of excessive fear and anxiety—with Melody Padgett and little Andrea—with widows Hilda Bainbridge and Hazel Buzbee, and anyone else who was (or felt) alone and lonely, including Buddy Osborne. He prayed that Thomas Rexford Jr. would be blessed with sufficient humility to be able to deal with the temptations that accompanied success, and that all the youth of the Fairhaven

Ward would be strengthened to resist temptation, including his own daughter, Tiffani. He remembered the missionaries throughout the world, and prayed for their safety and success, especially those serving in and from their ward. He prayed that Elder Rand Rivenbark would have the health, strength, and freedom from pain to be able to serve as he desired in the California Burbank Mission. His thoughts moved to those in the armed forces, and those dealing with the aftermath of the terrible events in New York, Washington, and Pennsylvania. He dedicated his period of fasting to all who were personally affected by those events, especially any in his own ward who were struggling with it, asking that all would be comforted and granted peace in their hearts. He prayed for protection for his nation and its people, and for wisdom and good judgment in its leaders, and that some good might come out of these difficult times.

"And, finally, dear Father, wilt thou continue to be my guide in all my dealings with the people under my care," he petitioned. "Thou knowest all my inadequacies, as a bishop, a father, and an employer—and all my responsibilities. Please bless me in times of need, put words in my mouth that these good people need to hear, and help me to be patient and untiring and sensitive to their needs. Please inspire and instruct all who teach or lead or serve in any capacity in our ward, that thy work may go forward and thy people be blessed. Help us all to humble ourselves and be repentant, so that we may hear thy counsel and the whisperings of the still, small voice of the Holy Ghost."

He remained on his knees, pondering and listening, for a while longer, then closed his prayer in the name of the Savior and arose from his knees to go to work.

He sat at his rolltop desk in the far corner of the dining room and began to prepare a short lesson for the Aaronic Priesthood on respecting priesthood offices and those who hold them. He was nearly defeated in his efforts by Samantha, Mallory's Siamese kitten, who at five months was leggy and lean and amazingly determined to pounce on the pen that obviously was being wiggled on the pad of paper for her amusement.

"Hey!" the bishop yelled, as one of her sharp claws caught his finger. "Which side are you on, anyway? Don't you think those guys need this lesson?"

Samantha paused in her attack and looked at him with the quizzical, cross-eyed expression that nearly always made him laugh.

"Seriously, cat, I need to get this done. Go play. Where's your mouse?"

She changed her mind about capturing the moving pen and sprawled across the pad of paper, giving her chest a couple of licks and beginning to purr. Carefully, he tried to ease the paper out from under her, but she opposed that idea, as well, curling her claws around the edge of the pad and holding on.

"Now, see? A dog wouldn't do this. A dog would just lie down at my feet and keep me quiet company while I do what I need to do. Then we could go outside and play catch, or go for a ride in my truck to do some errands. But you? No—you have to oppose every move I make. So what good are you, I ask?"

Samantha rolled over onto her back and stretched, her tawny body elongating impossibly before it contracted back into normal cat-shape. Once more, he tried to remove the pad of paper, and once more, quick as a mongoose, she grabbed it and held on.

"Okay, I get it. I see what you're for. You're here to remind me of Second Nephi two, eleven. There must needs be opposition in all things. Yep—good object lesson, Samantha. I got the point. Now, give me the doggone paper!"

CHAPTER FOUR

"MY REFUGE FROM MINE ENEMY"

Ralph, this is Bishop Shepherd. I'm coming out to visit you folks in a little bit. Is that all right?"

"Bishop, not a good idea to be out and about too much, right now. No need to come here, we're quite sufficient—got everything we need. Thanks, though. Stay home and protect your family."

"Ralph, I appreciate your concern, I really do. But you know, a bishop's in a kind of unique position. Sometimes, even if it isn't convenient, or even if things don't feel especially safe, he gets a prompting from the Spirit that says, 'go and do this, or that,' and he can't just say no to that, so he gets up and goes. And the Spirit's telling me this afternoon to get out there and visit with you and Linda, so here I come. Be ready to open the gate for me, okay? Bye, now."

He hung up before Ralph could protest again, left a note for Trish, who was shopping, and headed out in his truck. The afternoon was golden, with a deeper blue to the sky than summer had provided. October days could still produce plenty of heat, but the air began to cool appreciably in the late afternoons. It was, he thought, probably his favorite time of year. He loved harvest time. Even though it was the end of the growing season, and was often accompanied by a wistful sadness or nostalgia, there was also a sense of new beginning and new purpose. He wasn't sure how those two elements came together in his thinking, but there they were. This autumn, of course, the sense of sadness and loss probably outweighed the more joyful aspects of the season. His country was at war, a new kind of war, not the kind his father and uncle had fought, against known enemies, and usually for well-defined purposes—but one against hatred and terror and misunderstanding—and the opening salvos from the forces of terror had been delivered here in the homeland, in unexpected and horrific ways. It was a complicated situation, and he was still trying to work out in his mind how it had all come to be.

He wound his way through the back roads west of town to the Jernigan "compound," as he had come to think of it. Surrounded by tall fences of barbed wire, their house stood in an open field, with no trees or shrubbery around it to harbor those who might wish to do the couple harm. That these enemies existed primarily—or entirely—in Ralph's and Linda's imaginations made no difference. The fears were real, and he had some idea as to why that was so. The attacks of September eleventh had unnerved everyone to some degree, but to the Jernigans, they were the beginning of the end. The couple had not emerged from their sanctuary since that day. The bishop was here to try to change that, with the help of the Lord. He breathed a short prayer as he approached the electronic gates and gave two quick beeps with his horn.

For a minute or two, he was afraid that Ralph would refuse

to admit him, but then he saw the gate open just far enough for the three guard dogs to emerge and do their sniff test of his vehicle. Ralph's troops, as he called them—Corporal, Private, and Captain—swarmed around the bishop's truck, sniffing the tires and engine and exhaust, then running back to sit beside the front door. He knew the drill by now—the inspection was over, and Ralph would allow the gate to roll back and admit him to the property. He pulled in, parked, and got out, rubbing Corporal's head as the wolf-like dog came to greet him. For some reason, Corporal liked him. The other two animals stayed obediently sitting until Ralph tossed out a small treat for each of them.

"Just you, Bishop?" Ralph called cautiously, peering through the partially open door.

"Just me, Ralph. Glorious afternoon, isn't it? Harvest time. How are your pumpkins?"

The door opened barely wide enough to admit him.

"Pumpkins are still in the field. Likely rot there, this year."

"Oh, no need for that, is there? I'm hoping to get some from you for my store."

"Dunno, Bishop. Perilous times, and all that. Don't dare get out to harvest them. They'll last a while, anyway. We'll see how things go."

"What if some of the brethren from the ward came to help you get them in? We could finish it up in a hurry."

Ralph shook his head. "Wouldn't want anybody jeopardized on my account. Bad enough that you're here. Since you are, will you sit down?"

"Thanks, I'd like to. Linda busy?"

"Keeping an eye on the news. One of us does that, all the time, you know, to watch for developments."

The bishop could hear the low murmur of a television set coming from the kitchen.

"Doesn't watching it constantly get to you?" he asked. "It bothers me if I watch too much—plus, they repeat everything several times. I don't think you'd miss much if you turned it off once in a while, do you?"

"Can't do that. You never know when there'll be a breaking news flash, or a special report, or a warning of some kind. Need to be in touch, you know. For our own survival."

"I see. Well, speaking of keeping in touch, did you folks get to hear President Hinckley's talks last week, from General Conference?"

"No, sir. Keep it tuned to the news channels, all the time. Knew it was conference, one of the stations mentioned it, but we figured we'd read it in the *Ensign* when it comes out. I worried, though, about the people gathering in such large numbers—hope everything was okay."

"Everything went fine. And if you read the magazine, I'm sure you'll be glad you did. There were some wonderful, powerful talks. I don't know—I felt like I needed to hear all I could, especially this year. Searching for some answers, I reckon. It's hard for me to come to grips with what's happened. Sure took us all by surprise, didn't it?"

"Well, sir, not me. Expected it, sooner or later. Always have said those fundamentalist types are more dangerous than anybody—commies, organized crime, whatever. Ready to die, you see. Expect to die, in their attacks. Don't care. Hard to defend, against an enemy who wants to sacrifice himself to take you out."

The bishop nodded. "That's true, isn't it? It bothers me that they think we're the 'great Satan.' This country that's based on freedom of religion for all people, including theirs, and they want nothing more than to destroy us."

"Us an' the Jews. Enemy doesn't like us because we're allied with Israel. Bound to come to this. Armageddon, before we know it."

The bishop unfolded a piece of paper from his shirt pocket. "I unloaded—I mean, downloaded—this from the Internet," he said, with some satisfaction at having mastered that skill, with the help of Buddy Osborne. "It's President Hinckley's comments about the situation. Okay if I share some of them with you? Then I'll leave this with you, and you and Linda can read it all for yourselves. He says, 'Now we are at war. Great forces have been mobilized and will continue to be. . . . The terrible forces of evil must be confronted and held accountable for their actions. . . . It is the terrorist organizations that must be ferreted out and brought down.'

"Then he compares the terrorists of today to the Gadianton robbers in the Book of Mormon, who were vicious, bound by secret oaths, and bent on destruction of the Church and society. He says, 'We are people of peace. . . . But there are times when we must stand up for right and decency, for freedom and civilization, just as Moroni rallied his people in his day to the defense of their wives, their children, and the cause of liberty. . . . Religion offers no shield for wickedness, for evil. . . . The God in whom I believe does not foster this kind of action. He is a God of mercy . . . of love . . . of peace and reassurance, and I look to Him in times such as this as a comfort and a source of strength. . . .

"'Occasions of this kind pull us up sharply to a realization that life is fragile, peace is fragile, civilization itself is fragile. The economy is particularly vulnerable. We have been counseled again and again concerning self-reliance, concerning debt, concerning thrift.' Now, Ralph—you folks are a great example of preparedness and self-reliance, so you can know that the Lord will honor your efforts and grant you peace if you turn to Him, because in this thing, you've been more than obedient in what He asked of you."

Ralph looked downward, nodding, his lips pursed in thought. "Tried to, Bishop."

"Now, listen to this from President Hinckley. He speaks of the time to come in which the earth will be cleansed and there will be a lot of distress, but then he says, 'Now, I do not wish to be an alarmist. I do not wish to be a prophet of doom. I am optimistic. I do not believe the time is here when an all-consuming calamity will overtake us. I earnestly pray that it may not. There is so much of the Lord's work yet to be done. We, and our children after us, must do it. . . . Peace may be denied for a season. Some of our liberties may be curtailed. We may be inconvenienced. We may even be called on to suffer in one way or another. But God our Eternal Father will watch over this nation and all of the civilized world who look to Him. . . . Our safety lies in repentance. Our strength comes of obedience to the commandments of God. . . . He has said, "Be still, and know that I am God."

"'Are these perilous times? They are. But there is no need to fear. We can have peace in our hearts and peace in our homes.'"

Ralph was gazing toward the draped picture window of his living room, his expression sober, his mouth still pursed. The bishop wondered what Ralph saw in his mind's eye—what his inner reaction was to the words of the prophet. Finally Ralph spoke.

"Hard for me to do, you know. Hard not to fear. So many ways to be caught unaware, to get hurt. . . . Feel I need to be constantly vigilant."

"I know, Ralph. And—" He nodded slightly toward the framed photograph of the little blonde girl on the makeshift table of powdered-milk cartons. "And I know a little about why you feel that way. For very good reason."

Ralph looked startled, but didn't reply. The bishop took a deep breath and continued. "The thing is, my friend, we all feel a little threatened and insecure right now, and we need to band together for strength and comfort, and pray together for protection and peace. It would be a great act of faith if you and Linda could make it to sacrament meeting tomorrow. It'll be fast and testimony meeting, you know, and I imagine there'll be feelings expressed that you folks can really relate to. I know it'd strengthen me to have you there, and I believe you'd benefit, too."

"Don't know. Dangerous times—what we've guarded against and prepared this place for. So we never have to leave. Never have to feel so . . ."

He stopped, and the bishop nodded and continued for him. "So terrified, so vulnerable, so robbed and violated as you felt when little Jodie Lee was taken from you. Of course. I don't blame you one little bit. The Lord knows and feels and understands your pain, never doubt it. But, as President Hinckley said, this is probably not the time for a huge calamity to overtake us. It is a time of uncertainty, for sure—but in times like these, there really is strength in numbers, and I truly do believe you and Linda would feel better to come out into the sunshine, at least for an hour or two, and join with the other Saints to share our faith and testimony. We all need each other, Ralph.

We need you and Linda to be there—and you need us. We're supposed to share one another's burdens, remember? I think that's why the Lord sent me out here today."

Ralph's eyes were haunted, but his voice held steady. "Can't promise anything, Bishop. I'll talk to Linda—see what she thinks. She told you, did she?" He nodded toward the photograph.

"She did, a little. I wanted to know. Linda said she was never found. It hurts my heart, Ralph. I love you guys."

Ralph nodded, and walked to the door to open it for his guest. His lips worked, but he didn't attempt to speak. Nor did the bishop say any more. He left the paper with President Hinckley's talk on the makeshift table and patted Ralph's shoulder as he slipped past him and headed for his truck.

Jamie was sprawled on the family room floor with the sports page of the *Fairhaven Lookout* spread before him.

"Hey, Dad," he greeted, when the bishop came in. "Hey, what's a Mariner, anyway? Is it some kind of animal?"

"As in Fairhaven High Mariners?"

"Yeah."

"No, it's not an animal. It's a seafarer, a sailor. Related to the word *Marine*, I suspect."

Jamie frowned. "Well, how come the team gets called that? We're not anywhere near the sea."

His dad sat down wearily in his recliner and leaned back. "As I understand it, the town of Fairhaven was named for a plantation that was built here many years ago, by a retired sea-faring man whose wife wanted to get as far away from the sea as possible. I reckon she was tired of him being gone on a ship so much, or something. So I guess you could say he put into port here, and thought it was a 'fair haven,' meaning a safe and pretty place to settle and put down his anchor. Then when the town grew up, they decided to name it the same thing. And that's why you have the Fairhaven Mariners, with blue and white uniforms—the colors of the sea."

"Cool. I never knew that."

"Mrs. Martha Ruckman taught me that. Tashia Jones's grandmother, in fifth grade."

"Yeah? My age. Weird."

His father smiled tiredly. "Yeah. I was once in fifth grade. Weird."

There were no lengthy or awkward pauses in the bearing of testimonies in the Fairhaven Ward that Sunday. People stood up in groups, it seemed, one deferring to another until all had had a chance at the microphone. Bishop Shepherd listened carefully, both for content and for hints of unresolved problems he might need to address at a later time. Many of the testimonies were predictable—expressions of faith and gratitude that might have been offered on any fast day—but a few were remarkable.

Lori Parsons spoke, balancing her curly-haired baby on one hip and leaning toward the microphone. "Most of y'all prob'ly know that our little girl, Alyssa, was born profoundly deaf," she said. "Yet when my husband Joe blessed her, right here in fast and testimony meeting six months ago, he blessed her that she would have the use of all her faculties in her mortal life. I didn't see how that could ever be, but recently we got a call from our doctor, telling us about cochlear implants, which can help a deaf person actually hear. I'd never heard of such a thing, and neither had Joe. So we're looking into that for Alyssa, and it's real expensive. Our insurance won't cover it, but if it's the right thing for her, I know we'll find a way. Now, I'm not up here asking for donations! I just wanted to testify that the Lord hears the blessings and promises that are given through His priesthood, and honors them. So it wasn't just Joe's wishful thinking that made him say that, even though for a while he worried that it might have been. I just wanted y'all to know that we have faith in the power of the priesthood and in the gospel of the Lord Jesus Christ, and I say this in His name, amen."

"Amen," responded the congregation warmly.

About a third of the way through the meeting, Brother Levi Warshaw stood at the pulpit. Levi was one whose knowledge of the scriptures was enviable, making him an almost permanent fixture as Gospel Doctrine teacher, and the bishop was always interested to hear what he had to say. Levi's accent was not as pronounced as that of his wife, Magda, but it was enough to add a special emphasis to his message.

"Brothers and sisters, the events of this past month have sent me deeply into the scriptures to try to find some meaning to what has happened to our country. Most of you know that my wife and I were both little children in Europe during the Second World War, and saw some terrible things. We were very blessed to escape with our lives, but we both have memories that haunt our dreams, even now. This attack on the United States brings it all back to us.

"Also, as you know, there's no scarcity of war stories in the scriptures, from the war in heaven to prophecies of

Armageddon and the final conflict with Satan at the end of the Millennium, with plenty of wars and rumors of wars in between. But I came across one passage that spoke to me in a particular way, given what we've witnessed. It's in the book of Ether—which has never yet put me to sleep," he added with a strained smile. "If you'd like, look at chapter eight, beginning with verse twenty-two. This is Moroni, speaking about secret combinations. In Europe, you know, we Jews saw what evil could be done by secret combinations. And surely, if ever we have been besieged by secret combinations in this country, the likes of Al Qaeda qualify. We are taught to liken the scriptures to ourselves, so listen as Moroni says, 'And whatsoever nation shall uphold such secret combinations, to get power and gain, until they shall spread over the nation, behold, they shall be destroyed; for the Lord will not suffer that the blood of his saints, which shall be shed by them, shall always cry unto him from the ground for vengeance upon them and yet he avenge them not.

"'Wherefore, O ye Gentiles, it is wisdom in God that these things should be shown unto you, that thereby ye may repent of your sins, and suffer not that these murderous combinations shall get above you, which are built up to get power and gain—and the work, yea, even the work of destruction come upon you.

"'Wherefore, the Lord commandeth you, when ye shall see these things come among you that ye shall awake to a sense of your awful situation, because of this secret combination which shall be among you; or wo be unto it, because of the blood of them who have been slain; for they cry from the dust for vengeance upon it, and also upon those who built it up.

"'For it cometh to pass that whoso buildeth it up seeketh to overthrow the freedom of all lands, nations and countries; and it bringeth to pass the destruction of all people, for it is built up by the devil, who is the father of all lies.'

"Sorry, brothers and sisters, to quote such a long passage. Now, I never have thought to refer to myself as a Gentile." He smiled. "But I think you can see that we are the Gentile nation that is in danger from those who seek power and gain and destruction. There is no excuse for what these people have done to us, but I do feel that we need, as a nation, to repent and turn to the God who made us free and plead with Him to keep us free, and to grant us comfort and peace. That's what I'm trying to do. These evil men did 'get above us,' as the scripture says, in more ways than one, and I believe all Americans need to unite and plead with the God of this land to keep them from being successful again."

Brother Warshaw closed his testimony and sat down, to be followed by Sister Rosetta McIntyre, counselor in the Relief Society presidency, who quietly expressed her gratitude for the general conference that had been held the previous weekend.

"I remember, and most of you do, too, when we couldn't get more than about an hour of conference here, and it was so frustrating to me to know that there was so much more being said by such great leaders and I didn't have access to it. I'm grateful for the technology that allows us to participate as fully as we want to. I'm grateful, too, for the peace that only comes through the Lord Jesus Christ. He doesn't always give us the kind of peace that most of the world is hoping and working for, but He gives us individual peace in our hearts, if we trust Him, so that we can endure whatever comes."

After Rosetta, Sister Ida Lou Reams stood up and determinedly made her way to the podium. She held a little card in her hand, from which she read. "Dear friends, you know I have to read my testimony because if I just try to speak it, I get all tangled up and forget half of what I want to say. I love my Heavenly Father, and I know He loves me. He lets me know that, pretty regular, and I appreciate it. He answers my prayers, though sometimes I don't know why He should, but I'm glad He does. I know He loves each one of you, too, because He gives me love in my heart for you. If I've ever give any offense to anybody, I'm sure sorry. I don't never intend to do that, but sometimes it just happens in spite of all. I pray for all the folks who've lost loved ones in this terrible thing that's happened in our land, and I know they'll be blessed if they can just hang on and have faith. Things do get better, in time. I'm grateful for our dear bishop and his good wife, and all they do for us. I know this Church is true because it's built up on truth and revelation from God, and because Jesus Hisself and His Father brought it back to earth and give it to Joseph Smith. I don't understand all the scripture the way good Brother Warshaw does, but what I can understand, I sure do love. I say these things in Jesus' name, amen."

The bishop reached out a hand to shake Ida Lou's trembling one as she passed by him. He was grateful for her, too, and her simple goodness.

One of the Birdwhistle boys stood up to bear his testimony, all the while grinning at his twin in the third row. The bishop strongly suspected they'd had a wager or a dare between them as to who had the courage to stand up. It wasn't the best motivation, he thought, but it was a start. Then he saw something he had never dreamed of seeing. Up the aisle, from the overflow area, came Ralph Jernigan, plodding along with a look of dogged determination that would have been better suited to a man on his way to the guillotine. He nodded curtly in the bishop's direction as he climbed the three steps to the stand.

He took a moment to glance right and left before he cleared his throat and began to speak.

"Read somewhere that bearing a testimony makes it stronger. Here to test that idea. I need—I need to be stronger. Need to find that peace the lady just talked about. Here because our good bishop came to my place when I told him not to and read to me what our prophet said about the war and all. Bishop said it would make him stronger if I came today, and I owe him that much. Good man, our bishop. Knows what he's doing. I support him, me and Linda, too. We believe in God. Believe in the Church. Thanks. Um—amen."

"Amen," echoed the congregation in stunned surprise, and the bishop's amen was strong.

"Thanks, Ralph," he whispered, as the man retreated in almost unseemly haste from his ordeal.

There followed a few other testimonies, but later, Bishop Shepherd remembered little of them. He was flying high on the wings of one man's heroic effort to grow and show appreciation and gain the peace of the Lord that passes all understanding.

CHAPTER FIVE

"TO SERVE HIS CHILDREN GLADLY"

At the end of the testimony meeting, the bishop spotted Thomas Rexford Jr. talking to a group of admirers and fans as he migrated toward the foyer and, the bishop suspected, an escape route home or to a well-known donut shop not far from the meetinghouse. The bishop exited the chapel through the funeral door at the front of the chapel and intercepted T-Rex as the young man came out through the glass double doors of the building.

"Thomas Rexford!" He grabbed the boy's beefy hand and shook it firmly. "The mighty T-Rex strikes again! Man, that was a magnificent end to the game. Don't know when I've yelled so loud."

"Aw—you were there, Bish? That's so cool. Thanks for comin'."

"My pleasure. And Jamie's, and Buddy Osborne's. Thought those two were going to bring the bleachers down, they were jumping up and down so hard."

"Yeah?" Thomas grinned.

"Sure. They really look up to you. All the young guys do."

"Well, I'll do my best to keep giving 'em something to cheer about."

"You do that. We'll all be watching. Say, Thomas, which Sunday School class do you go to?"

"Huh? Well, you know—the one for my age group."

"Oh—Brother Birdwhistle's class?"

"Um—yeah. Only, I don't feel so hot, today. Thought I'd head home, rest up."

"Right. Boy, I'd love to do the same. Fasting's never been easy for me, you know? I get so hungry, and headachy and tired." The bishop sighed. "Funny thing, but I keep thinking about how when I was about fifteen, some of us guys would sneak out after fast and testimony meeting and make a donut run down to AM/PM Bakery. Can you believe that? We tried to justify it, you see, because testimony meeting was over, and we figured we'd done about all we could do in the fasting department."

T-Rex's face was an interesting study. He had gone red, starting with his neck, when donuts were mentioned, and he turned his head to one side, his eyes narrowed as he listened in disbelief. "Aw, Bishop—you didn't do no such thing!"

"Did, honest. I'm not proud of it now, of course, because I know the value of fasting, even when—or maybe especially when—it's hard. Plus, I learned not to buy things on Sunday unless there's a real emergency. But back then, it sure seemed like the thing to do!"

T-Rex looked down, his massive shoe squishing a bug on the cement step. His bishop suspected the young man felt about as trapped as that bug.

"Boy, those donuts were good. Never tasted better than they

did on fast Sundays. My favorite was the custard-filled with chocolate icing. Which one do you like best?"

The boy looked miserable. "Cinnamon twists, I reckon. Come on, Bish—how'd you know what I was gonna do?"

The bishop smiled. "I didn't, Thomas. But I guess the Lord did. Hey, if you've got a minute, why don't you come into the office with me, and we'll have a little visit? I wanted to talk to you about a couple of things, anyway."

Thomas followed him dispiritedly into the office and flung himself down in a chair.

"You didn't really go for donuts, did you?" he asked. "You just said that, to get me to admit where I was headed."

The bishop raised both hands. "Honest, Thomas, I did. Many times. Tell you what—you ask Brother Bill Nettles about it. He was one of the other guys who went. He'll tell you. He drove."

"How'd you get away with it?"

"Well, now, that had better remain my secret," the bishop replied with a grin. "Maybe we just didn't have leaders who cared enough to head us off. Not that going for a donut is some kind of major sin, Thomas, don't get me wrong. It's just that there's a better way. There are more important things than satisfying our hungers right away."

"I reckon, Bishop, but like you said, it's hard. I mean, I'm a big guy, and if I don't eat pretty regular, I don't have much energy, and my strength starts to go. Yeah, and I get headaches, too. I just don't feel good when I try to fast."

"I don't reckon anybody does, though some folks seem to do better at it than others. Or maybe they just don't complain. I try to think about the Savior, who fasted for forty days. Of course, we're not capable of that—and the Church suggests we not try for more than twenty-four hours . . ."

"Huh! No danger of that, with me!"

"Not for you or me, but some folks think the longer the better, especially when they're plagued with really tough problems, and begging the Lord for help."

Thomas shook his head. "Gotta confess, Bish—I don't really get this fasting bit. How come doin' without food and water's supposed to make your prayers go farther, or somethin'?"

The bishop nodded in understanding. "It's interesting, how it works. Seems like, most of the time, we feel pretty self-sufficient, like we can handle things ourselves. But when we fast, we begin to realize how dependent we are on our daily food, and then there's some kind of crossover that happens, especially if we're fasting for a purpose, and in the right spirit. We begin to realize how dependent we are on the Lord, for our lives and all we have—and how much we need His help in all our trials and temptations. In other words, it humbles us. Personally, I think that's why we see so many folks get tearful at testimony meeting. They've become humble enough that the Spirit of the Lord can touch them and make them realize how precious their lives and families are, and how meaningful their testimonies are of the Savior—his atonement and his gospel."

T-Rex leaned forward in his chair and dropped his head down, leaving the bishop only the top of his head to address.

"See, when things are going well, it's perfectly easy to sail through life and give little thought to those things. Fasting reminds us of what's really important—physically and spiritually. We need spiritual feeding just as much as we need physical food. Even donuts."

Thomas looked up and frowned. "Well, it just makes me hungry, and all I can think about is how soon can I eat again."

"Uh-huh, I used to feel the same. In fact, when I was a kid, fasting was the only thing I didn't like about the Church. But over the years, I've learned its value. You keep trying, Thomas, and I bet you will, too. I'll tell you one thing that helps, and that is to try to focus on a reason for fasting. It could be a personal problem, or wanting to strengthen your testimony, or it could be for somebody else—a loved one who's sick, or a friend who's having some trouble. Focus your fasting and prayer during that time on that problem, and try to believe it'll help. You'll be surprised."

"Huh."

There was that ubiquitous "huh" again. His secretary used it; his kids used it; and the young people of the ward used it. As he interpreted it, the expression seemed to mean, "I hear you, but I'm not agreeing or disagreeing, I'm just acknowledging that you spoke, and registering what you said."

"One other thing about fasting," he said. "And I know you've been taught this from Primary up—and that's the fast offering—donating the money you would have used for food to the Church for aiding the poor. When you begin earning your own way, you'll want to include that."

The boy nodded. "Makes sense. Yeah, I knew about that part. Went out a couple of times with the deacons to collect fast offerings from people."

"Right. Good. Oh—one other thing, Thomas. I wanted to tell you that the other night, at the game, I felt bad about what that young lady yelled at you. Thought that was totally uncalled-for."

"Man, I reckon! Dumb girl, she got me in trouble with Coach. He was mad, whoo-ee!"

"Is she somebody you've dated?"

"Angie? Took her out, once, is all. She's—um—she's . . ." Thomas made a little face and wiggled his fingers.

"Trouble?"

"Um—right. Nicest way to put it. Good work, Bishop."

"Hard to know how to respond to something like that, isn't it? What to say, or do."

"Yeah, but I just took it like a joke. Which it was—I guess."

"But girls like Angie—sometimes they say things in a joking way that they really mean."

"Well, I hope to heck she didn't mean that!" Thomas looked embarrassed.

"Keep away from her, Thomas. Don't even chance finding out what she meant. It's so important that you not get mixed up with that sort of girl. Date the young ladies in our ward, and treat them like something precious, because they are. Save the heavy stuff for later—much later. After you're married."

Thomas summoned a weak grin. "Seems like we've had this conversation before."

"Yep, and I expect we'll have it again, because it's very, very important for you. And you have an extra challenge that lots of guys don't have. You're popular, and admired, and that's great, except it brings out the girls who want to date you for all the wrong reasons. You know what I mean?"

"I guess I do."

"That's all pretty scary, and dangerous, Thomas. I'm glad I never had it to worry about when I was in high school. Nobody that I know of ever fought over me or suggested any inappropriate behavior. Certainly nobody ever offered to be the mother of my child! 'Course, maybe that was partly because I was too shy to look 'em in the eye. And maybe it was because I was a skinny, gawky kid who cared more about working on his truck than much of anything else. But you, Thomas! You've got an added burden in your life, friend. The burden of popularity. It's not an easy thing to carry."

The bishop almost chuckled as he watched T-Rex process this notion. He had obviously never regarded his popularity as anything other than a desirable and well-deserved blessing.

"Yeah, but . . ." he began, and stopped, confused. "Burden?"

The bishop nodded. "Popularity is a burden. Or at least, it can be. Think of the extreme example—entertainers and musicians and sports figures who can't go anywhere without being mobbed and followed. People try to get their attention, or steal from them, or haul them into court to sue them for big bucks. Half the time, they can't tell their friends from their enemies. Even in your case, you have to wonder about the motivation of any young lady who tries to get your attention. Then, you've got the envy of the other guys. How do you know who's really your friend, and who just wants to hang on to your jersey for his own benefit? It's tough duty, for sure. But, I'll admit, there is an upside to being popular. Can you think what it might be?"

"Bishop, you're like, messin' with my head!"

"I don't mean to do that, Thomas. I just want to show you all sides of the situation."

"Well, I reckon it's good to be popular because—um— shoot, now I can't think of why. I s'pose because everybody knows you, and talks to you?"

"That's not a bad thing, is it? And that gives you wonderful opportunities to get to know a lot of different people—all kinds of people, not just the ones in the 'in' crowd, or on the team and cheer squad. And the more people you know, and like, and who like you, the more good you can do, just by setting a good example and being decent to everybody. It's almost like a missionary opportunity. I don't mean you have to preach the gospel to everybody," he added, noting the slight panic in Thomas's eyes. "Just live it in how you treat people. Then your burden will become a blessing to you, and to other people, as well. Does that make sense, Thomas?"

T-Rex was quiet for a few seconds. Then he said, predictably, "Huh."

"So it's something to chew on, okay, Thomas? Now, tell me—how're your folks doing?"

"Mama's workin' more hours, now that Grandma's passed on. I know Mama, she sure appreciated y'all holdin' the funeral here, even though Grandma wasn't a member of the Church."

"No problem. Our privilege. I'm sure your grandma was a fine woman."

"She was real nice, back before—you know—her mind went, on her."

"Right. How's your dad? He found any work, yet?"

"Naw. I reckon he don't quite know what to do with himself. All he knew was the work he did at the base, all them years. He's kinda embarrassed, I reckon, to go for training in something new."

"I see. Well—thanks, my friend, for coming in to talk with me. Remember I'm here for you, anytime you may need me, okay? Also—just a few more Sundays, and I think we can get you ordained to be a priest. Speaking of which, I've got to give a little presentation to the combined Aaronic Priesthood in about ten minutes. Come on, I'll walk down there with you."

Thomas sighed, but the bishop smiled to himself. It looked

like the football hero would be staying for the whole three-hour block.

Y

Early that evening, on their customary Sunday stroll around their neighborhood, the bishop and Trish held hands and enjoyed the capricious little wind that swirled and tugged at leaves that were still reluctant to be detached from their twigs.

"So, how'd your presentation to the Aaronic Priesthood go?" Trish asked.

The bishop chuckled. "Better than I'd hoped, actually. The guys themselves brought up some things I'd wanted to address but was a little reluctant to, so it didn't all come from me. And that's good. It's better when it comes from them."

"Now I'm curious. What did you talk about?"

"Basically, just about respectful speech. How holders of the priesthood ought to speak of their leaders, of adults in general, and of girls and women—and how they should not. It's gotten to be a problem, recently."

"Was T-Rex there?"

"He was." The bishop smiled, recalling how that had come to be. "And I didn't even have to suggest that he not call me 'Bish,' or 'Bishie.' One of the young priests brought it up, himself. He didn't mention Thomas by name, which was good—he just said 'we' probably shouldn't use nicknames like that for our leaders. Then Sam Wright said, 'Yes, and I've always called Bishop Shepherd "Jim" because we were friends in the Fairhaven Ward, so I've had to watch myself, too, and call him "Bishop," now—not because he'd get mad if I called him "Jim," but out of respect for the office he holds.'"

"That was good."

"It was. And then we talked about how to refer to young ladies, and you can imagine that was interesting."

"I'll just bet it was."

"The young men came up with quite a list of terms that were less-than-flattering, which we shouldn't use, even if they seem to apply."

"And even if they're widely used on TV and among the school population?"

"That, too. And then, I was real proud of Ricky Smedley. He said, 'You know, some of us have called Brother Jernigan "Old Brother Hunker in a Bunker," but when he got up today to bear his testimony, I felt real bad about doing that, and I don't think we oughta do it anymore.'"

Trish smiled. "Even if it applies."

He squeezed her hand. "Even if. Maybe *especially* if it applies. You know, I've grown real fond of Ralph and Linda."

She nodded. "I know you have. And I think they know you care, which is most important. Bless their hearts. I was so proud of him, today. That had to be hard."

"I don't think we have any idea how hard."

"But it really was impressive of Ricky, to admit that hunker-in-a-bunker business, and speak out against it."

"Wasn't it? He's a nice young man. Plus, his dad has home taught the Jernigans for years, so maybe he's put in a good word for them with Ricky. It could be he's taken Ricky with him to visit them, for that matter. In any case, what he said today was a good start in—what do they call it?—raising everybody's awareness of respectful speech."

"Can't hurt."

They walked in silence for a few moments, then the bishop

asked, "What do you make of Tiff's prickly attitude when I was talking about that cheerleader's comment to Thomas?"

"I didn't hear all of that conversation, but I got the distinct impression that her nose was out of joint over something, all right. I don't know—maybe it's just the natural instinct to take up for her own age group. I know she disapproves of what Angie said, so it's not that she's defending that. She's been kind of defensive lately about a lot of things. I'll try to talk to her, and see if I can figure out what's going on."

"Thanks, hon."

"Oh, Jim—I forgot to give you this. It came in yesterday's mail," Trish said later Sunday evening, handing him an envelope. He nodded, looking at the return address. Elder Rivenbark, in California. He opened the envelope and drew out the letter.

Dear Bishop Shepherd,
    Things are going great here in the best mission in the Church. I have a new companion, Elder Bidwell, and we get along just fine. He's a big help to me, and I hope I can be helpful to him in some way. We are teaching two families and one young guy who is out here trying to become an actor. He's from Kansas, and seems really interested in the gospel, although sometimes I wonder if maybe he just likes us because we're close to his age. Anyway, he has promised to read the stuff we left him, so we'll see how things go. The families are neat. One is the Truman family—no relation to President Harry, I

guess, as they're a black family. They're really nice. They always want to feed us, and Mrs. Truman's a really good cook. They have two little boys who climb all over us and sit on our laps—even mine, once they got used to my wheelchair, which I use a lot, here. I think Mr. Truman might have a little trouble with the Word of Wisdom, but he also seems to be a man of faith, and I can tell he loves his family, so I have hope.

The other family is the Marchbecks. There's the mother, Agatha, and two daughters, Melanie and Jacqueline, who are in their late twenties or early thirties, it's hard to tell. They are always polite, but sometimes I think they are secretly laughing at us— especially Jacqueline—but their mother rules the roost here and makes them sit down and listen, and they obey her, out of respect or what, I don't know. The father died about a year ago, and I think the idea of an eternal family appeals to Agatha. She is reading the Book of Mormon, and finds it interesting. I don't know if the daughters have read any, yet.

I am really enjoying my mission, Bishop, and my testimony is growing more and more. I am less and less scared to bear my testimony anytime and anywhere, to anybody. I want to thank you for all your encouragement and letters of recommendation for me. Please pray for me and for our contacts, and say hi to everybody in the ward.

Sincerely yours,
Elder Randall Rivenbark

The bishop leaned back in his desk chair and watched through the dining room doorway as Trish tidied up the kitchen, but his mind was in California with two young elders, sharing their excitement and hopes for the people they were teaching. He hadn't served a mission, himself; maybe he could get a feel for the experience through the letters of those serving from the Fairhaven Ward. It was some compensation.

CHAPTER SIX

"THROUGH MISTS OF DARKNESS WE MUST GO"

Monday morning dawned dark and gray. The whippy little wind of the previous evening had ushered in banks of clouds that seemed ready to unleash a downpour. Bishop James Shepherd rather relished the prospect. Except for the somewhat adverse effect it had on the grocery business, he enjoyed a good rainy day now and then. People who really needed to shop for food came anyway, while people who could wait for clear weather to venture out did so, and all in all, it made for a rather cozy atmosphere in the store, with a little more time for employees to visit with customers or each other and to catch up on tasks that were set aside when things were busy.

He and Jamie left the house early, and after he dropped his son at school for a morning Space Club activity, he turned his truck in the direction of the ward meetinghouse, but instead of turning in at the usual parking lot, he continued on for four more blocks and stopped at the AM/PM Bakery and Donut Shop. He wished AM/PM would let him distribute their product, but they were adamant about keeping their business a strictly small, in-house, mom and pop affair. He ordered a half-dozen cinnamon twists in one box, and two dozen mixed varieties to treat his employees, then headed for the Rexford home.

Sister Lula Rexford opened the door. "Bishop! What in the world . . ."

"Morning, Sister Rexford. Is Thomas still here?"

"Well, he's in the shower, but . . ."

"That's fine. Would you please give him these, from me? It's a little joke between us. He'll understand."

"Sure I will. He loves these things. Thank you, Bishop."

"You're welcome. How are you and Tom doing?"

"We're gettin' by. I'm working more, now. Thank goodness we'd already paid off the house, or we'd be in a peck of trouble."

"Boy, that's a blessing most folks can't claim! Good for you. By the way, you might want to stop by the store Wednesday afternoon. Are you off work then?"

"I get off at two."

"Great. Come by, 'cause we're planning one of those unannounced buy-one-get-one-free sales between three and four o'clock. In case you're interested."

Lula Rexford chuckled, and he could see traces of T-Rex's smile in hers. "Can't be totally unannounced, can it, since you just announced it to me?"

The bishop smiled. "Oh, you know—preferred customers sometimes get a heads-up on these things."

"Well, thanks again, Bishop. Uh-oh—you'd better get back in your truck before you get drenched!" A dart of lightning pierced the clouds, followed by the expected thunder, and rain began to fall in earnest.

"See you!" he said, and sprinted for his truck.

That night, as his family gathered in the family room on the back of the house for their weekly home evening, he enjoyed the cozy warmth of the lamplight that illuminated the rain-streaked windows. Jamie was tinkering with an old puzzle cube he had found at a neighborhood yard sale, and Mallory, her platinum hair turned into an angel's halo by the table lamp above her, sat on the floor, arranging several Barbies in sitting position beside her. Tiffani yawned and kept reading her library book, waiting for the meeting to begin.

Under Trish's direction, they more-or-less sang a Primary song about an autumn day—not the kind this one had been, but one that was bright, and featured red and yellow apples. Jamie and Mallory sang along with their mother, while the bishop muffed most of the words, and Tiff, looking embarrassed, muttered along. Jamie gave the opening prayer, then Trish said, "And now we'll turn the time over to Daddy, who has the lesson."

He did? It was his turn? Why hadn't Trish reminded him? He thought fast. "Okay, gang, hang on for just a sec while I grab something from my desk," he said. As he climbed over Mallory and her dolls, he saw Trish mouth the words, "He forgot!"

"Daddy!" Mal's voice followed him. "You *forgot?* Mommy and I didn't forget the 'freshments!"

"Well, I'm sure glad of that," he responded, coming back with his briefcase. "Because I think that's just about the most important part. Let's see, now. In here . . ."

"Oh, no, the dreaded briefcase," Tiffani intoned. "Who knows what boring things may be lurking in there?"

Her father pulled out the notes from his discussion with the Aaronic Priesthood the day before. None of his family had been there, the subject was adaptable for children of all ages, and he breathed a sigh of relief when he threw out a couple of opening questions about speaking respectfully of and to others, and the children responded. Mallory opined that everybody should always say "ma'am" and "sir" when talking to grown-ups, and her father, having been brought up in that good Southern tradition himself, agreed.

"In fact, I still can't talk to some folks without doing that, myself," he admitted. "Mrs. Martha Ruckman will always get 'yes, ma'am' or 'no, ma'am' from me, no matter how old I get."

"Yeah, 'cause she'll always be older'n you, huh, Dad?" put in Jamie, grinning.

"I think it's 'cause she'll always be my fifth-grade teacher, and I have great respect for her. Same with some folks at church—Brother and Sister Mobley, Sister Bainbridge, Sister Strickland, Brother Tullis. He used to be my deacons quorum adviser. It never hurts to be a little too polite. It's way better than not being polite enough."

"My Mia Maid adviser said we could call her 'June'," Tiffani said. "But I have a real hard time doing that. It feels funny. So—should I call her Sister Ralston, or will that hurt her feelings?"

"What do you think, Trish?" the bishop deferred.

"I think if you're comfortable calling her Sister Ralston, then keep doing that unless she makes a point of wanting you to call her June. Sometimes younger women feel funny being called Sister somebody, all of a sudden, especially when they're young marrieds, like June is. It makes them feel old. I remember somebody calling me Sister Shepherd once, when your dad and I were first married, and I actually turned around and looked for your Grandma."

"Well, I sort of don't call her anything, most of the time. I just go, 'um—can we do this, now?'"

The discussion meandered, but some useful things were said—including the fact that the reason that we speak respectfully is that we are all children of God—and all in all, the bishop felt, as he enjoyed his pumpkin cookies and milk, that things had gone pretty well for a dad who had forgotten his assignment.

Early Tuesday evening, Bishop Shepherd inserted his key into the door of the bishop's office and let himself in. He was the first one to arrive, and when he turned the light on, a gray tithing envelope on the floor just inside the door caught his attention. He picked it up and could tell it was full of coins. In the upper left corner, in the space for a return address, was printed, "T-Rex."

He smiled and opened the envelope as he headed for the clerk's office. He couldn't wait. The donation slip inside listed a fast offering of three dollars and ninety cents—exactly the price of a half-dozen cinnamon twists. The bishop laughed out loud, stuffed the slip back into the envelope with the money, and left it for Brother Perkins to find.

He had two couples to interview for temple recommends— Don and Connie Wheeler and Gene and Frankie Talbot. The interviews were a pleasure; he wished every couple in the

Fairhaven Ward had the faith and determination to do right that these two couples had. Don and Connie were cheerful and uncomplaining in spite of their inability to have children and the seemingly endless adoption procedures they were going through. Gene and Frankie were solid, service-oriented folks who also declined to complain in spite of the rigors of bringing up five very active children, Frankie's calling in the Relief Society presidency, and Gene's job that took him away from home for days at a time. They were organized and energetic and somehow found time to do things for people. Word of their good deeds—only some of them, the bishop felt sure—filtered back to him from time to time. A lawn mowed or raked, a meal taken in to the sick or tired or elderly (though none had been asked for), a sack of school clothing, all properly sized, for a family without the means to provide their own—all evidence of the Talbots' love of God and fellowman.

His Relief Society president, Ida Lou Reams, popped in for a brief chat just as the Talbots were leaving.

"I declare, that little Frankie's got the most spunk and energy of anybody I know," she said, sitting in one of the chairs across the bishop's desk. "She sure keeps us on our toes in the Relief Society." A look of alarm suddenly crossed her face. "You're not taking her away from us, are you, Bishop? They weren't here about a new calling, were they?"

He smiled. "No, no, Ida Lou, no fear of that. They were just renewing their temple recommends. They're sure a fine couple, and so are the Wheelers, who were here before them. It does a bishop's heart good to be reminded that there are such good stalwart people in his ward. Now, how's the Relief Society doing? Anything I can help with?"

"Well, shoot, Bishop, after what you just said, I hate to give you my news."

"Uh-oh. What's the problem?"

"Well, I don't know why he come to me—I reckon because he thinks I might help, woman-to-woman, or that the sisters might could rally round her, and he said he hatn't talked to you about it, yet—but he said I could, iffen I thought it'd help, so that's why I'm here."

The bishop's mind raced like a search engine through the ward list, trying to match Ida Lou's words with any potential sisters with problems. He was concerned about Melody Padgett, of course, and Lula Rexford, with her husband's unemployment, and Sister Bainbridge, widowed and nearly blind, and Nettie Birdwhistle, homeschooling her ten children in her log house in the hill country, and others of slender means—but none of them seemed to fit what Ida Lou was saying.

"Who?" he blurted.

"Oh, didn't I say? Sorry, Bishop, reckon it addled me—it was Brother Lanier, talking about his wife. Says he thinks she's losing her testimony."

The bishop felt as if he had been blindsided. Marybeth Lanier, losing her testimony? Why hadn't he known? Why hadn't he felt it, when he looked out over the congregation, or had a prompting about her during his prayers?

"Why does he think so?" he asked.

"He said she's been questioning some things about the gospel for a long time. I don't know just what. She's a real smart lady, and I don't see how I could help her out, but I told him I'd pray for her. I think he's real concerned."

"I'll bet he is." Scott Lanier was a medical doctor—a podiatrist, actually—and a kind, quiet man who seemed to know the gospel well and to do his best to live according to its precepts. Marybeth, his wife, was also very quiet, but, as Ida Lou said, "smart," and very capable in anything she set her mind to do. They had been stalwarts in the Fairhaven Ward for a number of years, and he would have never imagined that she would be entertaining doubts about the Church or its teachings.

"Thanks, Sister Reams. I'll talk to Brother and Sister Lanier, and see if I can find out what it's all about. You do just what you said—pray for her—and ask your counselors and Trish to do the same, but remind them not to say anything to anyone else about the situation. You can just imagine how it'd make Marybeth feel to find out everybody was talking about her behind her back."

"That wouldn't help atall, would it?" she agreed. "Well, other than that, far as I can tell, the sisters are all perkin' along pretty good."

"You know, I wonder, when I go out to visit Sister Hazel Buzbee next time, whether you'd be able to ride along and get acquainted with her? Trish will be going, too."

"Reckon I'd like that. I have a real vague memory of her, but it's been so long, I cain't put a face to the name. I should know every sister in the ward, that's for sure."

"We'll be going on the first of November, so if that fits into your schedule, I'd be grateful. I'll let you know what time. Oh— and does Sister Lanier receive visiting teachers?"

"Well, there's some assigned, but I noticed on the report that they've had a hard time catching up to her, of late."

The bishop nodded. "Well, I reckon now we have some idea why," he said sadly.

Thursday evening Bishop Shepherd left work a little early and cleaned up a bit before going to visit another of the extra people he had assigned himself to home teach. Sister Elaine Forelaw was a lifelong member of the Church who had grown up in Mississippi and had married a fellow named Sergeant Forelaw there before they had moved to Fairhaven. It was a matter of speculation whether her husband had earned his name in service of his country, or his folks had given it to him as an honorary title at birth, or he had acquired it as a nickname because he behaved like a drill sergeant with his kids. There were Forelaws in Fairhaven; the bishop had gone to school with them, and he thought it was high time he found out what relationship there might be. Sergeant Forelaw was not a Latter-day Saint, that much was known. Elaine and the three children came to church now and then, but not with any regularity.

He pulled up in front of their house, which was quite an ordinary white frame house set on concrete blocks. The spacious yard was dotted with pine trees and enclosed by a chain link fence. He looked around carefully for dogs as he approached, but there appeared to be none, and there was no sign of children at play, either.

His knock on the door was answered by Elaine, a cheerful young woman with light reddish-brown hair and rosy cheeks.

"Bishop Shepherd? I thought that must be who you were, but I haven't happened to be at church when you were conducting, so I wasn't sure if you were the bishop, or if it was the man with black hair. How're you doing, tonight?"

"Fine, thanks, Sister Forclaw. The fellow with black hair is

Robert Patrenko, my first counselor. Second counselor is Sam Wright."

She nodded, smiling. "I know Brother Wright. He's a nice man. Won't you come in?"

"Is your husband at home? I'd be pleased to meet him."

"He's here, like he promised he would be. He's in the kitchen." She turned and called over her shoulder, "Sarge! Bishop would like to meet you!"

Sergeant Forelaw ambled into the room with an open can of beer in one hand. He offered his other hand to the guest.

"Good to meet you, Mr. Forelaw," the bishop said, shaking Sergeant's hand firmly and ignoring the beer. "I grew up with Jakey Forelaw. Is he—"

Sergeant nodded. "Jake's my cousin, and the reason we're up here in Alabama. I come up here to work with him in the tire business."

"Oh, tires—of course. Forelaw Tires, over on Second Street. Well, it's good to meet you. We enjoy Sister Forelaw and the children in the ward, and since I'm the new bishop, I decided it was time I got better acquainted with the family. I appreciate you letting me visit. Are the kids here?"

"Oh, they're in bed, already," Elaine said. "They go down at six-thirty."

The bishop tried to hide his surprise. He also tried to imagine getting any of his three in bed by six-thirty. Of course, the Forelaw children were mostly younger. "How old are they, now?" he asked.

"Eight, four and three," Elaine said easily. "Won't you sit down, Bishop?"

"Oh, sure. Thanks." He sat on the edge of a clean, but worn, blue sofa. The room was spotless—no toys, no mess, but also no books or magazines or needlework or plants or anything to show the interests of the occupants.

"Something to drink?" inquired Sergeant, lifting his can.

"Sarge," said his wife, with a slight hint of admonition in her voice. "Glass of ice water, Bishop? Or apple juice?"

"Neither, thanks. I'm fine."

"I'll be in the kitchen," Sergeant said and strolled slowly back in that direction. He was a large man with sandy blond hair and freckles under what appeared to be a perpetual sunburn.

"So you folks are both originally from Mississippi?" the bishop asked.

"Meridian," Elaine agreed. "Eastern part of the state."

He nodded. "Right." He knew where Meridian was. "Lived there all your lives?"

"Yessir."

"Well, Fairhaven's my hometown. Been here all my life except for a couple of years away at college. So I haven't gone far afield, but my wife, Trish, isn't originally from here. She was an Air Force kid. Her dad was here on special military assignment when she was a teenager, and we met then. Corresponded, finally got together again, and married. Lucky for me she likes it here. At least, she claims to." He smiled.

"I'll bet she does," Elaine said. "I do. It's a pretty town."

"Have you met Trish? She has dark hair, greenish eyes. She was teaching Primary, but now she's Relief Society secretary."

She shrugged. "Probably, but I'm not sure, sorry. I know I met the Relief Society president. I've met people whenever I've been to church, but it's hard to remember their names."

He nodded. "That does take a while, putting names with faces. And even longer to place children with their parents."

"That's true."

There was a momentary silence, which seemed to the bishop to stretch on and on. He was uncomfortably aware of Sergeant, sipping his beer in the kitchen, no doubt listening very carefully to the conversation between his wife and this Mormon bishop.

"One day, when I visit, I'll bring Trish along, if that's all right," he suggested.

"That'd be nice."

"So how are things going for your family?" he asked. "Is there anything we can help you with?"

"Oh, no—we're just fine. But thanks."

"Lots of folks are having some uneasy feelings after what happened on nine-eleven. Are your kids okay about that?"

"I don't think they even realize much about it. We don't let them watch much TV—and mostly just stuff like *Sesame Street* when they do."

"I believe that's wise. My ten-year-old son's been kind of upset about it. He had to write a paper for school about his feelings, and I think that helped him a little, to express his confusion and fear."

"I try not to think about it. I won't listen to all those lists of people who died, and the tributes to them. Makes it too real. I start feeling like I know them, and then I get sad."

"I understand. I surely do hope there's some good that can come out of all of it, but it's hard to see what that might be, except for the heroism of the police and firemen. That's been impressive."

"I'm just sorry they needed to be heroes for such a reason," Elaine Forelaw said. "Now so many of their best people are lost, and they have to try to replace them, and train new ones."

"It's tragic, all right, and a very tough situation for everybody. But President Hinckley said he doesn't believe this is the beginning of a huge, worldwide calamity. However, he did encourage all of us to do our best to prepare, to get out of debt, to put away our food supplies, and so forth. That's always been good advice, of course. I've known families who've pretty much lived on their storage food during times of personal problems, such as illness or job loss."

She nodded. "Sarge and me, we don't owe anybody except for our house, and a few more payments on his truck. I bottle whatever fruits and vegetables I can get cheap, and we've got a freezer for meats and such. Sarge hunts when he can, so we've got venison and pheasant in the freezer, as well as chicken and beef we've bought on sale."

"Sounds like you folks are right on track. I believe it's important, these days, to keep on hand the things we need and use the most. Be prepared, as the Scouts say." He raised his voice slightly. "Isn't that right, Mr. Forelaw?"

Sergeant Forelaw appeared in the door to the kitchen. "What was that?" he asked. "I wasn't listening."

"Bishop was just saying it's good to be prepared, like the Boy Scouts say. For emergencies, and all."

"Oh, yeah. I was a Boy Scout once, for a couple of years. Learned some good stuff."

"I was telling Sister Forelaw that it sounds as if you folks are on the right track, with no unnecessary debt, and food put away for the winter, or for hard times. The Church encourages us to do that, so that we can be as self-sufficient as possible."

"That's just good, plain common sense, seems to me," the man commented. "Don't know why a church needs to say so."

The bishop smiled. "It is good sense, but not as common as

you might think. I own a grocery store, and you'd be surprised how quickly the shelves empty out whenever there's a storm coming, or a trucker's strike or such. Seems like nobody keeps basics on hand like they used to. Anyway, I think the Church leaders encourage us to look out for our own needs by planning ahead, and then we won't be a drain on anyone else, be it the government or the Church or our neighbors. We might even be in a position to help other people out." He stood up. "Well, it's been a pleasure to meet you folks. Next time, I'll try to get here a little sooner, to meet the kids, too. Thanks for letting me come."

"Thanks for coming, Bishop. It's good to meet you," Elaine responded.

Sergeant Forelaw raised his can in salute. The bishop wondered if it was the same one the man had been sipping when he arrived—or did he go through several in the course of an evening? Could that be why the children were tucked safely in bed so early? That was an uncomfortable thought.

CHAPTER SEVEN

"COME UNTO HIM, ALL YE DEPRESSED"

R ain had fallen, off and on, for three days, leaving the air washed and cool and smelling of the sad-sweet fragrance of damp leaves. On Friday afternoon, the bishop sat in a patch of late sun on his patio, stealing a quiet moment, trying to deal with the news about Marybeth Lanier that had left him reeling with regret and confusion. He should have known something was amiss with Marybeth, he scolded himself for the hundredth time. Why hadn't he known? Had the Spirit tried to whisper something to him, and he'd been too busy, or too caught up in things like football games or reports of the war in Afghanistan to listen? And, more to the point, now that he knew—what should he do? He thought back over the meeting he'd had with Dr. Scott Lanier on Wednesday. Scott had agreed to meet him for lunch at a soup and salad restaurant that had recently opened downtown.

"Bishop, thanks for taking the time to see me," Scott had said. He was a slight man in his early forties with glasses over kind blue eyes, and hair that was just beginning to gray and to recede. He had a gentle manner and a quiet voice, but the bishop knew of his inner strength and testimony. He and Marybeth had one son, married and in graduate school at Duke University.

"Dr. Lanier, I'm glad for the opportunity," the bishop said.

The man shook his head. "Just Brother Lanier, between us," he requested. "Or, better yet—just Scott. Not enough people call me Scott, anymore." His smile was deprecating. "I guess I know why you asked to see me. Sister Reams spoke to you?"

The bishop nodded. "Let's get our lunch, and then we'll talk," he suggested, and once they were settled in a corner booth, he said, "Why don't you just give me some idea of what's been taking place with Marybeth? And, by the way, I apologize for not being aware of this."

Scott shrugged. "How could you be? I've only known for a couple of weeks—although now, with good old hindsight, I can see hints going back for months or more. For example, she started making excuses not to go to the temple with me. She didn't feel up to it, she couldn't take the time away from her house or yard work, or she was already committed elsewhere." He took a bite of salad and swallowed. "You may know she's quite active in a couple of community charities. She helps with the local March of Dimes effort, and she's very involved with the county shelter for battered women."

"Good causes," the bishop said.

"They are," Scott agreed. "And I didn't think much of it for a long time. I just thought it was hard to pick a good block of time for her to get away. Then, more recently, it began to be difficult to find a time to have prayer together as a couple, or if we did, she'd prefer for me to say it, never her. And if I came home late for dinner—which happens, with doctors, even podiatrists—she would keep a plate for me, and if I started to ask a blessing, she would say, 'Oh, it's already been blessed,' so I'd just say, 'Well, then, amen,' and go ahead and eat. Lately, I realized that I hadn't seen her open her scriptures for longer than I could remember, and I found them tucked away in a bookshelf in our study, instead of where she used to keep them, in her bedside table."

The bishop buttered a roll. "Have the two of you actually discussed what's troubling her?"

Scott nodded. "A couple of weeks ago we were having dinner in Birmingham, and she ordered a glass of wine. She looked at me, and said, 'So? Are you shocked?'"

"Mm. How'd you respond to that?"

"I just said, 'Well, I know you used to enjoy wine before you joined the Church, but I didn't know you'd felt the need for it, recently.' She said, 'I don't need it—I just want some.' So I said, 'I see.' Though I didn't, not really. The wine arrived, and she sipped at it, and I didn't say anything, and finally she said, 'I have to be myself, Scott. I can't just do what other people expect of me.'"

"Wow. So do you think it's a matter of agency? Is she feeling controlled, or somehow forced to conform?"

"I think it's partly that. She's always been quite independent and a bit of a feminist, though not excessively so. Just active and vocal about women's rights. I certainly haven't made any effort to control her or to tell her what she may or may not do. That goes against my grain, to begin with, and I know, with a woman like Marybeth, it would do no good to try, even if I wanted to."

"That's good," the bishop said, thinking for a moment of Jack and Melody Padgett. "I'm certainly aware of the fact that control and force have no place in an LDS marriage, or any marriage, for that matter. The scriptures make that perfectly clear."

"M-hmm. As in the one hundred twenty-first section of the Doctrine and Covenants, right? So I said to her, 'Would you like to tell me what's going on? How you're feeling?' She said, 'I doubt you'll understand. You're a believer.'"

"Meaning that she isn't?"

"Apparently. I said, 'Try me, honey. You know I'll listen.' She just said, 'I'm sorry, Scott, but I don't believe, anymore. Once I did, now I don't. It's that simple.'"

"Did she go into any detail, or give you any idea why she had stopped believing?"

"I pressed her a little. I said, 'What, exactly, do you not believe anymore?' and she said, 'I don't believe the Church is true. I don't believe in all that stuff about angels and visions and the Book of Mormon and modern prophets and temples and priesthood. I think it's all folklore. I'll grant you the Church is made up of mostly good people who are sincere in their beliefs. And I'll grant you that the Church does a lot of good in humanitarian aid—and those are the only reasons I've stuck with it for this long. But now I've decided that I can't continue to attend or support any group that I believe to be founded on false notions. I'm moving beyond it, Scott. I know you're not ready to do that, so I won't try to influence you, but I'm asking for my name to be removed from the Church records.'"

The bishop put down his fork. He tried to think what sort of impact it would have on him, on their marriage, if Trish were to hit him with that kind of bombshell. It was a sickening feeling. "My word," he said. "Did you feel as if the rug had been pulled out from under you?"

"That's about it," Scott agreed, nodding sadly. "All kinds of objections came to mind, all kinds of evidences and proofs and scriptures and testimonies, but I felt the time wasn't right to bring up any of that. So I asked her, 'What about the Savior? Do you still believe in Him? In the Bible? In God, at all?' She just said, 'I don't know. I'm working on all that. There isn't any other church that's wooed me away, if that's what you're asking.'"

"What do you think has wooed her away?" the bishop asked.

"Well, the adversary, obviously," Scott replied. "I'm still trying to figure out just how. She's a very intelligent woman, you know. I wonder if it's an appeal to her reason, to her intellectual abilities or sophistication. She reads widely, in many different fields."

"Normally, that would be good," the bishop mused. "I wonder if she's been reading some anti-Mormon literature."

Scott shook his head. "She says not. I asked her. She said, 'I don't need their kind of propaganda to tell me how to think or what to believe.'"

"I see. Scott, I've got to ask you—apart from this situation, how is your marriage?"

Scott frowned at a chunk of cauliflower on his fork, as if wanting the vegetable to speak for him. "I thought our marriage was good," he said. "Well, more than good—very good, maybe even outstanding. Marybeth can be a delightful companion, and she's usually warm and affectionate. She's been a great mother to John, and we've both wished she could have had a couple more kids. She's seemed content until recently, and I've gotta think it's this loss of faith business that's made the difference I see in her. She seems restless more often now, and sometimes even giddy."

"Have you talked this over with John?"

"Yes, I called him. He didn't seem unduly worried about it, seemed to think it was just some phase his mom was going through, like a passing hobby, or something. But I'm afraid it's far more than that."

They ate in silence for a few minutes, then the bishop queried, "How do you anticipate this problem might affect your marriage, if she continues to feel as she says she does?"

"Bishop, I honestly don't know. I'm sickened at the thought of losing her. On the other hand, I don't look forward to feeling—I don't know—maybe 'patronized' is the word, as she talks about having gone ahead, intellectually, and recognizing that I'm not ready, yet, to leave my faith—as if that's a normal and expected part of a person's intellectual progress! I just don't buy that, and I honestly don't know how I'll feel if she continues in that vein."

The bishop thought for a few moments. "You know, Scott—I've been told that, generally speaking, when a person begins to lose his or her faith and testimony, it begins with some transgression on the person's part. It could be a sin of omission or commission. Could be something as simple as neglecting to study scriptures, or pray. Or it could be something more deliberate, such as sexual sin or drinking, drugs, and so forth. Do you have any reason to believe Marybeth's slipped into any of those things?"

Scott's face was miserable. "Not that I know of," he said slowly. "Except for what I already told you—about her not wanting to say the prayer, or go with me to the temple. I assume she certainly wouldn't be saying personal prayers, in that case, although maybe I shouldn't assume anything. I doubt she's been reading the scriptures, as I mentioned. I certainly am not aware of any big sins of commission. She's pretty honest and straight-forward about things—like she was about the wine. I think she'd just come right out and tell me if there were—you know—someone else."

"Probably there isn't anyone else," the bishop comforted. "I just need to ask, to try to understand the full picture. Do you think Marybeth would come in and visit with me?"

"Maybe she would. If only to request that her name be stricken from the records." Scott bowed his head, and covered his mouth with his hand. Finally he looked up, and his eyes were red and wet behind the glasses. "I want an eternal family, Bishop. I thought Marybeth and John and I had a chance at that."

"Try not to despair, my friend. Maybe you still do."

There was one other difficult interview that week, and the bishop decided it might as well be another lunch meeting. On Saturday, he tracked down Jack Padgett at one of the automotive supply stores over which he was the area manager. He found him in the Anniston store, roundly criticizing the store manager for not displaying a set of advertising posters for the newest automotive stereo systems to best advantage. He glanced away from the manager when the bell on the door jingled and he caught sight of his bishop coming toward him, frowned and lowered his voice as he finished his harangue. The store manager quickly removed the posters from their place and hustled them toward the front of the store, his ears red as he said, "Be right with you, sir," to the bishop.

"No, no—I'm just here to invite Mr. Padgett out to lunch," the bishop assured him. "How about it, Jack? My treat?"

"Uh—sure," Jack said, quickly packing up his briefcase. "Travis, I'll be back in three or four days," he called to the man with the posters. "I'll expect to see those changes implemented."

"Yessir, they will be," the man promised.

"What'll we eat?" the bishop asked, as they emerged onto the sidewalk. "What's your favorite food, Jack?"

Jack shrugged. "Whatever. Doesn't matter."

"Barbecue? There's a good place not far from here."

"Sure." He trudged along like a condemned prisoner, his demeanor a far cry from that of the gum-chewing, over-confident man he had once appeared to be. "You know Anniston, do you?"

"My mom and sister live here," the bishop replied. "How about we take my car, and I'll drop you back here? It might be easier than following me." *And*, he thought to himself, *you won't be tempted to "accidentally" get lost along the way.*

"Okay."

Jack said little more until they were seated and awaiting their orders. The aromas of pit-barbecued beef and pork and rotisserie chicken with hot and sweet sauce was making the bishop's mouth water. He and Jack had both ordered the all-you-can-eat ribs with coleslaw and fries, buttermilk biscuits and honey. He would repent later. He would have salad for dinner. He would not tell Trish what he had eaten. Unless, of course, she asked.

"So, have you seen Mel lately?" Jack asked in an offhand manner, glancing off to the side as if the answer didn't really matter much to him.

The bishop nodded. "She was at church, last Sunday. She's doing pretty well, I think—just lonely."

"Why don't they let Andi go back home? Poor little kid, none of this is her fault."

"I totally agree with you there. And I'm trying to do everything I can to get her back with her mother. I'm not sure, but I may be asked to attend a session with the judge who has jurisdiction over the case, and if I'm allowed to speak, I'll certainly recommend that Andi be allowed to go home."

"I guess it'll be a cold day in hell before I get to see her again," Jack grumbled. "By now, she's probably convinced I'm the big, bad wolf, anyway."

The bishop refrained from reminding Jack that it was his own violent and impatient behavior toward his wife that had brought about his banishment from his family.

"Where are you living now, Jack?" he asked. "Last time we talked, you were pretty tired of that rooming house."

"Got a little studio apartment in Gadsden. It's not much bigger than the room I was in, but it's at least private. Not that I'm there, much—it's just a place to sleep and keep my clothes."

"It's not home, is it?" the bishop murmured, thinking how much he would hate being denied access to his home and family.

"Guess I don't deserve a home," Jack said, his voice low and bitter. "Looks like I forfeited that."

"Things can change. You can change, I'm sure of it. How are your counseling sessions going?"

"Oh, fine, if I liked being verbally poked and prodded and made to repeat things three different ways and talk about things I'd rather keep to myself. Not my idea of fun."

"Pretty unsettling, huh?"

"Putting it mildly."

"It's tough for all of us to face our weaknesses and mistakes, I know that."

"Not supposed to have weaknesses," Jack muttered, almost too low for the bishop to hear.

But hear, he did. And he had learned from past experience that Jack most often spoke the truth in such undertones.

"Not have weaknesses? Why not, man? Because you were a Marine? I know they do a great job in their training, but I never heard that they perfected people!"

Jack twisted his head to one side again, as if he were hoping to see their server appear with a laden tray and save him from this uncomfortable conversation.

The bishop decided to give him a short break. "Looks like your stores are doing well," he commented. "I see their ads in the papers."

Jack nodded. "Doing okay," he agreed. "In spite of doughheads like that Travis you just saw. That guy doesn't know a car horn from a cow horn."

The bishop grinned. "I expect you can teach him a few things, and work on lessons in patience along the way."

"That may be more than I can handle."

"No worries. I fully believe patience is a skill that can be learned, with practice. Some folks are naturally better at it than others, but that's true of all skills. Just hang in there, friend. Stay with the program."

Jack nodded. They both knew the bishop wasn't just speaking of Jack's career.

He stopped at his sister Paula's house before heading back to Fairhaven, taking advantage of the chance to visit her and their mother, who lived with Paula. He found the two of them watching a Lawrence Welk rerun on television in the plant-filled family room behind the kitchen.

"Son!" exclaimed his mother happily, and her joy made him feel guilty for not having visited for too long.

"Hey, Mama," he said, kneeling beside her chair to give her a hug. "How're you doing?"

"Good," she said emphatically. It was one of the few words she had mastered since the stroke that had changed her life two years earlier.

"She's doin' real fine, aren't you, Mama?" commented Paula, smiling. "We have us a fine old time watchin' the TV shows she used to like, don't we? The other day we were lookin' at Perry Mason, and she figured out who done it before he did. She pointed and said, 'bad one,' just as plain as anything. And she was right."

"Good job," he said, squeezing his mother's good hand. "Mama always was pretty sharp about people. Speaking of that, Mama—a week or so ago I drove out into the country and looked up a lady who used to come to church way back when we first joined. I bet you'll remember her—she remembers you. It was Hazel Buzbee."

His mother nodded slowly, and a corner of her mouth turned up.

"Old times, huh?" he said. "Want me to tell Hazel hello for you?"

She nodded again. "L-love," she enunciated carefully.

"Give her your love?"

She nodded.

"I'll do that. Know what she wanted me to bring her? A sweet potato pie. I said I would."

"Oh, that's what Trish wanted the recipe for, is it?" Paula asked. "I found it. I'll just send it on home with you, then."

"Thanks, Paula. That'll be great. Yep, Hazel said her oven doesn't work, and she'd been craving that pie. I'll tell you what, though—she about scared the daylights out of me. I was knocking on her door, and all of a sudden she came around the corner of the house toting a shotgun, yelling at me that whatever I was selling, she didn't want any!"

There was a sound from his mother, and he looked at her quickly. The sound was laughter, bubbling from deep inside, rusty but unmistakable. It did his heart good to hear it, and he and Paula joined in.

"So, was Hazel always like that?" he asked. "Kind of feisty and outspoken?"

His mother's head nodded again.

"What're you doin' in town, Jimmie?" asked Paula. "Reckon this isn't a regular visit, or you would've brought along the family."

"You're right, this is an extra little visit I get to sneak in because I had to meet a fellow here from my ward. I'm trying to encourage him to keep up his counseling sessions so he can overcome some spousal abuse issues and get back together with his family."

Paula raised her eyebrows. "Didn't know you grew that kind in your church," she commented. "Everybody I've met seems so nice."

"You know, most are, nice that is. This guy must've had a pretty rough upbringing himself, plus he was a Marine, and seems to think because of that, he always has to be tough and show no weakness, or something. I'm really hoping he can beat this thing—instead of beating his wife." He sighed. "We sure had a good upbringing, didn't we, Sis? Daddy was such a good man, and of course, Mama's the best."

"You're right on, there. Daddy was the kindest man I ever knew. He never spanked us kids—well, at least, not us girls. Don't know about you, Jimmie."

"Once, that I remember—and I well deserved it. But he couldn't bring himself to spank very hard, even then. And he hugged me afterward, for the longest time. And he was real good to you, wasn't he, Mama?"

She was nodding again, and both eyes were watering.

"I'm sure you must miss him," her son said softly. "I know I do."

CHAPTER EIGHT

"IT REQUIRES A CONSTANT LABOR"

D
ad, this is like really weird," Tiffani said as she took her place in one of the upholstered chairs across from the bishop's desk in his church office. "I mean, why can't we just do this at home? How come I had to have an appointment, like just anybody?"

"You hit the nail on the head, Tiffi. Just like anybody. I know it must feel weird, as you say, but the fact is, I'm your bishop as well as your dad—and frankly, I consider it a great honor to be able to interview my own daughter in these circumstances, just like I would anybody else."

"Yeah, but you know me too well. I can't hide anything from you."

"Do you have anything to hide?"

"No, but if I did, it sure would be hard."

"Well, good!" her father replied, with a broad grin. "Let's always keep it that way, okay?"

"Okay, cool—so can I go, now?" She made a playful move as if to leave.

"Not on your life, kiddo. Now, Sister Shepherd, I under-stand from the records, here, that you're soon to have your six-teenth birthday."

She giggled. "You know it's next Thursday."

"Ah, yes, so it is. So you'll be advancing to the Laurels class. That's wonderful. And are you preparing to take your driver's test?"

She rolled her eyes. "You know I'm taking Driver's Ed."

He frowned. "Who's Ed, and where are you taking him? Is he a nice guy?"

"Dad! You're being as silly as I am. I thought this was sup-posed to be a serious interview."

"Tiff, I reckon I feel a little strange, myself, though I've given you many an informal interview at home."

"You have? When? I don't remember any."

"That's because they were just daddy-daughter chats about how your life was going, and how you were feeling about things."

"Those were interviews? I thought you were just interested."

"I was. I am. More than ever. So let's just have one of those little chats now, and we'll call it an interview, okay?"

She gave him a look that plainly said, *Okay. If we must.*

"So how's school going?"

"Fine."

"Keeping up in all your classes? Not feeling overwhelmed? Getting along with your teachers? Making friends with good kids? Feeling safe and secure in the school environment?"

"Let's see. Yes, keeping up; yes, overwhelmed in sewing and geometry but plugging along; yes, teachers are all okay except Miss Leonard in keyboarding—she's too serious and prissy—um—what else did you ask?"

"Friends? Feel safe there?"

"I have friends. I mostly run around with Claire, as you know, and sometimes with Lisa Lou and some of the other kids from church. And Vanessa—you know Vanessa Rogers—I've known her since fourth grade. Oh, and a girl named Jenny Daniels, who just moved here last year. She's nice. I'd like to ask her to come to church with me, but I haven't had the nerve, yet."

"I see. Well, that would be a good thing. Just pray to know when and how to approach her. How about boys?"

"What about boys?"

"Well, as you know, when you turn sixteen, there may be some young men who are aware that you might be allowed to go out on group dates. There may be a line forming down the block from our house by Thursday afternoon. I just wonder what to do about it."

"Oh, right!" She smiled, but shrugged. "Honestly, I don't know anybody right now that I'd want to go out with. Not anybody special, I mean. I'm not like Lisa Lou, who's in love with somebody new every Monday morning."

He smiled. "And I'm glad of that. I'm sure I wouldn't be able to keep up with Lisa Lou. Who's her current favorite? Is she still sweet on Elder Rivenbark?"

"Oh, she wrote about fourteen letters to him, and sent I don't know how many batches of cookies and stuff, but she's only had one little thank-you note, so I don't think she still has much hope, there. I can't see them together, anyway."

"Hmm." The bishop couldn't, either—and he had figured that Lisa Lou's crush on the good-looking, handicapped missionary would perish of its own weight, sooner or later. "I see."

He took a different tack. "Tiffani, what are some of the goals you have set for yourself—either in conjunction with the Young Women program, or on your own?"

She wrinkled her nose, as if this were a difficult question. The expression so reminded him of Trish, at Tiffani's age, that he nearly laughed. Tiffani didn't really resemble Trish a great deal, either in coloring or in feature, but every now and then, an expression or a gesture appeared that was so very Trish-like that it caught him off guard.

"I—let's see. I want to get good grades, so I can go to BYU after I graduate."

"BYU's a long way from home," he said. "Lots of other good schools closer by have fine institute programs, with quite a number of LDS students, and you wouldn't have to travel so far."

She fixed him with a look. "Dad—are you being an overprotective father, again?"

He winced. "Yep. Sorry. Go on. You were saying . . ."

"BYU. And, in the meantime, I want to learn to quilt. I mean, real pieced quilts, not just tied ones."

"You do? I'm surprised. You don't seem to be enjoying your sewing class all that much."

"It's not at all the same thing. Well, I mean, you have to use the sewing machine for part of it, but not all. I like hand-sewing, like embroidery and stuff. And I love quilts, because they're so friendly, and cuddly—and colorful, and creative and all."

"That's great. What else?"

"Um—I do want to get married someday, but not for a long time. I think I'd like to work a while first, at something I really enjoy."

"Any idea what that something might be?"

"Maybe teaching kindergarten. I just love little kids Mal's

age. They're so sweet and real and honest, and I think it'd be fun to give them a good start in school. And I'm really into stuff like making bulletin boards and teaching aids and all that. And maybe, someday—I haven't told anybody else this, Dad, so you can't say anything—someday I'd like to write children's books."

She waited, watching as if for any flicker of doubt from her father.

"Tiff, that is so neat," he told her. "I can see you doing that, I really can. You read so much, yourself—you always have—that I'll bet you've developed a good feel for stories that kids would like. Go for it!"

She looked down, pleased and embarrassed.

"What else?" he prodded. "Any particular spiritual goals?"

"I want to get ready for the temple. Nana loves the temple so much, and you guys do, too. It makes me want to go. And, maybe, I'm not sure—I might want to go on a mission."

"That'd be wonderful, but it's not a decision you need to make right now. Preparing for the temple, though—that's something you can be doing, right along, by studying your scriptures, going to Seminary and your Sunday meetings, having personal prayer every day, and living according to the commandments the Lord has given to help us be happy."

"Yeah. Seminary's neat. I like Brother Warshaw a lot. He's a good teacher."

"How're you doing with your personal prayers and scripture reading?"

"I do them—almost every day. Sometimes I forget, or fall asleep before I do them, but most often, I do."

"I'm so glad, Tiff. Do you have a testimony of the Lord Jesus Christ?"

"Sure—I've always believed in Him. You and Mom taught

me to, all my life. Mom used to read me stories about His life from that big Bible with the pictures—the one that was Grandpa's. I've always felt like Jesus was real, and alive, and I know he died for my sins and was resurrected, so we all will be, too. There's a lot I don't know about the gospel, and the Church, but I'm learning, and I do believe in it. So—don't worry."

He smiled. "I'm not worried, honey. I'm really grateful for you, and your testimony. You just keep doing what you should, and it'll grow to be a strong and sure faith that you can stake your life on. Now—is there anything in your life that you should tell your bishop about? Any problem that hasn't been resolved?"

"Huh-uh, I don't think so. Except—look, Dad—I know I've been kinda grumpy, lately—like last week about that stuff that went on at the football game. I don't know why I acted like that. I don't even like Angie much—and I don't always like the way T-Rex behaves, either. There's no call for me to be taking up for them. So—I'm sorry if it seemed like I was."

"I knew you didn't like what happened. But I confess, I was a little confused about how you acted. Then your mom reminded me that young people often feel kind of lumped together as if they were all the same, so that one gets blamed for another's misdeeds, and naturally they get a little defensive and take up for themselves—and each other—when they think they've been attacked. I didn't mean to attack. It was just that one isolated behavior I reacted to."

She nodded. "I knew that. It just felt—well, like you just said. Like we were all being criticized or attacked for what Angie did."

"I think we understand each other, sweetie. Thank you. Now—could we have a little prayer together before you go?"

"I guess. Do you do that with everybody?"

He shook his head. "No, but when I feel a prompting to, I do. And I feel a prompting now."

"Okay—go ahead, then."

"Let's kneel by these chairs, shall we? And Tiff, would you go first, and express your feelings and goals to your Heavenly Father? And then I'll close."

It was a few long seconds before Tiffani's prayer began, and her earthly father noted a change in her voice as she expressed some of her deepest longings to the Father of her spirit. By the time she finished, there were tears, and her dad's voice wavered a bit as well as he expressed his love and gratitude for this daughter and asked for the Lord's protection and guidance as she went about the business of growing up physically, mentally, emotionally, and spiritually.

They stood up, and he wrapped his arms around her slight figure and held her tenderly for a moment. "The Lord knows and loves you, Tiff—and so do your mom and I."

"Thanks," she whispered shakily. "I love you guys, too—and Jamie and Mal. Even though I don't always act like it."

He grinned. "It's all in growing up. And you're doing that, just fine."

He was packing up his briefcase to go home for Sunday dinner when Sister LaThea Winslow sailed in and poked her head around the open door to his office.

"Bishop! Do you have a couple of minutes? I have the most wonderful news!"

"Well, sure, Sister Winslow. What news would that be?" He poked his own head into the clerk's office and sent an apologetic look to Dan McMillan, who was the last one there. Dan nodded, understanding that the bishop required someone else to be nearby for the sake of propriety when visiting with a sister alone, and went back to the desk chair he had just vacated.

"Well," began LaThea, perching on the edge of a chair as the bishop consigned his own weary posterior to another stint on polished oak. Maybe he should speak to Trish about getting him a cushion. "You remember my telling you about our son, VerDan, who's been attending the University of Utah? You won't have met him, yet, as he hasn't been home since the wards were combined, but he's decided to withdraw from school this semester and serve a mission! He just called last night and told us, and I am so thrilled! Harville and I have always hoped he would go on a mission, and encouraged him to, but of course it needed to be his own decision, so we haven't pushed. And now he's decided! He'll be flying home tomorrow, so I told him I'd hurry and make an appointment with you, so that you can get the ball rolling right away!"

"Well, well—that is good news," the bishop said, trying hard to remember anything he knew or had heard about the Winslow boy. There was nothing—only the impression he had that all the Winslow children had flown the nest. "How old is— uh—VerDon?"

"VerDan, Bishop. He was named for his two grandfathers, N. Verd Winslow and Daniel D. Compton. That would be of the good Comptons, of course—the pioneer stock—not the ones who came to Salt Lake later, from South Dakota. We're not at all related to them. Oh—and he's twenty."

"A-ha. I see." He had never heard of either family.

"Anyway, VerDan's ready to commit, and I'm so delighted I just couldn't wait to tell you, so you can start getting the paperwork ready for him."

"And I'll be delighted to get acquainted with him. If he's real anxious to get started with the process, I may be able to squeeze him in for an initial interview on Tuesday evening. Let me just check with Brother McMillan on that."

Dan McMillan assured him that he could probably shift the time of the bishop's last scheduled interview on Tuesday up by half an hour, to allow time for him to meet the young man, and this he duly reported to LaThea.

"Oh, Bishop, thank you. I knew I could count on you. I just want to strike while the iron—or the missionary—is hot, if you know what I mean."

He wasn't entirely sure he did. "Do you feel that—uh—VerDan—might change his mind about going?"

"Oh, no, not really. It's just that sometimes, you know, young men get cold feet if things drag on too long. I just know that VerDan will be a great missionary. He's a very confident, well-spoken young man, and he comes of great missionary stock."

"Well, I certainly look forward to getting to know him. Thanks for coming in to share your good news." He stood and came around the corner of the desk to offer his hand to her, but she stayed put.

"There's one other thing I wanted to run by you," she stated. "And that's about the ward social coming up in November. I've decided on a feast, based on the Jewish Feast of Booths, or

Tabernacles. That's a harvest festival, and I thought it might be really interesting to incorporate some of their ideas into our own harvest celebration."

The bishop thought so, too. He sat back down. He could say one thing for Sister Winslow—her socials were unique and interesting enough to bring everyone out. The first ward party, a celebration of ward unity among ethnic diversity, had been a rousing success that people were still talking about. There had been a ward barbecue and a swimming and ice cream social during the summer. Then, in September, plans had changed from a square dance to a special fast day followed by a ward prayer service and dinner, the proceeds of which had been sent off to Humanitarian Aid specifically for the needs of the September eleventh victims.

Now, in October, they were looking forward to something LaThea called a Trunk-or-Treat party on Halloween. They were to have a chili supper and a pumpkin-carving contest (with some of Ralph Jernigan's pumpkins), after which the families—in costume, of course—would repair to the parking lot, where car trunks would be opened (also decorated inside) to allow trick-or-treating from car to car instead of the more dangerous practice of house-to-house begging in their various neighborhoods. LaThea had admitted that this last had not been her original idea; her sister's ward in Bountiful, Utah, had done it last year with great success.

"Tell me more about this festival," the bishop invited.

"I'm still studying about it," LaThea confessed. "But I know the Jews used to build little huts or shelters, each family making their own, and use foods of the harvest. I have a vague idea about asking the families in our ward each to come and construct a little booth or hut in the cultural hall. It could be a tent, or something made of corn stalks, or cardboard—just any-thing—as long as it's their own, and their family eats together there. I'll let you know more when I've figured it out—but what do you think, so far?"

"I think it sounds great!" he told her. "What does your com-mittee say?"

"Oh, well, you know—I haven't had a chance to run it by them, yet—but they'll go along with whatever I decide. They always do."

The bishop raised his eyebrows. Did they have a choice? He wondered. LaThea had a powerful way about her. He also won-dered, in fact, how much of VerDan's decision to serve a mis-sion was his own, and how much might be attributed to his mother. Perhaps on Tuesday night he'd be able to get a feel for that.

On Monday afternoon he drove straight from work to the Rexford home, having called ahead to say he wanted to visit with the husband and father, Tom Rexford.

Tom met him at the door, frowning in anticipation—or dread—of whatever might have occasioned this visit from his bishop. He was neatly dressed, at least, in a checked, long-sleeved shirt and chino pants, and his hair was combed, and the bishop took heart from that. Tom, in the past, in warmer weather, had received him in shorts and an undershirt, sprawled in a lawn chair in the backyard from which he didn't rise, to greet or to bid goodbye to his visitor.

"How're you doing, Brother Rexford?" inquired the bishop,

sticking out his hand and expecting it to be shaken. It was, with a fair degree of heartiness.

"Aw, I'm good, Bishop. How're you, and yours?"

"We're just fine, thank you." The bishop moved into the Rexford living room, which was paneled in knotty pine and sported several framed photographs of T-Rex in his football uniform, as well as a clock face on a painted slab of wood featuring what appeared to be a flock of geese rising from a marsh. Red and black checked upholstery on the sofa and two chairs contributed to the general effect, which was warm and cozy but totally masculine, as far as the bishop could tell. Where was Lula's influence in this house? Maybe in the kitchen, or bedrooms? Well, probably not in the one she shared with Tom, he amended—and certainly not in T-Rex's.

"So, Bishop, what brings you out this evenin'? Checkin' to see have I got a job, yet?"

"Um—no, not at all, Tom—although my visit does have to do with employment. No, I'm here to invite you to accept a calling in the ward."

"Aw, no, Bishop—there's nothin' along that line I'd be good at. I'm no teacher or leader or nothin'."

"I think there is something you'd be good at, and apparently the Lord agrees with me, since he confirmed my prayer about you pretty powerfully. He wants you to be the ward employment specialist. I'm sure you know you folks are not the only family affected by all the changes that have taken place around here in the last couple of years. A number of our people are having trouble finding jobs. The stake puts out a list of job openings that come up in the area, and it's updated pretty regular. Your job would be to try to identify who needs work and what kind, and what they might need to do to train or retool for a new position, and try to match them with possible openings. You'd be working with the elders quorum president and the high priest group leader, visiting people with them and just doing whatever you could to help. Will you accept this calling?"

Tom Rexford studied the paneled wall across from him as if waiting for writing to appear there to instruct him how to answer. Finally he pulled his eyes away from this contemplation and asked, "I wouldn't hafta give a talk or nothin', would I?"

"Not if you didn't want to," the bishop assured him. "This could be a kind of behind-the-scenes, one-on-one kind of calling. Just casual, helpful phone calls or visits with folks you've mostly known for a long time. You'll know how to be sensitive to their feelings and how to gauge what somebody might be good at."

"Well, Bishop, I thank you for your confidence in me," Tom began, shaking his head. "But I ain't been any good at finding myself a job, so I don't rightly see how I could be of much use to other folks."

"One other thing, too," the bishop continued, ignoring the negative tone in Tom's answer. "You'd be the first to see the job list as it came through, and if something showed up with your name on it, so to speak, you'd be able to check on it, right away."

"Wal, wouldn't that be unfair to the other men?"

The bishop leaned forward and looked him straight in the eye. "Your family deserves your support just as much as anyone else's," he told him. "Circulate the list to others, of course, in a timely way—but don't hesitate to apply for anything of interest to you, as well. That's all I mean."

Tom chewed on the idea—literally, it appeared, as his jaw and lips worked as though he were chewing a wad of bubble gum or tobacco, which the bishop felt sure he was not—and finally said, "Wal, reckon I could give it a try. S'pose I owe it to you, Bishop, you been good to us, with T-Rex, and Grandma's funeral and all."

"It would be a great help, Tom. We've been trying to handle it in the bishopric, but we have plenty of other things to see to, and if we could count on you to carry this, we'd feel better about things."

"All right, then. I'll do it."

"Thanks so much, Brother. The Lord will bless you for it, I know. Now, we'll be sustaining you next Sunday in sacrament meeting, and we'll try to set you apart right after the block that same day. Lula and young Thomas can come in to the setting apart, too. In fact, I believe we'll be able to ordain Thomas a priest at the same time, since he's been attending his meetings much more regularly than he used to. Well, I'll be going now—unless there's anything I can do for you folks?"

"No, sir, thank you. Boy thinks a lot of you for goin' to his games, though. Wanted to tell you that."

"I can't get to all the out-of-town games, but I sure enjoy seeing him play when they're at home. He's a powerhouse, isn't he?"

Thomas Rexford cracked a smile. "He is that, ain't he? Don't know where he gets it from, but he's got a lot of grit, all right."

"Should help him get into college."

"Hope he'll do that—a man needs all the schoolin' and trainin' he can get, these days."

"That's the truth. Thanks again, Brother Tom. Have a good evening."

He climbed into his truck with a sense of great satisfaction.

"Yes!" he exulted. "Thank Thee, Father! Please bless Brother Rexford for this decision, and help him carry out his duties well. Bless his family that they may have all their needs met and their testimonies increased."

To his knowledge, this was the first church calling that Brother Tom Rexford had ever accepted. He didn't know how Tom felt about that, but he felt wonderful.

CHAPTER NINE

"ALL THOU SEEST AMISS IN US"

VerDan Winslow, tall and handsome as his parents, as might be expected, strolled into the bishop's office fifteen minutes later than the time agreed upon, and reached across the desk to shake the bishop's proffered hand.

"Welcome, Brother Winslow," the bishop said cordially. "It's great to meet you. We sure think a lot of your folks here in the ward, and I was glad to hear that you're considering a mission. Have a seat, and let's get acquainted."

The young man ran the fingers of his right hand through longish brown hair streaked with blond, and tossed his head back to arrange it, then crossed one ankle over the other knee and looked expectantly at his new spiritual leader.

"I understand you've been at the University of Utah?"

"Yep." The young man nodded. "For two years."

"What are you studying?"

"Mostly general requirements, with a business emphasis."

"Great. And then you decided it was time to plan a mission?"

VerDan nodded. "That's about it," he agreed.

"Seems like this must have been a sudden decision," the bishop prodded. "Hadn't classes already started, this term?"

"Yeah, but I got most of my money refunded. I needed a break from school, and from Utah, and I figured a mission would be as good a thing to do as any."

"I see. Why'd you figure that? Is a mission something you've always planned on doing?"

The young man shrugged, smiling lazily. "Well, off and on, I'd thought about it. You know, like every good little Mormon boy. But the time never seemed right—till now."

"Okay. Help me out a little, here, if you will. Why does the time seem right, now, so suddenly that you dropped your classes and came home? What's your motivation for wanting to serve a mission, other than needing a break from school?"

"Uh, well—you know—I think it's a cool idea to go out and help people, and stuff. Lots of my friends have done it, and they said it was a great experience. I guess I could develop some skills along the way, you know? Leadership skills, getting along with people, stuff like that. And probably by the time I got back, I'd have a better idea of what I want to do with my life—for a career, I mean. Right now, I'm not sure, and it seems dumb to spend a lot of money and effort on school when I'm not sure where I'm heading."

"So you see a mission as a kind of stopgap? A time to get your head together and figure out what you want to do afterward?"

VerDan shrugged. "Sure. And Dad and Mom—especially Mom—want me to go, and I think it'd be a good thing to do, too."

"Uh-huh, I see. How do you feel about the Church, VerDan?"

"The Church? It's cool. It's good. I was in a good student ward at the U. We had lots of fun activities, and a great bishop."

"That's good. What was his name?"

"Huh? Um—Bishop Vale. Ronald Vale. He's a history prof."

The bishop wrote that down. "Fine. And what was the name of your ward, and your stake? I'll give them to Brother Perkins, so he can have your records transferred here."

"It was—um—the Twenty-fifth? No, the Twenty-sixth Ward, I think. I've got it written down in my scriptures at home. I don't remember the stake, but I'll call you with it."

"Okay. VerDan, how do you feel about the Savior, Jesus Christ?"

VerDan looked surprised. "Um—good. Good, of course. What do you mean?"

The bishop looked steadily at him. "Bear me your testimony."

"Um—well, I—um—know the Church is true. I know God lives, and Jesus is His Son, and all. Joseph Smith was a true prophet. I love my family and friends. In the name of Jesus Christ, amen. Is that what you wanted me to say?"

The bishop smiled at him. "What I wanted to hear were your true and honest feelings about the Lord you would be going out to represent and teach about if you were to be called on a mission. You may be aware that the Brethren in Salt Lake are calling for better-prepared missionaries with strong testimonies, ready to go out and really testify to the truth. Now, let's talk for a few minutes about your moral preparation, all right?"

VerDan raked his hair with his fingers and tossed it again. "Sure," he said in a small voice.

"One of the first things we need to establish about a prospective missionary is his moral worthiness," the bishop explained. "You'll need to be absolutely truthful with me about these things. There've been far too many young people go to the MTC, or even out into their mission fields, and then they've found themselves stricken with guilt over unconfessed sins. Often, they have to come home, and that can be a sad and embarrassing situation. It's far better to take care of any unresolved problems ahead of time. I'm sure you can understand that."

The young man nodded. His eyes were round and apprehensive. *Oh, boy,* thought the bishop. *I think there's something there. Help me, Father, to be sensitive and understanding if there is.*

He began to question VerDan, who answered all his inquiries with the replies any bishop would wish to hear. He was morally clean, he didn't have any unresolved sins or misdeeds, he didn't smoke or drink or do drugs, he was honest in his dealings with others, he honored his priesthood, he supported the leadership of the Church—everything sounded fine. Why, the bishop asked himself, didn't he feel that the boy was being totally honest with him?

"Do you have a girlfriend, VerDan?" he asked, smiling.

"Oh—not really," VerDan said, shaking his head. "Just dated around, you know. Lots of cute girls in my ward."

"I see. Well, I'll tell you what—let's get your records transferred here, and you start filling out these papers. You'll see that there are some health and dental exams that need to be taken care of, as well as other forms to complete. So you go ahead and start on these, and we'll talk again soon, all right? Thanks for coming in. It's a pleasure to meet you, and I'll look forward to getting to know you better."

"Okay. Thanks!" VerDan stood and took the papers. The

bishop stood, too, and watched the young man saunter out of the building. He shook his head. Something was definitely not right.

Thursday, Tiffani's sixteenth birthday, dawned bright, but with a haze that burned itself off by noon, leaving a gloriously blue sky as a foil for the yellow and orange leaves that still clung to twigs and branches. Tiffani's father remembered the morning of her birth—a very different day from this anniversary—laden with roiling clouds and an unremitting downpour that had seemed to drain all color from the day. Trish had had a difficult labor for many long hours, before the doctors had been able to coax the red, squalling little Tiffani into the world. Her father had chuckled at her fury, then melted as she quieted in his arms and looked up at him. He was sure she had looked at him, though Trish said the baby really couldn't have focused much. It was no matter what the weather was doing outside; inside, the sun was shining straight from heaven.

The joy of fatherhood had broken over him like a warm Caribbean wave, and in spite of all its realities and responsibilities, it hadn't disappointed him, yet. The fact that it was rather difficult for Trish to conceive only made the children more precious. If the two of them had had their wish, there would have been at least one other child between Tiffani and Jamie, and another in the five years between Jamie and Mallory. But he couldn't complain—wouldn't ever complain—not when thinking of the couples he knew who had no children—or whose child, like Ralph and Linda Jernigan's daughter, Jodie Lee, had been taken from them. As nervous as he might be about Tiffani beginning to drive and possibly to date, he was thankful she was alive, well, and able to do so.

In keeping with the family tradition, the birthday celebrant was allowed to choose a restaurant for dinner or a favorite meal at home. They discussed the matter a few evenings before the big day. Tiffani changed her mind several times about the food, but was adamant that she wanted Claire Patrenko to be invited along.

"Sure, that's fine. And what about Lisa Lou?" Trish asked.

Tiffani made a face of pained indecision. "I don't know," she said. "I like Lisa Lou, but she—she's kind of different from Claire and me."

"I know," Trish agreed. "But she's the only other girl in your age group at Church, and I'm afraid she'd find out and feel left out."

"Look, Mom—if there were fifteen girls in my group, would I have to invite them all?"

"Of course not. But there aren't. And I know Lisa Lou's already in Laurels, but you're right behind her, and the two of you have come up from Primary, together. I just think she'd feel hurt."

"Why would she have to know?" Tiffani muttered.

"She'd know," Trish assured her. "Sooner or later. Well, I'll leave it up to you, honey. I don't want to force you to invite her, but just think about it."

The bishop decided to put his two cents in. "You could think of it as an effort to help unify the ward," he said brightly. "You and Lisa Lou from the former First Ward, and Claire from the Second. Besides, I like for Lisa Lou to associate with you and Claire—it's good for her."

"Dad, she gets bored with us, 'cause we don't talk boys

nonstop, like she does. We actually talk about other things, sometimes. And she turns everything around to guys—clothes, movies, music, seminary, books, school, whatever—pretty soon it's guys, again. I'll tell you, the girl's got a gift for it! I'd think you'd be worried we'd take after her."

"Mmm. No, I have great faith in you and Claire. Why don't you play a secret little game, the two of you? Call it 'heading Lisa Lou off at the pass and changing the topic of conversation before she can take charge.'"

Tiffani rolled her eyes at the weird ideas of parents. "All right," she said, resigned. "She can come."

Trish frowned. "Honey, not if it upsets you. We don't want your birthday dinner to be ruined."

"Oh, really?" asked Tiffani dryly. "I could've sworn you were more worried about the feelings of dear little Lisa Lou than about mine."

"Well, we're not," Trish said quietly. "That is, we are concerned about her feelings, but we're more concerned about yours. So you do whatever you think best. Just let us know."

Tiffani huffed off to her room, and her parents looked at each other.

"That didn't go so well," her father murmured.

"Hm-mm," his wife agreed. "It's not easy, being sixteen."

"Or green," he added with a small grin.

"Who's green?"

"I think we are—we're greenies at parenting sixteen year olds, anyway."

"Just imagine—I was sixteen when we met."

"Maybe so, but you were way older than Tiff."

"In some ways."

"Way older," he insisted. "I'd never have fallen in love with a little girl like Tiff, so you must have been."

She smiled wisely at him. "But you were just a little boy."

"Not! I was wise and mature beyond my years."

"Right. About like Ricky Smedley."

"No way!"

"Way," she assured him, adopting the children's retort.

He wound his arms around her. "Of course, Ricky is a nice young fellow. Seems to have his head on straight, even if he does act a bit silly around the girls."

"Uh-huh. We were just their age, Jim, when we started liking each other."

"So, if Ricky Smedley starts looking fondly at Tiffi, I should worry?"

"Right now, I think he's looking fondly at Claire. But that can change."

"I never changed, once I started looking fondly at you."

"Well, you're remarkably loyal—and a little bit shy."

"That helped, too, I reckon. Wow, that's scary. It still seems like I had some pretty grown-up and serious ideas about you, even when I was too dumb to know how to express them. And Tiff and Ricky and Claire and Lisa Lou are that age, now. Do you think Tiff ever has such ideas about anyone?"

"Not that I know of—and not that I would know, anyway. I suspect she'll be pretty private about any romantic feelings she may have—unlike Lisa Lou, who tells everyone who'll listen."

"What were you like?" he asked. "Did you tell your Mom about me?"

"I didn't say much to anyone. Roxanne and Kathy were gone from home by then, but Merrie would've broadcast it nationwide, and teased the life out of me, and Mother and Dad would have been all concerned and curious, no matter who it was that I liked, so I confided in my diary and one or two friends. I suspect Tiff will be kind of like me, in that respect. Did you tell anybody?"

He shook his head slowly. "Well, ultimately, I told Mac. We didn't have very many secrets from each other. But he didn't tease, or spread the word. No, I kept you kind of secret and special. Mama may have suspected, but if Daddy did, I wasn't aware of it. We just didn't talk about things like that at home. I don't know if he ever knew who it was that sent me that first letter at the store."

"I was so scared you wouldn't answer."

"I almost chickened out—but that didn't seem polite, and even though you were a couple of thousand miles away, I really wanted to stay in touch, somehow. Glad I did, by the way." He ruffled her hair, and planted a kiss on her forehead.

"Me, too. Jim, I hope our kids find good people to marry! It makes such a difference."

"It makes all the difference," he agreed with a sigh, thinking sadly of those he knew whose choices may not have been quite so favored. "That, and *being* good people to marry."

He knew he needed to meet with Sister Marybeth Lanier, but beforehand he fasted, prayed, and visited with Stake President Walker about the situation, and, thus fortified, met with her on Wednesday evening, when the Church was not busy with auxiliary meetings. His second counselor, Sam Wright, busied himself in the clerk's office adjoining the

bishop's. He left his hall door open, hoping it would seem inviting. Marybeth walked in promptly, smiled, and sat down.

"Well, I'm sure Scott's told you my position," she stated
brightly. "We might as well get down to business. I want my
name removed from Church records."

Bishop Shepherd looked at her for a moment, wishing he
had known her better before all this began. She was a slender
woman with fair skin and short, nearly black hair in a fringe of
bangs above blue eyes. She seemed younger than Scott, but it
was hard to tell.

"Sister Lanier, I was so sorry to hear about that," he began.
"Can we discuss your feelings a little bit? Why have you come
to this decision?"

"There's no reason for you to be sorry, it's nothing you or
anyone else has done. I don't feel at all sad about it—in fact,
I've never felt such relief. I simply don't believe anymore, that's
all."

"But you once did?"

She shrugged. "I thought I did. I tried to make myself, but I
was always uncomfortable with the notion of angels and gold
plates and visions and so forth. It always seemed a little like a
fantasy novel, to me."

"Did you ever make it a matter of sincere prayer?"

"Well, frankly, prayer's another thing I've never felt totally
at home doing. I mean, you know—talking to somebody you're
not at all sure even exists doesn't sound like the sanest thing to
do, does it?"

"So, you're not entirely certain that there is a God who
hears and answers prayers?"

"I'm pretty certain there's not."

"Many millions of people believe and testify that there is.

Does that make you wonder if you might be missing something?"

She shrugged again. "Not really. I wondered, for a while, but then I decided that most people don't really think for themselves, and simply believe what others who are more persuasive or have stronger personalities tell them. I've quit doing that. I think it's important to be intellectually honest with oneself."

"I see. You know, there are many very intelligent people in this Church—excellent scholars in every field you can imagine—who are still people of faith."

"That's their right, if they want to buy into the Mormon mindset, and see the world from that perspective. But once an honest person steps outside the box, so to speak, and begins to see reality more clearly, then he—or she—can't continue to be honest if he stays with an organization that represents something other than truth as he sees it."

"So I take it you reject Joseph Smith as a prophet?"

"I reject everybody who styles himself a prophet, from Adam and Moses right on down to the present."

"And Jesus Christ?"

"An interesting person. A thinking person, and a fine moral teacher, in his day. It's too bad he was killed so young, it would be interesting to know what more he might have said and how his ideas might have changed as his thinking matured."

"But he knew God, Sister Lanier! Knew, in fact, that he was God's Son. What was the source of his fine moral teachings, if not God, Himself?"

"Please don't call me 'Sister,' all right? We are not related. No offense, of course, I wouldn't mind if we were, but we're not. And I believe several authors and scholars have shown that

Jesus' ideas weren't his alone, but found earlier in other documents, Jewish and Greek and Egyptian."

"Could I possibly persuade you, Marybeth, to experiment once again with scripture and prayer? Do you recall the King in the Book of Mormon who prayed, 'O God, Aaron has told me there is a God, and if there is a God, and if thou art God, wilt thou make thyself known unto me, and I will give away all my sins to know thee'? Do you think you could bring yourself to try once again, to read the Book of Mormon and pray in that vein?"

"Book of Mormon! Trust me, if I don't believe the Bible to be of divine origin, why should I believe the Book of Mormon?"

"Because the whole purpose of its existence is to bring you—and everyone else—to a knowledge of your Savior and Redeemer, so that you can be enlightened and . . ."

"And what, Mr. Shepherd—saved? Now you're sounding like a Baptist. Don't want to do that, do we?"

"You know, Marybeth, you're closing off the windows to the greatest source of light and truth and intelligence and love there is. It saddens me to hear you talking like this—and I know it's breaking Scott's heart."

"Scott will survive. He's strong. Not strong enough, just yet, to see things as I do, but strong enough that this won't destroy him, so don't worry about us, all right? Now, I didn't come here tonight to argue, or to be persuaded to believe against my will. Haven't you heard the old saying? 'A man convinced against his will is of the same opinion, still.' The same's even more true of a woman."

"Of course it's true. And I couldn't convince or convert you any more than a barking dog could. But I know that the Holy Ghost could speak to your heart and spirit and confirm the truth of the scriptures to you if you'd sincerely study and sincerely pray and ask—first, about whether Jesus is truly the Christ, and the Son of God—and second, whether the gospel taught in this Church is true. You could know. Can't I get a promise from you that you'll try, one more time?"

She shook her head. "I don't think so. I respect your concern and sincerity, but I'm just not interested."

"Let me make you a suggestion, then. If the time comes when you feel down—that something's missing in your life—that things might not be just as you think they are, after all—will you promise me that you'll pray for help at that moment, in the name of Christ?"

"Oh—I don't know. Maybe. Maybe. I can't promise. Anyway, I'd appreciate it if you'd take care of the matter of my name removal in a timely way."

She stood. So did he, and he looked her in the eye.

"Marybeth, I want you to know that I know that there is a God, and that you're His spirit daughter, and He knows and loves you beyond measure. He wants you to know Him, and He's just waiting for you to turn to Him with a sincere heart and a real desire to know, and then He can bless you in ways you've never imagined, not the least of which is an increase in the intelligence, light, and truth which you admire and hold dear. I testify to you that He made and ordered the heavens and the earth through His beloved Son, Jesus Christ, who is your Savior. He knows your concerns and doubts and problems, your strengths and weaknesses, and He can work with you to make far more of your talents and abilities than you can do on your own. You and Scott and John are bound by eternal covenants and ordinances that will allow you to advance throughout the eternities, together as a family. I know there is forgiveness of sin, on condition of repentance. These things are real, Marybeth, and I testify of them to you as your bishop and your friend, and in the holy name of Jesus Christ."

She was looking at the floor, and her smile had vanished. Her voice, when it came, seemed diminished. "Well, I can't say 'amen,' but thank you, anyway. You've done your duty. Good night."

She walked quickly out the door, and the bishop sank into his chair, surprised to feel his hands trembling and his shirt damp with perspiration. He bowed his head. "Father," he prayed, "I know the things thou gavest me to say are true, whether Sister Marybeth Lanier knows it or not, and I thank thee for this knowledge. I pray thee to continue to strive with her and help her open her mind and heart to the truth. Please comfort and strengthen her husband according to his needs, and help him cope with this trial. Please protect others in our ward that they may not be affected adversely by Sister Lanier's attitudes. Help us all to be strong in the face of dissension. Bless us, Father, in our many varied situations and areas of need. We need Thee, every hour of every day." He continued praying, mentioning a number of ward members by name, until he was weary but calm, and able to lock the building and walk out into the cool night with his counselor, thankful for him and for that greater Counselor whose advice he so sorely needed each hour.

CHAPTER TEN

"THOU, WHO KNOWEST ALL OUR WEAKNESS"

Tiffani's birthday dinner, an expedition to her favorite pizza place, went off without a hitch, except for some eye-rolling on the part of Tiffani and Claire as Lisa Lou was describing her latest crush—a boy named Billy Newton at school whom she felt sure she could convert to the gospel because he was so nice. The bishop refrained from inquiring about the state of her recent affection for Elder Rand Rivenbark. For all he knew, there may have been a couple of other crushes between Rand and Billy. It was hard to keep up with the affairs of Lisa Lou's heart.

On Saturday afternoon, with the warmth almost approaching that of a summer day, the bishop took the opportunity (said opportunity having been pointed out to him by his good wife) to clean out the rain gutters and to give the lawn its fall feeding, so that by March it could spring to life and grow rapidly, thus affording him an early start at mowing. He couldn't wait.

Trish and Tiffani had gone shopping, leaving the two younger children with him, and he was contemplating inviting them for a clandestine trip to the Dairy Kreme for a milkshake when the two of them came running across the yard with obvious purpose.

"Dad, you've got company," sang out Jamie.

"It's that hamburger man," chimed in Mallory.

"Hamburger man?" he questioned, picturing a delivery of warm sandwiches.

"It's just me, Jim," came a deep voice, as Big Mac—Peter MacDonald—came around the edge of the patio and strode toward them.

"Well, hey, Mac! You're back. Are you here for good?" They shook hands warmly.

Peter MacDonald chuckled, and reached out to touch Mallory's cheek playfully. "Whether it's for good or not, in any sense of the word, varies according to who you want to ask," he replied. "My little Ruthie and I think it's for good, time-wise and otherwise, but Ruthanne and Petey aren't so sure on either count. But yes, we're here, and in the middle of arranging and rearranging all our stuff at the new place. Seems we should have got rid of about a third of it before we came. Man! What a job. In case anyone asks, I'm at the hardware store right now, buying picture hangers. What're you folks up to?"

"I've dutifully cleaned out the rain gutters, and still have to feed the lawn, but I was just contemplating a run to the Dairy Kreme with these two. Want to come?"

"Yes!" exulted Jamie, and Mallory jumped up and down.

Mac consulted his watch, then shrugged. "Why not? Sure—

haven't been to the Dairy Kreme in years. Is it still where it used to be?"

"Same spot, same great cholesterol specials. Shall we crowd into my truck? Trish has the car."

"Oh, let's take my car," offered Mac. "Room for all. Just excuse the leftover gum wrappers and junk in the backseat. Haven't cleaned it out since we arrived."

Mac's car was a nearly new Lincoln, shiny and elegant. The bishop surreptitiously checked the soles of his children's shoes for mud as they clambered into the back. The ministry in Atlanta must have paid well, he thought. He hoped the family wouldn't suffer a huge downturn in their personal economy by moving to Fairhaven.

"This is a cool car," Jamie said, as they floated along the streets.

"Well, thanks, my friend," Mac responded. "My wife picked it out, and she has pretty good taste, I guess. Now, what grades are you kids in?"

"I'm in fifth," Jamie said, "and Mallory's just starting kinder-garten."

"I can say it my own self," Mallory objected. "Kindly-garden," she repeated.

"Is that right? That's special, the very first year. My kids are so big, now. Petey's in eleventh grade, and Ruthie's in seventh."

"My sister's big," volunteered Mallory. "She's in eleventh grade, too."

"Good—they'll probably get acquainted! And we'd like to have all of you over, just as soon as we're settled in a little."

"Seems to me we ought to be the first to have you folks over, to welcome you home," the bishop said. "How about Sunday dinner, tomorrow? Could y'all come about three o'clock?"

"That's really nice of you, Jim, and it would save Ruthanne having to try to come up with something. I'm not sure we'll get to the grocery store before tomorrow for much besides bread and milk and lunch meat. But hey, buddy—hadn't you better check with Trish?"

"Ah, Trish's a good sport about things like that. Anyway, she always cooks a ton for Sunday—usually on Saturday, so it makes Sunday easier. She'll be tickled to have you."

"You *what?* For tomorrow? Four adult-sized people, with no notice? Jim Shepherd, you can't do these things to me! It's eleven P.M. What if I only have five pork chops? What if I've made five little individual tarts for dessert? What am I supposed to do, then?"

"Are we having pork chops? 'Cause I know how to disarm the burglar alarm at the store, and I could run over and get anything you need . . ."

"No, we are not having pork chops, lucky for you—we're having a nice, big pork roast. It's marinating in the fridge right now."

"But what about the tarts? Hey, maybe the kids would just as soon have ice cream."

"I didn't make tarts. I made two lemon pies, so we'd have leftovers. Jim, don't you get it? It's the principle of the thing! You know how I am—I have to plan, I have to have time to get ready for these things. I'm not one of your spur-of-the-moment entertainers who can whip up a gourmet meal in ten minutes using only ingredients from one shelf of the pantry!"

"Now, babe, be reasonable . . ."

"Oh! I absolutely hate it when you tell me to be reasonable. You're the one who hasn't been reasonable, expecting me to put a Sunday dinner for nine on the table when I was planning a simple family meal! And then you forget even to mention it until nearly midnight!"

Her husband retreated. "You're right. You're absolutely right, honey, and I'm very sorry. Mac warned me that I should check with you, first, and I didn't even realize what a big deal it would be for you. I just said, 'Oh, Trish's a good sport—ya-da, ya-da— it'll be fine.' Now, I see it isn't fine, at all. Tell you what—I'll call Mac first thing in the morning and explain. I have his cell number. So just relax, babe. We'll do it another time."

"No, we will not! You can't do that—can't take back a dinner invitation, when those poor people are barely here, and not even prepared to fix meals, yet. We'll just do the best we can. I'll bake some apples along with the roast, and do extra potatoes. I can add more stuff to the salad, and we have plenty of carrots and beans. What else? Let's see—I'll use my grandmother's china, and I'd better run check on the green tablecloth and see if that gravy stain came out. If it didn't, I'll have to use the beige one, but it's not as pretty . . ."

The bishop watched as his wife went into action. He followed her downstairs to the linens cabinet in the dining room.

"So, let me get this straight," he said softly. "Things are going to work out okay after all, but I'd just better be sure I don't pull this stunt again?"

"That's about it," she agreed with some asperity, and then turned to face him. "It's not that I'm not glad to entertain your friends. It's just that I—oh, Jim, you know how I am—I panic if I can't plan ahead and be orderly about things like this. Rolling with the punches has never been my favorite form of exercise."

He reached out for her, and after a brief hesitation she came into his arms, clutching the green tablecloth. "I'm so sorry, babe, I truly am. I don't ever mean to cause you panic or distress of any kind. I'm just so proud of your cooking—and of you, period—I like to show you off a little. I'm sorry I threw you for a loop—whatever that means."

She leaned against him. "You know, if you came in and said, 'Trish, we need a couple of dozen sandwiches out here for these hungry people, I'd just go to work and make sandwiches. But Sunday dinner should be special. Not that I believe in working much on the Sabbath, but I like to get it done ahead of time and just put the finishing touches on it on Sunday. And these people—you know I don't know them as well as you do—but I know they're city folks, used to really nice things—and I just can't relax unless I've done my best to make things nice as possible here."

He tilted her chin up and looked into her eyes. "Seems like I've heard this somewhere before," he remarked. "Or something very much like it—when your folks and Merrie were coming to visit. Remember? You worked yourself ragged, and everything was perfect, but it didn't need to be. They just wanted to be with you. You're not feeling inadequate, somehow, around Ruthanne, are you?"

"Well, of course I am! She's way more sophisticated than I am. Where's she from, anyway—wasn't it Charleston? Someplace where manners and etiquette and style are really important, and see, if we come across like country bumpkins, what will she think of the Church? That we're all just as ignorant and provincial as she's been told?"

He looked at his wife in consternation. "Are appearances really that important?"

"It's not just appearances—it's how we really are. It's—well, yes, appearances are important, to some people, and I think Ruthanne's one of them."

He shrugged. "I always thought she was a pretty nice gal."

"Of course you did! That's because she has lovely manners and knows how to put you at ease. Manners are based on graciousness, and graciousness is based on being truly nice and warm and kind, even to people you regard as your social and spiritual inferiors."

"Then you're about as gracious as they come, sweetheart, because you make everybody feel at ease and welcome here, and you're super-nice." He frowned. "But it's me, isn't it? I'm the one that's ignorant and provincial. I'm sorry, honey. I'll try to be on my best behavior around her. Mac knows me about as well as anybody—he and I've been buddies practically since we were little kids. I reckon he's attained a degree of polish that I don't have, but I think he still likes me. But you, honey—you could entertain the queen. You're all spit-polished and shiny-faced and elegant. Sorry I'm not."

Trish shook the green tablecloth across the dining table and examined it in the light of the chandelier. It apparently passed inspection, because she tugged and straightened it so that it could shed any wrinkles from being folded. Her lips were pressed together. Finally she spoke.

"Jimmy, I'm so sorry. I'm not criticizing you—you're wonderful. The best man I know. I don't know why I say things like that. I'm probably just—hormonal, or something."

"It's okay, babe. I know my limits, and in matters of social niceties, they're pretty constricting. Listen, we'd better get to bed. I've got early meetings in the morning."

"You go ahead. I'll just see to a few things, then I'll be up."

"Want to have prayer here, then?"

"Sure, I guess."

They knelt beside two of the dining room chairs. He prayed. He had intended to ask Trish to be voice, but somehow he didn't want to risk having her refuse. Maybe he would feel too much like Scott Lanier in that case. He already felt properly chastised and smarting.

During sacrament meeting, looking out over the congregation, he prayed silently for discernment regarding the members and their needs. He was still troubled by the fact that he hadn't known of Marybeth Lanier's loss of faith. What else should he know? His eyes paused here and there, lingering on the faces of Tom and Lula Rexford and young T-Rex. Lula's face looked strained, and Tom was frowning. He knew they were struggling financially, but they were proud people, especially Tom, and reluctant to divulge the extent of their troubles or to accept help. He spotted Tashia Jones, sitting with the Arnaud family, smiling happily just to be present. How could he help her achieve her goal of baptism, and obtain the agreement of her spirited grandmother, Mrs. Martha Ruckman, who had been his fifth grade teacher? Mrs. Ruckman was a devoted Christian and a member of a largely black congregation whose pastor she greatly admired. It was a wonder of some magnitude that she allowed her young granddaughter to attend services here at all.

The Jernigans were in attendance, and he was glad to see that they had made the effort to leave their fortified home and mingle with the Saints. They needed strengthening and reassurance and fellowship to help combat their fears and paranoia.

Next to them sat the stalwart and faithful widow, Sister Hilda Bainbridge. Elderly and nearly blind, she nevertheless remained cheerful and willing to help in any way she could. *Constant* was a word that came to mind when he thought of Hilda. Ida Lou Reams sat beside her. Another stalwart, this beloved Relief Society president combined love and unstinting service in her approach to her calling, all the while worrying that her lack of formal education would hinder her abilities. He knew she yearned to attend the temple, but her non-LDS husband, Barker, had so far not agreed to that privilege for her.

His eyes rested on the Smedley family, and he was grateful for their dependability and goodness. Likewise, he appreciated Brother and Sister Warshaw, and the Birdwhistle family, who always brought a smile to his face when they trooped in and made their way to the front. By common consent, the same row was always left vacant for them, even if they were late, because everyone knew they would be coming—usually all twelve of them, from Ernie and Nettie, the parents, and elder children Pratt, Moroni, and Rebecca on down to two-year-old baby Emma. Pratt would be mission age, soon. The bishop promised himself a visit to them in their log home in the foothills. An expedition to church was a matter of a sixty-mile round trip in two vans, and they fell under the jurisdiction of the Fairhaven Ward because it was logistically easier for them to travel there than to other wards in the stake, and because they had always done so. He worried a bit about the children because of their isolation—home schooled and unable to attend many of the youth activities of the ward, they depended upon each other for company and upon their parents for most of their education, temporally and spiritually. He hoped it would be adequate, in both cases. The Birdwhistles came as close as anyone he knew to being self-sufficient, independent pioneer types. He just hoped the children would be sufficiently socialized that they would be able to fit in the world, go on missions and to college without undue stress. These times weren't exactly the same as the days in which a young man would be allowed to build a cabin on the edge of his father's land and take a wife from a neighboring family and settle down to raise a crop of children of his own. The Birdwhistles grew hogs, corn, and soybeans as well as children, and did well enough, but their land wouldn't support all seven of their sons, even if the boys wanted to fol-low their father's line of work, and the price of land and farm equipment was escalating. He hoped plans were in progress for the boys—and the girls, for that matter—to get training in areas of their interests.

Melody Padgett slipped in just after the sacrament had been passed and sat alone by the exit that led to the Primary area. He wished she would associate more with the sisters of the ward. She was so embarrassed by her family situation that she was even more reclusive now than she had been when Jack had deliberately isolated her. He would speak to Trish, see if there was any way the sisters could help her.

Scott Lanier kept his head down, apparently studying the Sunday School lesson he would shortly present. He sat against the wall, and the rest of his pew was occupied by Frankie and Gene Talbot and their family. He needed to speak to Scott— maybe just after the block of meetings, unless someone else claimed his attention. He looked at his own family. Trish sat on the same row that her family had most often occupied when she was a teenager. Mallory was beside her, then Jamie, who appar-ently was drawing pictures to amuse his little sister. Tiffani sat on the aisle, looking the other direction, almost as if intentionally distancing herself from the family, her gaze toward the opposite wall. He sighed. He knew that children needed to go through a process of separation from their parents, and that it was often a painful process for both sides, and he dreaded it—hoped it could be as painless as possible. He looked at the pew he had always tried to occupy when he had been secretly in love with Trish—slightly closer to the front than hers, and to one side, so that he could turn a little sideways and steal glances at her.

His heart swelled with love and gratitude that the Lord had blessed him with Trish for his wife—a blessing for which he had hardly dared hope. He only wished he understood her a little better, so that he would never cause her stress or worry. The niceties of polite society were so foreign to him that he rarely gave them a second thought. His code of dealing with others sprang from the gospel—each was your sister or brother, one of God's children, and deserved to be treated as such. Sometimes, when you were in a position of authority, such as that of a parent or a boss—or a bishop—you needed to be firm, but always you were loving and kind and helpful as possible. If you offended, you apologized; if someone apologized to you, you accepted the apology graciously. Beyond that, the finer points of propriety and etiquette were a mystery to him. He supposed he ought to read up on such things. Trish seemed to know them, innately, and that was good—hopefully she could pass them along to the children—but he kept unwittingly bumping his head against a barrier he didn't even know was there. Of course, he knew to open doors for women, and to allow Trish to precede him into a room or a row of seats, and he knew he should walk on the street side of the sidewalk, and begin eating with the outermost fork when there were more than one—but beyond that, he was clueless. It was something to look into. A bishop should know his manners.

He caught Scott Lanier's eye after priesthood meeting and beckoned to him.

"Could we have a word?" he asked, and Scott nodded, accompanying him through the halls to the bishop's office, his head down, avoiding speaking to people they passed.

"Well, you know I met with Marybeth," the bishop began, as they seated themselves in the two chairs before his desk.

"Thank you for trying," Scott said. "I know it must not be easy for a bishop to hear of someone's testimony disintegrating like that."

"It is tough," the bishop agreed. "But I'm only her bishop. I can't even imagine what it must be like for you."

Scott started to speak, then covered his face, and his shoulders began to shake. The bishop waited, a lump in his own throat.

"I'm sorry," Scott said at last, clearing his throat. "I'm fine, except when someone's kind to me," he added, trying to muster a laugh.

"Don't even apologize. This is certainly worth crying over, even more so, in my opinion, than if Marybeth had died."

"She is dying, spiritually. She's so—changed. So—I don't know—flip, or something. And she seems so unconcerned about my feelings on the matter, or John's."

"Boy, that must be hurtful. She told me she feels relieved. I imagine that's pretty common, for folks who have felt that the gospel is restrictive—just a bunch of rules to hold people back from enjoying life. She's apparently never had a testimony of prayer, and now she isn't even sure that God exists. I tried to get her to say she'd make one more attempt to read the Book of Mormon and pray about it, and about the existence of God and the divinity of Christ—but I'm sorry to say she declined. So then I suggested to her that if the time ever comes that she feels depressed, or that something's missing in her life, she should pray for help in that moment, and she'd get an answer. That was all I felt I could say, at that point. I'm sorry, Scott, that I wasn't able to make much difference. All I did after that was to bear my testimony to her, and she thanked me and left, with the request that we take care of her petition in a timely way. I'm so sorry. But I haven't given up, either. Let's continue to pray for her and to love her, and see how things go."

Scott shook his head. "She's adamant about leaving the Church," he said sadly. "And I don't think she has a clue what she's giving up."

"I didn't feel that she's had a really clear understanding of the gospel, either, which is strange, considering how bright a woman she is."

Scott nodded. "She is bright, but she tends to see things through her own preconceived filter, if that makes sense. She's perfectly capable of filtering out truths that don't support her view of things. It makes it hard to reason with her, quite honestly. I'm just beside myself, Bishop, trying to see what I should do next."

"I would be, too. I know one thing's extremely important—and that is for you to remain staunch and strong in your own testimony, and not allow yourself to be pulled away into her view of things. You can't help her up the ladder unless you're a step above her and reaching down, if you'll excuse a homely and simple example. So you just keep on keeping on—attending your meetings, whether she comes or not, and I guess she won't—studying your scriptures and praying for the strength to deal with this problem. As I said, we'll continue to pray for Marybeth, too, but as someone said, you can't pray away another person's free agency. So you might concentrate your prayer efforts on finding out what the Lord wants you to do in this situation, and asking His help and comfort. That would be my suggestion. He'll lead you, I know He will."

"He already has, Bishop, to a great extent. In fact, that's the only reason I'm not completely around the bend. But it surely is hard. It's like having my whole right side cut away. It's tough even to find topics for conversation that don't have any bearing on the Church, or on spiritual matters. The gospel's so much a part of my life and thinking that sometimes I'm at a loss for what to say."

"That'd really be uncomfortable," the bishop agreed. "And you probably already know that things aren't just as simple as my removing Marybeth's name from the Church records as she's asked. I looked into it. If she's really intent on doing as she says, she'll need to write a letter to me, expressing her desire. Then I'll need to complete a Report of Administrative Action form and forward the file to the stake president. Before I do any of that, though, I'm obligated to write a letter to Marybeth, detailing the consequences, informing her that if she goes ahead, she will forfeit the effects of her baptism and confirmation and have her temple blessings revoked."

Scott shook his head, as if he couldn't believe what was happening, then looked at Bishop Shepherd with pain-filled eyes. "There won't need to be a church court, will there?"

"Not unless there is evidence of a serious transgression that would normally result in a disciplinary council. That failing, such a request is basically a self-excommunication, though it won't be called that."

"That's good. She'd be very resentful if that happened. She feels like she's done the honorable thing by talking to you."

"I see. Well, I hope she'll be willing to read and consider the letter I'll be sending her. Maybe seeing the consequences actually spelled out will have an effect on her and cause her to reconsider. I hope so." He sighed. "But I reckon we'll just have to see how things develop. Personally, I'm still hoping for a miracle!"

"We could use one," Scott agreed, with a ghost of a smile. "Thanks so much, Bishop. You're a good man."

"Well, you're another. Let's not give up just yet, okay?" He patted Scott's shoulder as the man nodded and headed out the door.

CHAPTER ELEVEN

"CALL LIFE A GOOD GIFT,
CALL THE WORLD FAIR"

The dining room was resplendent with Grandma's floral china, Trish's best silver, crystal goblets of water, an arrangement of fall leaves and flowers, and tall white tapers. A smaller, round table had been pressed into service for Jamie and Mallory, and it sported an orange cloth and a ceramic Halloween witch among the leaves. That left seven people at the large table, which could accommodate eight with the extra leaf inserted, so there was plenty of room, but the younger MacDonald child, Ruthie, sitting dutifully by her mother, cast occasional longing glances at the smaller table.

Twelve was such an in-between age, pondered the host. Not yet a teenager, but not as young as Jamie, Ruthie didn't really fit with either age group. She sat with downcast eyes as Trish brought in the pork roast surrounded by succulent baked apples.

"Ah-h," approved Mac. "That looks terrific, Trish! So much better than bread and milk."

Trish laughed. "I'll just get the vegetables and rolls, and then we can start," she said, and her husband followed her out to the kitchen, saying he would help. While there, he told her what he had observed about Ruthie, and she regarded him worriedly.

"Oh, rats! It didn't occur to me that she might rather be with the little ones," she said. "She does kind of seem young for twelve, doesn't she? I'll ask her. She'll be embarrassed, but at least she'll have a choice."

She did ask, and Ruthie's voice was tiny when she replied, "I don't know. It doesn't matter."

"Well, we can easily move you over there if you'd rather," Trish said warmly. "I'm not real sure that when I was your age I'd've wanted to listen to the grown-ups' conversation. But you're probably way more mature than I was."

Ruthie laughed a little. "No, I'm not," she asserted, and glanced up at her mother, who shrugged and indicated that the choice was up to her. Ruthie pointed shyly to the children's table, and the bishop sprang up to move her chair and place setting.

"Cool," muttered Jamie under his breath, as if ashamed to approve too heartily of anything a girl might do, but Mallory was more vocal.

"I'm so glad you're eating with us! Do you like to play Barbies?"

Ruthie smiled at her. "Sure," she answered. "Which ones do you have?"

The bishop happened to be looking at the MacDonalds' son, Petey, a tall, altogether-too-handsome boy who looked at Tiffani with an expression that obviously communicated the thought, *Kid stuff. I'm glad we're beyond all that.* Tiffani smiled slightly and looked down at her plate.

The bishop invited Mac to bless the food and immediately

wondered if it were some unknown breach of etiquette. He threw a hasty glance at Trish, but she was merely bowing her head along with everyone else. He hoped that was a good sign. Mac's sonorous voice expressed thanks for the kindness of friends and the good things of life and the boundless love and mercy of Christ Jesus, in whose name he prayed. Amens seconded his sentiments.

"Your daddy prays funny," whispered Mallory to Ruthie.

Ruthie scrunched up her face and leaned over to reply. The bishop leaned over, slightly, to hear. "It's because he's a minister," she explained.

"What's a min'ster?"

"Don't you have one in your church?"

"Huh-uh, do we, Jamie?"

"Hush, silly—we have a bishop instead, and that's Dad."

"Do you got a bishop in your church?" Mallory inquired.

"No, but we have four in our chess game," answered Ruthie, which sent Mallory into a peal of giggles.

At the adult table, there was much appreciation for Trish's dinner, and praise from Ruthanne for the beauty of the table and the antique china. The bishop hoped Trish's insecurities might be salved. There were questions about the local schools, and Petey inquired about the basketball team and which teachers were good, which questions Tiffani was pleased to answer.

"If you want, I'll introduce you to some cool people," she offered, and her father suddenly realized what prestige it would bestow on Tiffani, to be the first to know the handsome new boy in school. He hoped the prestige (and Petey) wouldn't go to her head. He also hoped she wouldn't introduce him to Lisa Lou. A follow-up thought reminded him that she wouldn't need to—Lisa Lou would undoubtedly take care of that little matter herself.

"It went okay, didn't it, babe?" he asked a few hours later as he and Trish walked hand-in-hand on their customary Sunday evening stroll through the neighborhood.

"I think so," she said slowly. "I couldn't tell what Ruthanne really thought, and that's because of her impeccable manners and good breeding. I think she was kind of testing me when she asked what organizations I belonged to around here. And you know me, I'm not much of a joiner. I mean, the Church and the PTA keep me plenty busy. But she seems to be a very social type—in a Christian way, of course."

"So what'd you tell her?"

Trish smiled. "I said I belonged to one of the oldest women's organizations in the world—the Relief Society."

"Good for you. Was she impressed?"

"Who knows? She hadn't ever heard of it, so I told her a little about our aims and ideals. She seemed interested, but that was probably just her politeness. I also told her that I have friends who go to garden clubs and Bunko groups and reading groups and charitable organizations, and that I was sure there would be some Christian women's groups she might enjoy. I'll ask Muzzie; she's more of a joiner and socialite than I am. She'll know."

"Did you think Tiff was impressed with Petey?"

"Of course. He's a hunk! I hope she wasn't too impressed, though."

"Me, too. I'm just not ready for her to begin the Lisa Lou routine."

"She never will. She's not that type."

"Keep telling me that."

"I do, all the time. Try to keep it in mind."

"So, did you get the impression that Ruthanne wasn't too excited to be here?"

"Again, she would never say so—to me, a local. Mac probably hears plenty about it, though."

He looked at her. "Are you saying her beautiful manners stop short of applying to her hubby?"

"Who knows? He'd tell you about that, if he told anybody. I think it's neat that your friendship has continued all these years. He's a genuinely nice guy, isn't he?"

"He's a very good guy. Very sincere about his work in the ministry. Loves the Lord, loves his family. I'd sure like to see him accept the fullness of the gospel, and take that family to the temple—but I just try to trust the Lord to lead him. He does a lot of good; maybe he's needed where he is, for now."

"Well, we'll try to be good examples. And hope that any other members they meet will do the same."

Late Wednesday afternoon, a few brethren from the elders quorum went with Bishop Shepherd and Robert Patrenko out to the fortified farm of Ralph and Linda Jernigan to harvest the last of his pumpkins. Brothers Smedley and Patrenko—and, of course, the bishop—had been there before, and so were accustomed to the rituals with the dogs, but the other two brethren were openmouthed to witness that everything they had heard about the Jernigan homestead was true. Ralph joined them as they tramped out to his field with wheelbarrows, sporadically scanning the skies as if watching for enemy aircraft.

"Glad you can use these pun'kins," he said, straightening up from cutting a large one from its vine. "Didn't have the heart to harvest 'em this year, you know. Didn't feel it was safe to be out here, either, of course. Still not sure—but I guess the Lord'll bless you—you're on His errand."

"So, Ralph, are you gonna come and see what folks create with these, tomorrow night?" asked Brother Smedley.

"No, no. Halloween's not a good time to be out and about. We don't observe it. Hope all goes well, though. Suppose it's a safer thing to do for the kids, than having them wandering house to house. Never did feel good about that."

The bishop remembered with great fondness his and Big Mac's forays into the neighborhoods of their childhood, their collection sacks old pillowcases, their costumes thrown together at the last moment—overalls stuffed with newspaper, an old straw hat, or a worn-out sheet with holes for eyes and mouth. There had been no worry about crime, only an admonition from their parents to watch for cars and frightened dogs, and to be responsible around smaller kids. It was sad to think that those times had vanished. Sad that children, and their parents, had to be wary of so many awful possibilities in the world, even here in Fairhaven. Of course, some things had changed for the better. There was more comfort, amazingly advanced technology, and the Church was growing by leaps and bounds, and temples being built so many places that he couldn't even begin to name them all. Wonderful things—but still, the loss of innocence was a high price to pay.

The Halloween dinner and Trunk or Treat party was a great success, as all of LaThea's productions had been. The best costume prize went to Lehi and Limhi Birdwhistle, who came as Tweedledum and Tweedledee from *Alice in Wonderland*. Privately, the bishop felt the family should have won a prize just for making the effort to show up, all more or less in costume. Second prize was awarded to Brother Tuapetagi, who walked around barefoot in a lavalava and a lei, with a headdress of some kind of exotic leaves. There were the usual witches and princesses, clowns and superheroes. Even T-Rex put in an appearance, not dressed as a dinosaur, but, predictably, clad in his football gear, with smears of black goop under his eyes and several colorful bruises painted here and there. Some of them may have been genuine; the bishop wasn't sure.

Trish had seen to their costumes, of course, saying that it was incumbent upon the bishop to join in the fun. She had turned under the sleeves and pant legs of an old black suit of his, so that it appeared several sizes too short for him. He wore a loud, crooked tie, a round straw hat, white socks, and his ugliest old hiking boots. Jamie was a young hayseed with overalls and a checked shirt, and Trish and the girls wore gingham aprons and huge matching bows in their hair.

The pumpkin-carving contest had begun before the rest of the party, to give the artists time to complete their masterpieces and not miss out on the other activities. Some were funny, some beautiful or scary, but the bishop's personal favorite was a tall, narrow pumpkin that wore a turban squash on its head and looked remarkably like a certain near-Eastern terrorist whose picture was constantly in the news.

After the dinner and the judging, the group moved to the parking lot, where car trunks and the backs of pickups had been decorated and lit according to the owners' whims, and the children went from one to the other collecting goodies. The bishop had only one pang of sorrow at the party, and that was when he thought how much little Andrea Padgett would have enjoyed being there. He hoped she was doing something enjoyable with her foster family, whoever they were. His heart was saddened, thinking of Melody opening her door and handing out candy to other people's children. He wondered if she even bothered.

The bishop took Friday afternoon off from work, picked up Trish and her glossy brown sweet potato pie, and the two of them collected Ida Lou Reams before heading off to Hazel Buzbee's place. He hoped Hazel remembered that this was the appointed day for their visit—but then, if she didn't, what difference would it make? Where would she go? It didn't appear that she ever went much of anywhere.

He had been sure that he could find the place again, and it only took correcting two wrong turns on red clay roads that all looked identical for him to get his bearings and arrive at the little greenish cottage.

"My land o'livin'," said Ida Lou. "She lives way out here, all by her lonesome?"

"She does that, and seems to like it that way," the bishop replied, getting out of the car to open doors for the ladies. He scanned the house and yard, interested to see that the garden had been tidied up and the ground plowed, ready for next spring's planting.

"Hello!" he called, then remembered Sister Buzbee's hearing problem and reached back inside the car to sound the horn a couple of times. It was a country tradition to announce your presence as soon as you could and not "sneak up" to the front porch and surprise people. He supposed the custom gave folks time to pull on a shirt or hide the jug of white lightnin' from their visitors.

Hazel heard the horn. She emerged from the house, peered carefully to see who was there, then came down the rickety steps to greet them, followed by her faithful hound.

"Well, I swanny! I didn't rightly think you'd remember, Bishop, but here you be."

"Here I be indeed, Sister Buzbee, and this is my wife, Trish, and Sister Ida Lou Reams, our Relief Society president. She wanted to come along, too. Couldn't let us have all the fun. How've you been?"

"Oh, I'm mean as ever. Is that my sweet potato pie I see there?"

Trish held out the pie. "I hope it's the way you like it, Sister Buzbee," she said.

"You have to yell, she's pretty deaf," the bishop told her, and Trish repeated herself a couple of decibel levels higher.

"Reckon I'll like it fine, if your husband remembered about the nutmeg," Hazel yelled back.

"Oh, he told me," Trish assured her.

"All right, then, y'all come on in. Iffen you don't mind, I'm gonna cut me a piece of this right now. Anybody else want some?"

They all politely declined, and found straight chairs to sit in while Hazel took her treasure to her kitchen table to serve her-self a generous slice. The front room had the three chairs they used, and one cushioned rocker that was obviously Hazel's accustomed seat. It also held a bed against one wall. The bishop recognized the high, lumpy look of it as a feather bed. His grandmother had owned one just like it. The small house smelled of kerosene and pork fat and old wood, but was scrupu-lously clean and neat. A small shelf on one wall held a clock in a wooden casing that had darkened almost to black over the years and a few books. He recognized a Bible and a Book of Mormon, and wondered if Hazel could see to read either of them, anymore. Two closed doors were located to the left of the bed, and he assumed they probably led to another bedroom and, since he hadn't seen an outdoor privy on the property, a bathroom.

Hazel came in and sat down with her pie and a cup of coffee, which she placed on a small table beside her chair.

"I done told you I drink coffee," she reminded the bishop.

"Yes, ma'am, you did," he agreed. She nodded, and put a forkful of pie into her mouth.

She frowned, chewed slowly, and swallowed.

"Now, I told you about the nutmeg," she said. "About how you cain't put too much nutmeg in the pie, for me?"

Trish leaned forward. "I only put a little bit," she said loudly. "Not more than half a teaspoon, honest!"

"Wal, no wonder I cain't taste it! Pah! I'm sorry fer yer trouble, honey, but no half-teaspoon of nutmeg's gonna give a whole pie the flavor I like! I'm real sorry, but I cain't eat this. Y'all just take it on back home with you—maybe somebody else'll want it." She took a sip of hot coffee.

The bishop looked at his wife, whose cheeks had grown very

pink. She opened her mouth to speak, but no sound came out. He had no idea what to say, certain that whatever he came up with would be wrong. Ida Lou came to the rescue.

"You know, Sister Buzbee, I reckon we've got ourselves a little messed-up communication, here," she said. "Now, you told Bishop that we couldn't put too much nutmeg in your pie, is that right?"

"That's what I told him, plain as day," Hazel agreed.

"And what you meant was that it just watn't possible to put too much in for your taste, because you like it so much, is that right?"

"Wal, yes, of course." Hazel frowned, her chin jutted out defensively.

"Well, see, I think the bishop took it to mean we shouldn't put in too much, because you didn't like it that well—and that's what he told Trish, here."

"I never said no such of a thang!"

"I'll tell you what. We're agonna make you another sweet potato pie, and it'll be plumb chuck-full of nutmeg. How's that?"

"Oh, I cain't ask y'all to do that. Jes fergit it. I'll git along 'thouten it."

"Tomorrow afternoon," Ida Lou told her. "It'll be here, you can count on it."

"I'm awfully sorry," Trish finally said. "It was just a misunderstanding. I really meant to make it the way you wanted."

"That's all right, honey, it weren't *yer* fault."

"It was my fault," the bishop owned. "I just didn't get the message right. We're sorry, Sister Buzbee."

"Wal, you're fergiven, I reckon. But I sure did have my mouth set for that pie."

"Tomorrow," repeated Ida Lou. "Just a few more hours."

The bishop managed to get in a little message regarding the Lord's love for all his people, and the hope that we have in Jesus and His atonement, which Hazel leaned forward and listened to hungrily.

"Are you able to read your scriptures still, Sister Buzbee?" he asked, nodding his head toward the shelf.

"Naw, I tell you, Bishop, I cain't make out the words no more. Now I wisht I'd committed a bait of 'em to memory, back when I could've done. Now, all I get is the Tabernickle Choir on Sundays. That's my church, and it does pretty well by me. But I'd be pleased to hear you read a verse or two when you come, iffen you don't mind."

"I'll be delighted to, no problem. Now, is there anything we can do for you, before we go?"

"Reckon not, iffen that thar pie's any indication," she said with asperity, but the bishop was learning to read her dry, cynical humor, and saw the tightening of the lips that meant she was teasing.

"Okay, now, Sister Buzbee, the Lord says we need to forgive poor fools like me," he scolded, grinning, and she leaned forward and slapped his knee.

"You're fergive, the both of ye," she told him, and they rose to leave.

Walking out to the front porch, Hazel looked Ida Lou up and down. "I do admire your dress, Sister," she remarked. "It's shore hard to get house dresses, anymore. Even the catalogs don't carry 'em much. Ever'body's gone to wearin' pants like a man, but I cain't cotton to that. Did you mailorder yer dress?"

"Well, no—to tell the truth, I made it up, out of some scraps of fabric I had on hand. I do love to sew."

"You done a good job. It's real purty. Wal, 'bye now, and y'all come to see me whenever you can, all right? Bishop, when can I expect you next?"

The bishop consulted the small calendar he carried in his pocket. Trish had tried to get him to buy a palm pilot, but he preferred his calendar. "How about a month from today— December first? I might get out here sooner, but that day, for sure."

"I'll plan on it," she agreed, as if her schedule were so full that she had to pencil it in. "You got the pie? Good—take it on home and feed it to whoever'll eat it."

They got the car turned around and headed back toward the lane before the laughter erupted. Trish began to giggle first, then Ida Lou, and then the bishop joined in. They laughed until tears formed, and then sighed from the relief of it.

"Babe, I am so sorry!" he gasped. "Honest, those were her exact words—you heard her—you can't put too much nutmeg in it! I never dreamed she meant the opposite! I wouldn't . . ." He broke off into another chuckle.

"That rascally old lady! For a second there, I wanted to smack her!" Trish confessed. "Isn't that awful? But it made me so mad, after I'd gone to the trouble to find a recipe and make it up the way I thought she wanted! Oh! I haven't been that mad in a long time. I'll have to repent, for sure, and make her another one, so nutmeggy it's bitter, if that's how she likes it!"

"She'll get her pie," Ida Lou said. "And you're not to make it, my dear. It's my turn. I'll make one in the mornin', and Barker and me'll ride out here and bring it to her. The pore little thing, I don't reckon there's much pleasure in her life, and her heart was plumb set on that pie. But, oh, my, that was funny! Trish, honey, your cheeks were that red, and your eyes were just a'snappin'! Now, let me make some notes as we go,

Bishop, on how to get back out here, 'cause I do want that pie to be fresh when we arrive!"

"Anybody want a piece of this?" Trish asked, looking at the pie in her lap. "It's going cheap."

The bishop offered his pocketknife, and they all munched sweet potato pie as they drove through the autumn afternoon. It was delicious.

CHAPTER TWELVE

"THE HOPE OF THINGS TO BE"

Bishop Shepherd was at work at Shepherd's Quality Food Mart on Tuesday afternoon when he was paged to the telephone by Mary Lynn. He gave her a questioning look as he entered the office, and she shrugged. "Some lady," she mouthed to him.

The lady was Mrs. Parkman, Melody Padgett's caseworker, inquiring if he might be available to attend the formal hearing regarding the possible return of Andrea Padgett to her mother.

"Yes, you bet I will," he responded eagerly. "Just tell me when and where."

"It's scheduled for Friday, November sixteenth, at eleven A.M. in Judge Williams's chambers. Her courtroom is being renovated, and the others are busy, but we're delighted that the judge feels this is important enough to go ahead with, that she's willing to hold it in chambers."

"A lady judge?"

"Yes, sir. Judge Teresa Williams."

"Is she—that is, do you think she'll be sympathetic to Melody's cause—and Andrea's?"

"I can't speak for her, of course, but she is known for being pro-family and fair in her judgments—and the fact that she's going out of her way to include this in a timely manner gives me some reassurance. Thank you, then, Mr. Shepherd, and we'll hope to see you there."

"I'll be there. Thank you."

He replaced the receiver. Mary Lynn flicked her brown hair over her shoulder and looked up at him. "That the case about the little girl who was taken away 'cause her daddy was abusive to her mom?"

The bishop sighed. Mary Lynn probably knew altogether too much. "That's the one," he agreed. "I'm really hoping the judge will allow the little girl to go home to her mother. I can't see any reason why she shouldn't."

"Was it you that reported the abuse?"

"No! No, it wasn't me. I was trying to head things off and get some help for that family before things had to come to this pass."

"Who narked, then?"

He regarded his secretary with interest. Sometimes her choice of words surprised him. He supposed it was the influence of television.

"Well, nobody's saying, of course, as it's all supposed to be confidential, but personally I think it was the day-care lady. Andi exhibited some pretty telling symptoms at her child-care center, and the lady got suspicious that things weren't just right with the family. She even discussed it with me, shortly before Andi was taken."

"Likely it was her, then. Hard to know what to do in a case

like that, idn' it? Whether you'll make things better or worse, I mean."

He nodded. "If somebody else hadn't notified the authorities, I might've had to, before long, and I reckon the results would've been about the same. But I'm glad it didn't have to be me, because it makes it a little easier, now, to try to counsel with each of the parents—they don't have their present misery to hold against me, at least. It's a sad situation."

"Got a lot on your plate, ain'tcha?"

"Oh, it varies from day to day. Minute to minute, sometimes." He grinned. "But it's good to be able to make a little difference, now and then. Help people out."

"That's cool. That you want to, I mean. That you care."

He did care, and that was why he called Melody right away.

"I have a good feeling about this, Melody," he told her. "And I'm planning to fast the day before the hearing, in case you'd like to join me. I'll invite Trish and Ida Lou and the brethren in the bishopric to do the same, if they can. I fully believe in the efficacy of fasting and prayer."

"I'll do it, Bishop, bless your heart, and thank you! I just don't think I could live through the holiday season without Andi. Halloween was bad enough. I just turned out the lights and pretended I wasn't home. I don't even know what she did, or anything! Sister Hallmark tried to get me to go help out at a shelter for battered women and children that evening, but I didn't have the heart for it. It's like, I don't know—like I still hurt too much, myself. Someday, though, I'd like to do that. When I'm stronger."

"Is Sister Hallmark seeing you regularly?"

"She sure is. Once a week, plus I can call her, anytime I need to talk. She's a sweet lady. And she's given me a couple of books to read, so I can maybe understand a little better what was going on in our family. You know what, Bishop? It just plain makes me sick and ashamed that I ever let things get to the point they did. I see, now, that I didn't have to take that kind of treatment! But I just kept making excuse after excuse for Jack, when he didn't deserve any of them."

"I'm glad you're sorting some of these things out. How do you feel toward Jack, these days?"

"Furious, that's how I feel! Mad as all get out. How dare he treat me that way! I didn't do one thing to deserve any of it. I can't believe I let him get away with it."

The bishop thought her anger was the most rational feeling he had ever heard her express toward her husband. It had taken a while, but all the hurt and fear she had experienced had finally morphed into anger and indignation, and he thought, in this case, that was probably healthy.

"I can't say I blame you," he told her. "Melody, what do you know about Jack's upbringing and childhood?"

"Now, Bishop—don't you go trying to get me to feel sorry for him, or even try to understand him, just when I'm working up a good head of steam!"

He chuckled. "No, I'm not trying to do that. It's just that it's part of my job to try to understand, literally, where he's coming from, and I wondered if you had any insights."

"Well, Jack's always been real closemouthed about his family and his childhood. I know both his parents are dead, and he and his brother don't keep in touch very often. He grew up in

Wilmington, Delaware, and joined the Marines about a year out of high school."

"Has he ever talked about his folks?"

"Not really. I used to ask him, but he never said much, except once he said, 'Look, they're not the best memories, all right? So let's drop the subject.' I didn't dare ask much more, after that. The only other thing I remember is that sometimes when we were buying something for Andi—a swing set or a playhouse, or something—Jack would say he wanted her to have the stuff he never had as a kid. So, I assume it wasn't a real happy situation."

"I see. Thanks, Melody—that helps some."

"Have you—seen Jack, lately?"

"A couple of times, to try to encourage him to stick with his therapy and counseling sessions. He isn't liking them, much. Other than that, I know that he's very lonely, and that he misses you and Andi and your home. He's working hard, but he's just kind of bitter and lonely."

"I don't reckon he gave you any kind of message for me?"

"No, he didn't—and frankly, if he did, I probably wouldn't deliver it, nor one from you to him. That'd put me in an uncomfortable kind of go-between position, which is not where I want to be. I will tell you that he seemed afraid that Andi would come to think of him as the big, bad wolf, I believe is the way he put it."

"I wouldn't make her think that. I've thought a lot about it, and I already figured out that it wouldn't be fair to her to poison her thoughts about her daddy. Even if I'd be tempted to, to get back at him! It just wouldn't be good for Andi."

"I believe that's wise of you. And I imagine the child services people are careful about that kind of thing, too."

"I sure hope so. But how can I know? I have no idea what that poor little thing thinks about either of us, or what she's been told."

"I know. But hopefully it'll only be about ten more days, and the judge will allow her to come home. We'll pray for that, Melody. Okay?"

"We sure will. Thank you, Bishop. I'm sure grateful to you. By the way, I know now who it was that reported us to the authorities. It was Mrs. Marshall at the day care. Andi was acting funny there, and she suspected. I talked to her. She felt bound by the law to let somebody know, like you said. So I'm trying not to hold it against her. I suppose it did need seeing to."

"Probably so. Well—take care, all right? And try to believe that things will work out for the best, eventually."

"I hope and pray you're right on that."

So did he.

When he arrived home that evening, a smiling Trish flung her arms around him.

"Guess what, guess what, guess what?" she said with an enthusiasm more often seen in Tiffani or Mallory than in their mother.

"What, what, what?" he returned, squeezing her tightly, grateful for whatever it was that had made her so buoyant.

"Meredith called. She said that she and Dirk are trying to decide between a Noah's ark theme and Winnie the Pooh for decorating their nursery!"

"Merrie's expecting? All right!" He hugged his wife off her feet and spun her around. "That's great news!"

He thought of Merrie's tearful confession to him on her last visit to Fairhaven that she was unbearably lonely, rattling around in the lavish Phoenix mansion Dirk had built for her, while he spent nearly all his time immersed in his work. Apparently something had changed, and he was glad. Merrie had gone home with a determination to lay things on the line for her husband, letting him know that she needed his company and that it was time to start their family, which would be difficult to do if he were always absent.

There were so many lonely people, he reflected. Old and young, together or apart, too many suffered from isolation of one kind or another. It certainly was not a problem that currently afflicted him, however. He valued a few moments of privacy and solitude now and then. They were hard to come by—but he wouldn't want a calendar filled with them.

Tuesday evening was Home, Family, and Personal Enrichment meeting for the sisters, and after one setting apart and two temple recommend interviews, he kept his office door open in case anyone needed to slip in for a private word. The Relief Society was featuring a tasting table of pumpkin recipes, so he and his counselors were each brought a plate of goodies for their supper.

"This is a casserole that was baked in a pumpkin," explained Sister Rosetta McIntyre, the second counselor to Ida Lou, pointing to a rice and meat mixture. "This one's pumpkin soufflé, and that's pumpkin gingerbread. I sure hope you brethren like pumpkin!"

He smiled at her. "If we didn't before, I'll bet we will, after this. Thanks so much, Sister McIntyre."

He settled behind his desk with his plate of pumpkin delicacies before him and opened his scriptures, hoping for a chance to catch up a little on his reading, which had been neglected of late.

"Bishop?" asked a tentative voice. He looked up. The voice belonged to Connie Wheeler.

"Hey, Sister Wheeler—come on in," he invited.

The young woman slipped into one of the chairs across from him. "I'm sorry to interrupt your dinner—go ahead and eat. But I've just got to tell you our news!"

He smiled. He knew what the news must be. "What's that?" he inquired, anyway.

"We've been chosen by a birth mother, to adopt her baby when it's born!"

Sister Wheeler's face was glowing with excitement, though it also looked as if she might suddenly burst into tears.

"That's wonderful! When's the baby due?"

"In just two or three weeks. In her letter, she said she took her time choosing from all the prospective couples, because none of them seemed just right. Then one night she had a dream, and she saw the faces of a couple, playing with a baby in some grassy place like a park, and a voice said, 'These will love your child.'" Connie bent her head and touched a tissue to her eyes. "A couple of days later, the agency gave her three more couples to choose from, and she said she recognized us from her dream, even before she read anything about us!"

The bishop put down his fork. He had to swallow a lump in his throat, along with his pumpkin soufflé. "That's really remarkable, Connie. And a tribute to her faith, and yours."

"We're so grateful, and so excited! We aren't supposed to tell anybody yet—but I knew you'd probably know about it, anyway."

He smiled. "I just knew that Social Services called, recently, checking to be sure that I still felt you and Don were worthy to be adoptive parents. I figured something was in the works, and I'm glad to hear it is! Congratulations."

"Thanks, Bishop. We're driving to Atlanta this weekend to meet her and get acquainted. She lives near there. I'll tell you— one minute, I'm so nervous I can hardly stand it, then the next, I'm all calm and happy. And I feel such love for that girl! I sure hope she'll like us."

"Sounds to me like she already does. I'd say this is probably the beginning of a sacred partnership—one that was forged in the heavens, you might say."

"It really strengthens my testimony, and makes me know for sure that the Lord is aware of us, each one."

"Mine, too," he agreed, and after Connie left, he whispered a prayer of gratitude.

He returned to his reading, and had nearly completed one section in the Doctrine and Covenants before Sister LaThea Winslow peeked around the door jamb, knocking lightly.

"Bishop? May I come in?"

"Sure, Sister Winslow. Have a seat. How's everything?"

She pulled a paper from her purse. "Here's VerDan's bishop's name, and the name of his ward and stake at the U. He said you needed that, to start the mission process going."

"Well, good. Thanks. Yes, you see, since VerDan hasn't been

here in the ward, and I don't know him very well, I'll need to talk to his former bishop about his attendance and so forth. Plus, we need to have his records transferred here, so I appreciate you bringing this by."

She leaned forward eagerly. "So—what'd you think, Bishop?"

"About—VerDan? Well, he seems like a fine young man."

"Can't you just see that he's great missionary material?"

"Well, we surely hope he will be."

"Oh, it's in his blood, Bishop. He can't miss. His grandfathers were both wonderful missionaries, and on his Winslow side, his ancestors were notable missionaries to the British Isles, where their own people had migrated from. I kind of feel that's where VerDan will be sent, too, don't you think? That would be so appropriate. In fact, can you put a bug in somebody's ear to help that along a bit?"

"Well, one of the questions on the papers he took home asks about where he'd like to serve, so—"

"Well, but you see—*he* thinks he'd like to serve in Hawaii, or Florida, or the Caribbean. Someplace warm and sunny, you know? He doesn't care for cold weather. But he's young—what does he know? Once he's in place in the British Isles—preferably England—he'll feel the rightness of it, and go to work and serve a wonderful mission, just like his ancestors."

"Um, well—we'll have to see how the Brethren feel. Often the assignments surprise everybody, although it does seem that in some families, folks are sent to the same area over the generations."

"That's how it'll be for VerDan, I'm certain of it."

"Sister Winslow, has VerDan expressed to you his deepest feelings about serving a mission?"

"Oh. Um—let's see, what did he say when he called with the news? Something about how it was clear to him that the time had come for him to go. We'd prayed and prayed, you know, for a long time, that he would feel the need to go and serve, because we knew he was meant to, and we knew he'd be successful at it. But it had to come from him, Bishop. We didn't want to push him."

"Mmm—that's wise. Well, we'll go to work on this, Sister, and tell VerDan that I'm available to him. Anytime he might like to talk with me, I'll try to see him. And thanks, again."

"Thank you. He's a wonderful boy, you know. He always planned to serve a mission, during his growing up years. We used to ask him where he wanted to serve, and he'd always say, 'Disneyland!' Isn't that the cutest thing? He was such a doll."

The bishop smiled. He wished he could dispel the feeling that the California Disneyland Mission, if there had been one, just might have been well-suited to prospective Elder VerDan Winslow.

When he arrived home from the store on Wednesday, there were two letters for him on his desk in the corner of the dining room. One was from Elder Donnie Smedley in Brazil, and the other from President Walker, the stake president. He opened Donnie's first.

Dear Bishop,
Hi there. I sure hope everything's going good with the ward and that everybody is ok. Things are great here in Sao Paulo as far as the work goes, but

it sure breaks my heart to see the little street kids who run wild and beg for food or money. I'd like to pack them all up and send them home to my mom to raise but I guess she's got enough to handle with my bros. and sis.'s. Thanks for your letter. I'm glad to hear Elder Rivenbark's doing good in Cali. I don't know him real well, cuz he moved to town when I was a senior, and was in the hospital a lot and stuff, but he seems like a real nice guy. I've got some real promising contacts. One family, the Fernandes family, they're real good people and I think they'll be baptized. It's funny, it's like they already know the stuff we teach them, and we're like just reminding them of it. They're golden. Then we've got Ricardo, he's this young guy who drives a bakery truck and lives in a little shack behind some members' house. They let him live there cuz he brings them bread and cake sometimes. His family is all broken up and moved to different places, and he's lonesome. I think that's why he lets us come and teach him, but who cares why, as long as he does. He's a cool guy, and seems interested in what we tell him, but he sure loves his coffee and I hope he can give it up. He doesn't often drink other stuff, cuz he says he doesn't like the feeling of being out of total control of himself when he does. My new comp, Elder Wittenbeck, is a real greenie and scared to try to speak the language, so I get to do most of the talking. Anyway, that's what's goin on. My mom writes that you're a real good bishop, so I look forward to getting to know you better in five months! I really want to work hard, this last part of my mission. I don't want to be a trunk-sitter, if you know what I mean. Thanks for writing.

Your friend,
Elder Don D. Smedley

The bishop smiled. He looked forward to getting to know Elder Smedley, too. He wondered if the elder knew that the Jernigans were helping to fund his mission. It touched the bishop's heart to know that, and he hoped the missionary's heart would be touched as well. He didn't think the Jernigans were wealthy, by any stretch of the imagination. Ralph was retired from factory work and supplemented his retirement with the produce he grew, so the bishop suspected that it was a bit of a sacrifice to donate a goodly portion of Elder Smedley's financial needs each month.

The letter from the President Walker caused him a little concern. It requested a stake choir for conference in February, and suggested that each ward that had not already done so, should form a ward choir to perform in sacrament meeting on a regular basis, including a Christmas program. Then the choir director was to select several men and women to participate in the stake choir for February third. This request had come from the area authority, who would be presiding at the February conference, and President Walker would appreciate timely cooperation on the matter.

The bishop leaned back in his chair. The Fairhaven Ward had been remiss for some time in the matter of special musical numbers for sacrament meeting. The Primary children had sung for Mother's and Father's Days and Easter, and Claire Patrenko had played a rather impressive piano solo once, and other than that, they had gotten along with an additional congregational hymn between speakers. Did they have anyone in the ward with experience in directing or even singing in a choir? He had no idea.

"Trish! Hey, babe—who do you know in the ward who sings well, or does a good job directing music?"

Trish came in from the kitchen, drying her hands, and sat on one of the dining room chairs. "Well," she said slowly, "let's see. Sister DeNeuve used to be really good as Primary chorister, before she became Relief Society president. I don't know how she'd do with other age groups. What position are you needing filled?"

"Choir director."

"We're going to have a choir? Fun! I can't remember when our ward has ever had a choir. Are you sure you want to do that?"

He grinned. "Not at all. But President Walker has directed every ward to put one together, and to contribute some singers to a stake choir for February conference. So—help!"

She laughed. "Well, let's see. Tiff and I both sing soprano. We're not great, but we can carry a tune. There are a number of good altos, I hear them harmonizing in Relief Society, but I'm not sure who they are. As far as men go—I think Brother Detweiler is a pretty good bass, and last week, the Rivenbarks sat behind us, and I thought Brother Rivenbark had a nice voice. Who sings tenor? Hey, how about Brother Tuapetagi? I think he might. As for directors, I don't know. Better just make it a matter of prayer."

It made him feel good—confident, somehow—that Trish assumed if he made it a matter of prayer, the right person's name would be provided. It had happened that way already, of course, in several callings, while others he had puzzled over for some time.

"Thanks, honey. That helps," he told her, and extracted a copy of the ward list from his desk drawer. Trish went back to her dinner preparations, and he said a quick prayer for inspiration, then examined each name with music in mind. He would try to find a director, he decided, then put out an invitation for all interested singers to join the choir. It shouldn't be hard to get this thing going.

Half an hour later when Trish called the family for dinner, he was still contemplating names of potential directors. Practically everyone in the ward already had a calling, and it looked as if this would have to be an extra responsibility for someone. Who would be able and willing to take on something else? Or should he choose someone to be choir director, and release that person from whatever position he or she already held, and let someone else, possibly, double up? A number of folks already held more than one calling. Some had both stake and ward callings, though that was discouraged unless necessary. He went to the table in the kitchen pondering the problem.

Trish had made lasagna and salad. The children chattered about school and friends, while he was uncharacteristically preoccupied with his own thoughts.

Trish put a piece of hot garlic bread on his plate. "Who'll be the accompanist?" she wondered aloud, and he looked up, stricken.

"I reckon I just thought Sister Tullis would," he said slowly. "But maybe that's too much to expect, you think?"

"I don't know—you'd have to ask her. She is getting a little older, though, and she mostly plays the organ. You might want a pianist for this."

"For what?" asked Tiffani.

"We're going to have a ward choir," her mother informed her brightly. "Isn't that fun? You and I can sing soprano, right?"

"Sure, I guess," Tiffani said doubtfully. "So you're looking for a pianist?"

"Well, I reckon I obviously should be," her father said. "All this is kind of beyond my ken. I don't know who's good at what, musically."

Tiffani shrugged. "What about Claire?" she asked.

"Is Claire that good?" he inquired.

"Claire's great," she said staunchly. "She wants to major in music, and she helps to accompany the school choir. She'd love it."

"That's a thought," the bishop said. "In fact, that's a great thought. Thanks, Tiff." If Claire Patrenko, who currently held no position in the ward, could serve as accompanist, that would mean that Sister Tullis, or someone else, wouldn't have to double up. "So—who do you know who would make a good director for the choir?"

But that question stumped Tiffani, as well as her mother.

"Well," the bishop said with a sigh, "I reckon I'll have to be patient and wait to see what the Lord thinks on the subject."

CHAPTER THIRTEEN

"TOUCH AND HUMBLE, TEACH AND BLESS"

The next Thursday evening was set aside in the bishop's pocket calendar for home teaching visits, and he accordingly presented himself at the Forelaw home, earlier this time, in hopes of meeting the children of the family. Sure enough, there they sat in a row on the sofa, all scrubbed and shiny and in their pajamas, looking at him curiously with bright, china-blue eyes. The older two, a girl and a boy, were redheads, and the younger boy was blond.

"Hey, Bishop," Elaine greeted him. "I kept the young'uns up so you could meet 'em this time. This here's Katie, then Carter, then Arnie."

He shook hands with each of them, amused by their embarrassed smiles at being greeted in such a grown-up way. Little Arnie rolled over backwards on the sofa and tried to hide behind his siblings, and the bishop indulged in a moment of Peek-a-boo with him, which brought out the giggles.

"All right, now, y'all young'uns run jump in bed," their mother instructed in a voice that brooked no nonsense.

"Tell you what," the bishop called as they scampered away. "Next time I come, I'll bring a story for you."

"That's nice of you, Bishop. It's not necessary, though."

"Well, I like kids," he told her. "It'd be fun for me. I should've thought to bring one, tonight. So, how're you folks doing, Sister Forelaw? And is Sergeant about?"

"I'm here," came a deep voice from the kitchen. "Just eatin' a late supper, if y'all will excuse me."

"You go right ahead. So everybody's well?"

Elaine sat on the sofa, and the bishop took a chair. "We're all doin' fine, thank you."

"Wonderful. I brought you a short message this evening from the general conference that was held last month. There were lots of excellent talks, but I finally chose this one by President Boyd K. Packer, because his message struck a chord in me and was about something I hold very dear—the Book of Mormon."

Elaine nodded. He wanted to ask her if she had read the book, but hesitated to embarrass her if she had not. He decided to proceed as if she had. He spoke just loud enough that he hoped he might be heard in the kitchen, where there was an occasional clink of dishes or cutlery.

"As you know, the Book of Mormon is a second witness of the Lord Jesus Christ. It supports and sustains the Bible in its message that Jesus Christ really is the Son of God and the Savior of the world. In addition, it holds answers to so many questions people have about life after death, the Resurrection, the place of justice and mercy in obtaining forgiveness for our sins, and many, many more things. I know one of my favorite parts is in Third Nephi, where the Savior was appearing to the people on this continent after his resurrection and ministering to them and to their children. It never fails to touch my heart to read that. I always picture my own little ones among that crowd, and I can feel the great love of the Lord for all His children.

"People from all over the world bear witness to the truthfulness of the Book of Mormon, and the impact it's had on their lives. It's now been translated into sixty-two languages, and parts of it into another thirty-seven languages, with many more translations in progress. In fact, I read recently that it's second only to the Bible in the number of copies that have been published and distributed. In his talk, President Packer tells of his first successful attempt to read it all the way through. It was when he was on a ship, headed into war in the Pacific. He had decided that he would find out for himself if the book really was true, as he'd been told. He says he 'read and reread the book, and . . . tested the promise that it contained. That was a life-changing event.'

"You see, Sister Forelaw, the book comes with its own way of proving its truthfulness. Pretty neat, huh? Remember what it is? It's a promise in Moroni . . . that if we read it, and ask God sincerely in the name of Jesus Christ if it's true, then the Holy Ghost will manifest the truthfulness of it to us. Can't beat that, can we? That's what President Packer did, and millions of other folks, too. I did it, myself, when I was about seventeen, and I had a wonderful warm and peaceful feeling come over me when I prayed about it. I'd never felt so loved in my life—and I had good folks who loved me a lot. But this was different. This was Godly love—beyond my comprehension, but it sure was real, and it included a reassurance about the reality of that book. So I've known, ever since then, that the book was true, and I've loved studying it. I love the Bible too, and the way they fit together to provide a more complete picture of things.

"One amazing thing to me about the Book of Mormon is that Joseph Smith translated it in only a very short time—short enough that most folks would have a tough time reading it in the same length of time, let alone translating it from an unknown language! Joseph's wife, Emma, said that she sometimes wrote for him as he dictated from the plates, and he would always take up exactly where he left off after a break, with no repeated words. I know he could only do that through the gift and power of God, and I bear testimony that the book is a treasure and a gift, to lighten our burdens and enlighten our minds. Have you had any particular experiences with the Book of Mormon that you'd like to mention?"

Elaine Forelaw gazed at him as if bemused. "I—it's been a while since I studied it," she confessed. "I don't get a whole lot of time to read. But I remember I always had a good feeling when I read in it. To tell the truth, I never got all the way through it, but I know the part about Nephi and Lehi and those guys traipsing through the wilderness, being led by—what's the name of that gadget the Lord gave 'em?"

"The Liahona."

"That's right. See, I kept starting over, so I read that part a dozen times or more. I need to just skip over that, I reckon, and start further in and keep going."

"Do that, why don't you? That'd be great. And when you come to the Isaiah passages, don't quit if you don't understand everything. Just plow on through, and pretty soon you'll understand it better. And I'd be glad to answer any questions you might have, or the missionaries here in town could answer them, too."

"You know, I like to read to my kids from some little Bible story books, about like Adam and Eve, and Noah and the Ark, and Joseph and his coat, and stuff. Is there any storybook for kids about the Book of Mormon, like that?"

"There are several. I'll search that out for you, and maybe bring one or two next time. Will that be okay?"

"Sure, that'd be fine. Well, thank you for coming. I appreciate you taking the time."

"Oh, my pleasure. And I really do think it adds so much to our lives to read in the scriptures when we can. There's just no better source for the truth about things. Don't you agree, Brother Forelaw?"

There was a scraping of chair legs from the other room.

"What's that?" he asked, poking his head around the door jamb.

"I was just saying there's no better place to find out the truth about things than in the scriptures. Don't you agree?"

"Reckon so. The Bible, at least. I'm not fermiliar with this other book you're talkin' about."

"It's a companion volume to the Bible—about God's dealings with his people on the American continent, instead of over in the Holy Land. Same Lord, though—same gospel."

Sarge Forelaw nodded politely. It was hard to tell what he was thinking. The bishop took his leave, rejoicing in the knowledge that Sarge had, at least, been listening from his supper table. He had given himself away by mentioning "this other book" that was being discussed.

"Thank you, Father," the bishop prayed, as he headed for his next appointment. "Please bless Sister Elaine Forelaw to be able to teach the truth to those sweet little children—and bless her husband, Sergeant, with a curious spirit, that he'll want to look into the Book of Mormon for himself. And please bless him to keep eavesdropping!"

Y

The evening was early enough, still, that he decided he could squeeze in a visit to Buddy Osborne. He knocked on the door of Twyla Osborne's mobile home. It was opened by a tall, well-muscled fellow in an undershirt and denim shorts.

"Yeah?" the man asked suspiciously.

"How're you tonight?" the bishop said pleasantly. "I'm looking for Buddy—is he home?"

The man shrugged. "I dunno," he said, with an emphasis on the "I," as if to say, "I have no interest or responsibility for the kid." He turned and looked over his shoulder. "Buddy here? Some guy wants him."

"Who?" asked Twyla, coming to peer from behind her companion. "Oh, it's you," she said ungraciously. "Come on in, I reckon. Buddy!" she yelled down a hallway. "Buddy, the bishop's here to see you. Get out here!"

She sat down on a sofa beside her friend, flipping her rather dried-out looking blondish hair over her shoulder. She was a slender woman, dressed in slacks and a shirt that emphasized her figure. She had Buddy's eyes, which she focused on the television set. She turned up the volume.

"Sit down if you want," she said.

"Don't let me interrupt your program," the bishop said, taking a seat near the hallway to Buddy's room.

"We won't," Sister Osborne said, smiling at the man beside her. They were watching some video with a great deal of unrealistic-looking action in it. The bishop picked up a small model of a Nascar racer. The man on the couch eyed him as if he suspected him of planning to steal it.

The bishop caught his eye. "This Buddy's?" he asked, holding up the small car.

"Buddy's! Hell, no, the kid ain't into Nascar. I collect 'em."

"I remember when Dale Sr. drove the original of this one at Talladega."

The man stared. "You into Nascar?"

"I sure am—at least, I follow it when I can."

"Yeah? Who do you like for—"

"Shh!" Buddy's mother interrupted. "Watch the movie, hon—I'm not gonna turn it back for you. This's the good part."

Buddy appeared, silent as a ghost, at the opening to the hallway.

"Oh—hey, Bishop," he said quietly. "Um—wanta see my room?"

"You bet. Excuse me," he said to the couple on the couch, who appeared not to have heard him, and followed Buddy into a small bedroom. It was surprisingly neat. Buddy had made shelves and cabinets for his books and belongings out of orange crates, and wherever the walls weren't covered by these home-made shelves, they were papered with drawings and paintings. The bishop stared in amazement. He'd known the boy liked to draw, but he'd had no idea of the scope of his gift. Buddy was good. There were charcoal sketches of people and animals of all descriptions, and watercolors, mostly of plants and southwestern scenes. One oil painting, of a red rock mesa surrounded by some kind of stunted pines, featured dramatic use of shadow and contrast. One could almost smell the pines in the warm, dry air.

"Wow, my friend. I'm really impressed," he said to the boy, who shrugged and looked downward. "You've been blessed with a real talent, Buddy! I mean, I figured you'd be good, but—I'm overwhelmed."

"I just like to do it, when I don't have anything else to do. It's no big deal."

"I think it is. What do your art teachers say? You are taking art in school, aren't you?"

"I took all the art classes I could fit in, already. They—they liked my stuff, I reckon. I got good grades."

"Well, I should hope so. Have you done other oils?"

Buddy shook his head. "Mama won't let me use oil paint here. Says the paint and linseed oil stink too bad. I done that one in school, last year."

"I see. Buddy, you should really keep on studying and painting. I'll bet you could get a college scholarship in art."

Buddy shrugged again. "Deddy says I don't need college to make a livin'. He didn't have any. And Mama—I reckon she's just waitin' for the day I turn eighteen so's I can get out and not bug her."

"Oh, surely—" Surely not, the bishop had started to say, but couldn't force the words past his lips. He was afraid they would be a lie.

"I think art will be your best ticket to a better and more fulfilling life," he said instead. "No kidding, Buddy! This is not a gift you want to waste or throw away. I'm not a critic, but hey—even I know something great when I see it."

"Well—reckon I'll have to see. Wanta sit down? You can sit on my bed." Buddy folded himself onto the floor, his arms wrapped around his knees. "Oh—hey. Maybe you'd like to see this one." He reached for a sketch pad and flipped it open to a charcoal sketch of a brawny young man in a football uniform, grinning from under his helmet. It was unmistakably T-Rex. The sketch was done as if from the point of view of a small child looking up at the powerful athlete.

"That's terrific," the bishop said, with a grin. "T-Rex would be so flattered. You oughta show it to him."

"Oh, no," Buddy said, shaking his head. "I wouldn't dare. But you can have it, if you want. You know—for taking me to the games with you and Jamie."

"Really? Seriously?"

"Sure. I can do another, if I want. Go ahead, just tear it out."

"Thank you, my friend—so very much. I'll treasure it."

Buddy looked embarrassed, but pleased. The bishop didn't give him a prepared message, but just talked about talents for a few minutes, and the fact that all talents were gifts, and valuable to enrich people's lives—the giver and the receiver. "See, you and T-Rex have totally different talents," he concluded. "You might not be able to do what he does on the football field, but I'm certain he can't come anywhere close to doing what you do with pencil and paper and paint! And frankly, I believe your gift is the greater one, because it can last your whole life long and bring joy to you and to anyone who views your work, while T-Rex, although he entertains and amazes us right now, will only be able to play for a part of his lifetime—less than half of it, most likely. And then there's me—I'm still looking around to see where I misplaced whatever talent I was given, 'cause I sure don't know what it is."

"Reckon I do," said Buddy shyly. "You got a talent for makin' folks feel good, like they're worth somethin'."

The bishop swallowed. "Well, you know, everybody is worth something. We're each worth a whole lot, to our Heavenly Father. He said 'the worth of souls is great in the sight of God.' And you can count on that to be true. Your soul, Buddy Osborne, is great in God's sight—and in mine, too. Now—do we have a date for tomorrow night? Last home game?"

"Sure—if you really want to go."

"Oh, I do—and even if I didn't, Jamie'd make my life miserable if I didn't take him. So I'll be here about six, if that's okay."

"Sure. Thanks."

"Thank you."

He said goodnight to Buddy and crossed between the couple on the sofa and their video as quickly as possible. "'Night, now," he said as he let himself out the door. There was no response.

Arriving at home, he didn't immediately see Trish but supposed she was involved doing something with the children. He consulted his watch. Nearly nine o'clock. In Salt Lake City, Utah, it would only be eight P.M., not too late to make a call to the bishop of VerDan Winslow's University of Utah student ward. He found the number LaThea had given him and dialed. Fifteen minutes later, he ended the call and sat in deep thought. Bishop Ronald Vale had been helpful, to some extent, and would have been more so, except that he felt he didn't really know VerDan Winslow as well as he would have liked. VerDan came to meetings—some of the time. He paid tithing, yes, but the bishop wasn't entirely sure it was a full tithe, because VerDan hadn't made it to tithing settlement. He didn't really know of any particular problems or transgressions VerDan might have; the boy wasn't one to confide in him. He had friends, but they were all of a seemingly casual nature. He really couldn't say who the young man's friends might have been. Even VerDan's roommate hadn't been especially close to him. No, he hadn't ever applied for a temple recommend in the two years he'd known him. Yes, the young ladies did seem to like him; he was, after all, very personable and nice-looking. And yes, the bishop certainly had been surprised when he'd heard that VerDan had withdrawn from school and gone home, presumably to serve a mission. He would have liked to work with him on preparing for that, had he known VerDan was leaning in that direction.

The cat, Samantha, leaped into the bishop's lap and settled against his stomach, purring.

"I don't know what to think, Samantha," he confided in her. "This kid gives the right answers, and his record seems to be at least pretty much okay. But something bothers me. D'you reckon something's rotten in the state of Denmark? Or Fairhaven?"

She reached a paw up to investigate a button on his shirt, patting it to see if it could be removed.

"Follow my heart, you say? But see, the thing is, we have a kind of honor system in the Church. If VerDan Winslow insists to me and to the stake president that he's worthy and ready to serve a mission, and we don't have a shred of evidence to the contrary, what do we do? Then, too, his mother's pushing like crazy, wanting to get him on his way before he gets cold feet— or is it before we discover he really shouldn't go? I don't know, yet. Reckon I need to have faith, and keep putting it before the Lord. Though I don't want to weary Him, either. Maybe this is one of those situations where I'm supposed to exercise my own judgment. If I were to judge what's best right now, young Brother Winslow would head back to school, or go to work for a while if he's tired of formal education." He thought of the letters he had received from Elders Rivenbark and Smedley, then tried to imagine what kind of letter he might receive from an Elder Winslow. He couldn't.

Samantha purred louder and narrowed her blue eyes to mere slits, apparently pleased that one of her humans was talking to her in such soft tones. He stroked her velvety back and closed his eyes, letting his head fall back against the overstuffed headrest. Together, they slept—one in pure contentment, the other in sheer weariness.

"Jim!" Trish's voice, low but urgent. "Jim, wake up."

"What? Ow!" he muttered, sitting up from his slumped position in the chair, his lower back complaining at his mistreatment of it. Samantha slid to the floor and padded away, her tail switching in feline annoyance. "What's wrong?" he asked. "Are the kids okay?"

"Kids're fine, I'm fine. But listen, Jim. Muzzie's here, with her girls. They needed a place to go for the night."

He frowned. "Why?"

Trish's lips tightened. "It's Dugie. She can't take anymore. She's leaving him."

He blinked. "Wow. That's too bad. I didn't see her car outside."

"It's in the garage. I closed the door and parked ours in front of it. I don't think he'll bother to come looking for them, at least not tonight. I put Muzzie and Chloe in the guest room, and Marie's bunking with Mallory. Tiff has more room, but I didn't want to get her all awake and upset, 'cause she has seminary in the morning."

"So, what's going on with Dugie?"

Trish shook her head. "It's a long story, and not a pretty one."

"Don't tell me if she doesn't want you to."

"It's not that. In fact, I think she'd like to talk to you about it."

"Muzzie? Talk to me?"

"Don't look so scared! It's just Muzzie."

"Trish, there's no such thing as 'just Muzzie.' That woman has scared me to death all my life."

"Well, she thinks you're wonderful, and she knows you're a bishop. So . . ."

"She's not even LDS. Doesn't she have a pastor, or something?"

"Not really. Not anybody she trusts enough to tell what's going on. You've known her forever."

"How about Big Mac? He's known her forever, too."

"He's been away all these years. You've been here. You know Dugie."

"Not well."

"Not as well as you will when Muzzie gets through talking to you, that's for sure."

His curiosity surfaced. "Has he hurt her or the girls?"

"Yes and no. Not physically, not like Jack Padgett. And probably not the girls—at least, Muzzie hopes not. But he's expected things of her—things she's not willing to go along with."

"Oh, boy."

"And he's heavily into porn."

"So what am I supposed to do—go over there and call him to repentance? I have absolutely no jurisdiction over Dugan Winston. We're not even really friends—just acquaintances."

"I think it's more that Muzzie wants you to counsel her about what she should do."

"Aw, babe—bet you could do that just as well as I . . ."

"It'll hold more weight, coming from a man—a clergyman, at that."

He sighed. "You'll have to be with us, anyway. I can't talk to Muzzie alone."

"I will. But don't be all nervous about it. She's so embarrassed and confused and—and weary. She's been dealing with this for quite a while."

"Seems like it wasn't too long ago she said something to me at the store about their marriage—that it wasn't as good as ours, or something? I can't remember, exactly. But I sure didn't get the impression that it was in serious trouble. I'm real sorry to hear it."

Trish nodded. "Me, too." She looked at him appealingly. "I had to let them stay, Jim."

"Oh, I know. You're her best friend. Shows she has good taste in friends, I always thought." He shook his head. "No, you couldn't do anything other than invite them to stay. But honestly, Trish, I hope it won't be for too long. Maybe I'm just being jealous of our privacy as a family, but you know how it is. Having anybody stay for very long just—I don't know—changes the fabric of the family, somehow."

"I don't think they'll be here long. We'll help her work something out."

"I'm sorry, Lord, to be so selfish about this," he prayed a short time later. "But I thought I had enough on my plate right now. Please forgive me if I was less than gracious. It just took me by surprise. Please bless Trish and me to be of genuine help to Muzzie Winston and her little girls. Help me to overcome my nervousness and fear around her, and see her as Thou seest her, as one of Thy dear daughters. I need Thee, Heavenly Father, every hour of every day. I know I'm nothing on my own. Please strengthen me."

CHAPTER FOURTEEN

"HERE BRING YOUR WOUNDED HEARTS"

He arose early the next morning and spent some time reading the scriptures and in prayer. Thus fortified, he went down to breakfast in time to see Tiffani off to early morning seminary at Brother and Sister Warshaw's home.

"Have a good day, sweetie," he told her. "Learn a lot."

"Right," she agreed wryly, shrugging into her backpack. "Don't I always?"

Her father winked. "Hope so. That's why I'm paying for free public education."

She gave him a funny look, but waved as she spotted her ride and headed out the door.

"Nobody else is up yet," Trish told him, giving him a kiss. "Can you be late getting to the store this morning, or come home early, or what? I'm sure Muzzie'll be fine with either one. She's keeping the girls out of school today so that Dugie won't be able to find her—or them—there. She just doesn't know, yet, how he's going to react to their leaving."

"Did she leave while he was gone? And what did she bring

with her? Does she have any money—do they have a joint account? Is this something she's planned for, at all, or was it a sudden, impulsive move meant to shake him up?"

"She said she went by the bank and withdrew several thousand dollars from the savings they had together there—about half of whatever there was. I don't know what other assets they have. Probably plenty. But she just wanted enough money to live on for a while—to take care of the girls while things get settled."

"So she's set on divorce?"

"It sounds like it. She's pretty disgusted with Dugie, and I can't say I blame her."

"Then—why does she want to talk to me? Why not a good divorce lawyer?"

Trish considered the question. "You know what I think? I think she wants somebody sensible, and outside the situation, to hear her story and validate her feelings."

"Well, again, a lawyer—"

"I know, but . . . it's almost like she wants someone to give her permission."

He sat down at the kitchen table. Muzzie Evans Winston, who had always had the aura of the pretty, the pert, the popular, the super-assured, around whom he had felt gawky, ignorant, and nerdy since third or fourth grade, wanted *his* permission to leave her husband? Life was just getting too weird.

"Want oatmeal?" Trish asked. "I made a big pot of it."

"Sure," he said distractedly. "And stir in a spoonful of fresh courage, would you?"

"Happy to," she said, and gave his shoulders a hug as she set the bowl before him and poured him a glass of milk. He mixed brown sugar and a pat of butter into the cereal, the way he had learned as a child from his grandfather, a way which Trish found exceeding strange, but had learned to live with, just as she had his banana sandwiches and his penchant for fried vegetables— okra, green tomatoes, eggplant, squash, even corn. It was, he had told her, a Southern thing.

"I'd better go get the kids up and running, or we won't have time for scriptures," she said.

"Okay. I think it'll be best if I take a little time off this morning, but I'll call Mary Lynn when she gets to the store to be sure I haven't forgotten anything."

"Thanks, sweetie."

Mary Lynn agreed with him that morning would be best, today, for a little time off, so he enjoyed reading in the Book of Mormon with Trish and the little ones while they ate. Reluctantly, they had decided that trying to get in weekday scripture reading that included Tiffani was next to impossible, and hoped that she would get enough with her seminary studies and on weekends. The bishop could envision such family activities getting more and more difficult to plan as the children grew and acquired different schedules. Fortunately, it would be a few years before that became much of a problem with Jamie and Mallory.

Chloe and Marie, ten and seven, wandered in while they were finishing up.

"Oatmeal?" Trish asked brightly, but they both politely declined, saying they didn't like it. They looked happier when Trish brought out a box of cocoa-flavored cereal.

"I didn't know we had any of that," Jamie said accusingly.

"You can have some after school, or tomorrow morning," his mother promised. "Better scoot, now, or you'll be late. Chloe, is your mom awake, yet? Not that there's any hurry to be—I just wondered."

"Yes, ma'am, she's awake. Do you want me to go get her? She doesn't usually eat breakfast."

"No, honey—you just eat yours. I'll go talk to her in a minute. Mallory, are you done? Go brush your teeth, and get your backpack. I signed the paper your teacher sent home, so you can go on the field trip to the zoo next week. Be sure to give it to her, okay?"

The bishop walked outside with his son. "Jamie, it's best you don't mention at school that Chloe and Marie spent the night at our house, okay?"

"Like I would!" Jamie said. "But how come they did, anyway? I heard 'em when they came last night, but I don't know what's going on."

"Well, it looks like their mom and dad are having a serious disagreement, and she wanted a place for them to get away from him for a little bit, while she decides what's best to do about it. So we just won't tell anyone about it, okay, chum? And we'll try to be patient while they're with us."

"Aw, man—two extra girls? I've already got two sisters!"

"I know. It's you and me, pal. We'll stick together. And don't forget the ball game, tonight. You and me and Buddy."

"Yeah, cool! Go, T-Rex! Go, Mariners!" Jamie hopped on his bike and was gone.

Exactly, thought the bishop. *But I have miles to go before I can relax and enjoy watching T-Rex do his magic.*

"Who's taking me to kindlygarden?" asked Mallory as he went back into the kitchen.

"I will, in my pumpkin carriage," he volunteered. Kindergarten classes started half an hour after the other grades, which was not terribly convenient for parents with children on both schedules, but he liked the idea of the bigger kids being in class when the little ones arrived.

"Daddy, your truck can't be a punkin. It's not or'nge."

"That's true. It's more like a—what?"

"A snowball. It's white."

"Very good. A snowball carriage. Did you brush your teeth, like Mom said?"

"Not yet, but I will. Aren't Chloe and Marie going to school?"

Chloe looked up from her cereal. "Not today," she said. "Mommy doesn't want us to."

"Why?" demanded Mallory, not able to comprehend such a Mommy.

Chloe shrugged, apparently reluctant to talk about the situation.

Marie looked up from her breakfast. "It's cause we're hiding here from my daddy," she explained unselfconsciously. "He's been doing some naughty things, and we might not live with him, anymore."

The bishop steered his youngest toward the stairs. "Hurry, now, sweetie," he encouraged, before she could ask more questions.

Trish and Muzzie were seated at the dining room table when he returned, and sounds from the family room indicated that Chloe and Marie were occupied there. Muzzie looked smaller than usual—somehow diminished, he thought—as he pulled out a chair and joined them. She had a mug of some kind of fragrant, steaming herbal tea in front of her, which she was slowly turning around and around with her hands as if the action would help it to cool. Her eyes were red and puffy, and she looked miserable.

"Hey, Muzzie," he said softly. "Trish tells me you're having some troubles."

She glanced up briefly and nodded. "I'm so sorry to bother you guys, and interrupt your lives like this," she said. "But Trish is the person I trust most in my life. She knows everything about me—always has, since we were fourteen, and she's such a great friend."

"She sure is," he agreed. "She even knows everything about me, and keeps me around."

Muzzie attempted a smile, but couldn't quite achieve it. "Y'all are so sweet," she whispered. "I'll find a way to get even, someday. Thanks for letting us barge in."

"No problem," Trish assured her. "Want to tell Jim what's been going on?"

"No," she answered honestly. "I hate telling anybody, and that's why I never have, till now. It's so . . . mortifying. All along, I kept thinking it would get better, you know? That Dugie'd get hold of himself, and stop acting that way. But it's just . . . he's just gotten worse. And I finally just had to leave. He won't listen to anything I have to say, even about the influence he's having on the girls. He said—said it'd be good for them, teach them early how life really is, and how to enjoy it." She ducked her head and began to cry in earnest. Her hosts waited patiently for her to gain control.

Once she did, Trish spoke, patting Muzzie's arm.

"Why don't you tell Jim how it all started," she suggested,

and Muzzie nodded. She gave him a quick glance from reddened eyes, then looked down again.

"I won't go into any gross detail," she promised. "We had a good marriage, for a number of years, we really did. We loved each other when we got married. I loved him, anyway, and I think he loved me. Then things started to change, about—oh, when Bradley was about eight, and the girls were six and three. Dugie started traveling once in a while, to conventions and shows of boats and RV's. We all went with him once, to Atlantic City, and it was okay, though some of the guys were a bit rowdy, I thought, for a convention that people brought their kids to."

"Excuse me," the bishop interrupted. "But where is Bradley, anyway—not here, I take it?"

Muzzie nodded. "I talked Dugie into putting him into a private boarding school in Atlanta this year. I told him it was because they had such a great reputation for prepping kids for college—and they do—but it was really because I wanted Brad out from under Dugie's influence. It's a Christian school, too, and they're really strict about standards and—what do they call it? Comportment. Heaven knows I miss him—I could hardly stand to leave him there—but I felt I had to."

"I see. You were brave to do that."

She shook her head. "Not really, just desperate. I mean, it's one thing if Dugie wants to go off the deep end and throw his life away, but he's not taking our kids with him."

"What's he doing to throw his life away?"

"First, he started drinking. Well, he'd always enjoyed drinking a little—just social stuff—but it got more serious, more regular. And then one day I found him in the family room, watching a porn flick. I laughed, at first—it seemed so ridiculous—and told him to turn that junk off. He got really angry with me. Said he—he needed that, to feel any interest in me. He started wanting me to watch the stuff with him. I tried, to please him, but it was so gross, and so demeaning. I hated it.

"Then, he found this place in the Caribbean—a really nice resort, I thought—until I found out you were supposed to not wear bathing suits on the beach. He liked to take me there, and watch other guys look . . ." She started crying again.

"It's okay," the bishop told her. "You don't need to tell me any more. I get the picture, loud and clear. I'm so sorry, Muzzie. I had no idea you were going through this kind of thing."

"I tried to hide it, but it just got worse and worse. Do you know there are even people here in Fairhaven—couples—who get together on weekends and—well, you can guess."

He was sickened to hear it. "Reckon evil and corruption are everywhere," he said.

"Exactly. But then on Monday morning, they pretend to be so—such upstanding, good citizens! And that's how Dugie is. I wouldn't go to those parties, so—I'm not sure—but I think he's been taking someone else." She straightened her thin shoulders. "He's given me three wonderful kids and a lovely home. But I just can't accept the other stuff he's been trying to give me! It's not my style, and I'm actually embarrassed to have stayed with him as long as I have."

"You've openly discussed all this with him? He's known how strongly you feel about his activities?"

"Oh, yes. He knows. I've made it clear, many times. He calls me a prude and a sissy. One time he said I was nothing but an aging cheerleader with nothing left to cheer about. I told him that sure was true, if he was on the team."

"What'll you do, now?" the bishop asked.

"I don't know. I've got the names of several lawyers who're all supposed to be good. One is a woman, and I think I'd feel more comfortable telling all this garbage to her than to a man. I mean, there's lots more, guys—I've only sketched an outline for you."

Bishop Shepherd frowned. "I'm not familiar with the various grounds for divorce in Alabama, but surely there's something to cover a moral disintegration like you've described in Dugan. You shouldn't have to live with that, or expose your children to it."

"You think it's all right, then, for me to go ahead? I mean, y'all are religious, good people, and I know your church doesn't approve of divorce, but I figured maybe there's an exception?"

Bishop Shepherd sighed. "Unless Dugie can be brought to his senses, and repent of his sins and really change his ways, I don't see that you have much of a choice. His changing, of course, would be the ideal solution."

"So far, he doesn't think he's doing anything he needs to be ashamed of. He thinks it's unreasonable for anyone to expect people not to explore pleasure to its limit." She shrugged. "I reckon maybe he'll even be relieved to be rid of me, since I'm such a prude, and the kids and I must be a drag on his lifestyle."

"Does any of his family know what's been going on?" asked Trish.

"His folks are both gone, now. It's just as well, 'cause they were nice people and they'd be horrified at how he's carrying on. His sister lives in Montgomery, and I don't know if she's picked up on anything, or not. I haven't told her. And my dad's so old and fragile I don't want to tell him all this stuff. He knows I'm not real happy, but not why. Mama's gone, of course. So you're closer than my own sister, Trish—that's why you guys got so

lucky, today!" Muzzie laughed shakily. "And Trishie, you really
are *so* lucky, to have a decent guy like Jim. I wish there were
more like him around, but I don't expect to find one. Anyway,
I'm prepared to be a single mom, rather than take a chance
again."

"Well, don't make that decision just yet," Trish told her
gently. "Let's take one thing at a time. What are you going to
tell the kids?"

"I may not have to tell them much. They've heard some of
my tirades, and some of his insults. I dread saying the big 'D'
word to Brad, though. He cares for his dad. And I don't even
know what I'm willing to go along with in the way of visitation
rights."

"You know," the bishop said, thinking of Melody Padgett's
situation, "the judge may well have something to say about that.
Your attorney will know how it works."

Muzzie took a deep breath. "So I guess that's my next step."

The bishop thought of something. "Muzzie, is Dugie the
kind to try to get the kids away from you? Would he pull anything underhanded? Like, would he try to get to Brad?"

She gazed at him for a minute, then comprehension
dawned. "I'm calling the people at Brad's school, right now," she
stated firmly. "That's exactly the kind of thing Dugie would do,
to try to keep Brad's affection and allegiance!"

Trish's eyes widened. "He could go there and withdraw Brad
from school, couldn't he? And maybe even put him in another
school, without your knowledge! Could that happen?"

"It could. Excuse me, will you? I have the number in my
wallet. I'm calling right now."

Bishop Shepherd and his wife looked at each other as
Muzzie ran to get her purse. Trish shook her head in sympathy

with her friend, then reached to cover her husband's hand with her own.

"Muzzie's right," she whispered. "They don't make many like you—and I'm very, very lucky. Thanks for listening, honey."

He left and went to the store, where he concentrated on working extra hard to make up for the time he had taken off. The day went by quickly as a result, and he rushed home to collect Jamie and head off to pick up Buddy and get to the game. Tiffani was already with Claire, and Trish wasn't at home; Jamie said she and Muzzie and the little girls had gone to talk to some lawyer somewhere and would be back before bedtime.

"Okay, fine," he responded, glad that Trish was being supportive of her friend. "Are you ready to go? Did you feed the cat?"

"Well, yeah, you know how it is. You can't not feed Samantha when she decides she wants to eat, or she climbs your leg with her claws."

"Oh, right. Good. Okay, my friend, let's go cheer T-Rex and the Mariners on to victory!"

They tried to do just that, but in spite of all sorts of heroic attempts from T-Rex and his teammates, the final home game went down as a defeat in the annals of Fairhaven High. Jamie hung over the side railing of the bleachers calling out encouragement as a dispirited team headed back to their locker room.

"Good try, Mariners. Great work, T-Rex! It's been a great season, guys!"

Several players, smarting from the loss, snarled up at him, but T-Rex looked up and reached up a beefy hand to high-five his staunch little supporter. "Thanks, Jamie. Hey, Buddy," he said, tiredly.

"Hey, T-Rex," Buddy replied. The bishop thought of the drawing Buddy had given him. No way was he going to part with the original, but T-Rex deserved to see Buddy's heroic depiction of him. He would make him a copy.

"Bishop, you can just drop me at Deddy's house," Buddy said, once they were in the truck. "It's his weekend to have me, and it'll save him havin' to pick me up, or Mama to drop me off, 'cause her and Jeter are in a hurry to head outa town for the weekend."

"Okay, sure. Here we go."

There were no lights on at the small house owned by "Deddy"—Gerald Osborne.

"He musta gone to bed, already," Buddy said. "If the door's locked, I'll just knock and wake him up."

"We'll wait, to be sure you get in," said the bishop.

"Oh, you don't need to, it's okay."

"No trouble," he replied, moving the gear shift to neutral.

Buddy took his duffel bag and ran up to the front door. He reached to to knock, then pulled a folded piece of paper from the screen door. He tried to read it by the light of a moon that kept being obscured by shreds of fast-moving, high clouds, but finally walked back out to the truck.

"Looks like he left me a note, but I cain't see it for nothin'," he said. The bishop switched on the overhead light, and watched as the boy perused the writing and frowned.

"Shoot," Buddy said. "Says he's gone outa town, too—had to go down to Biloxi to fetch somethin' for work. He tried to call me, but nobody answered. Well, reckon I c'n just get in a window, and be fine, but I might hafta break it to get in, and Deddy won't like that."

The bishop reached around his son to pat Buddy's shoulder. "Tell you what, Buddy, why don't you just come on home with us for the weekend?"

"Yeah!" agreed Jamie. "We got way too many girls right now, and we need you, bad—huh, Dad?"

"That's for certain," his dad agreed. "You can bunk with Jamie, and he'll get you to play all his computer games."

"Aw, I shouldn't do that," Buddy objected. "But the fact is, I don't got a key to neither house—don't ask me why not—and I don't reckon neither of my folks'd cotton to my tryin' to break in. I just don't know where else I could go, right now. My grandmas are too far away, lessen I was to hitchhike . . ."

"And you'll do no such thing as that. Go get your bag, my friend, and we'll be on our way home."

Trish looked up from a batch of dough she was kneading, her face tired, but not too tired to show surprise at the presence of Buddy Osborne coming in with her husband and son.

"Hey, sweetie," her husband said, coming to kiss her cheek. "Buddy's locked out of two houses, due to some miscommunication, so he's going to bunk in Jamie's room tonight."

"Oh, I see—well, fine! Of course he is."

"Hey, Sister Shepherd," Buddy said, in his deep but timid voice. "I'm real sorry about this. I tried to figure somewheres else I could go . . ."

"What for, Buddy? You're perfectly welcome here. Jim, why don't you get Jamie's sleeping bag, and I'll grab an extra pillow, and you boys can go to sleep dreaming about these cinnamon rolls I'm making for breakfast."

The bishop had never loved his wife more than in that moment.

"Yum!" cried Jamie. "I tell you what, Buddy—you ain't never tasted cinnamon rolls as good as my mom's. You like raisins in 'em, or not? She does some both ways, with and without."

Buddy smiled faintly. "I like raisins," he said. "I like most things, fer that matter."

The bishop fetched the sleeping bag, his wife found a pillow, and they saw the boys off to Jamie's room with goodnight wishes. Then he turned to her and opened his arms.

"House-party weekend?" he asked, enfolding her in a warm embrace.

"Why not?" she said, with a small, smothered giggle. "Come one, come all!"

CHAPTER FIFTEEN

"THERE'S A MULTITUDE
OF CHILDREN ALL AROUND"

On Saturday morning Trish organized a work party consisting of all the young people present in her household. Fortified by her delicious cinnamon rolls—with and without raisins—plus juice, cocoa, and scrambled eggs, they could hardly decline. She also dangled the carrot of tacos for lunch, followed by a movie if all necessary chores were completed, whereupon she had a corps of willing slaves. She directed Tiffani and Chloe to clear up the breakfast clutter and vacuum the living and dining rooms. Mallory and Marie were to straighten and dust the family room, and the boys accompanied Trish outside to pull dead flowers and learn to plant fall bulbs.

Muzzie, thus relieved of the care of her girls for the day, betook herself to visit the lawyer she had contacted, who felt it important enough to meet with her on Saturday.

The bishop, too, had plans for the day, and so was especially appreciative of his wife's organizing skills and way with young people. He called Ernie Birdwhistle to ask if he and his counselor,

Sam Wright, might drive up to visit the family in the early afternoon. One of the Birdwhistle daughters answered the phone, and asked him to please wait while she found her father. It was some time before Ernie came on the line, and the bishop had begun to wonder if the young lady had gotten distracted and forgotten about the call.

"Brother Birdwhistle, I'm sorry to interrupt your morning," he said. "I imagine you were busy."

"Oh, just flogging a lad," Ernie Birdwhistle said cheerfully, sounding rather out of breath.

The bishop blinked. Surely there wasn't an abuse problem with the Birdwhistle family! He hoped and prayed there was not. He hardly knew how to reply.

"Oh, I'm sorry. Um, is—is everything all right?"

"Right as rain, Bishop. The boy deserved it, and admitted as much. All's well. What can I do for you?"

"Brother Sam Wright and I have a little time this afternoon to make some visits, and we wondered if it would be all right if we drove up to see you folks?"

"Be a pleasure, Bishop, glad to have you," he agreed heartily.

Bishop Shepherd spent a little time at his desk, organizing his thoughts in preparation for the next day's bishopric meeting and priests quorum discussion. One of the items on his list for his counselors was the question of ward choir director. He was leaning toward Linda DeNeuve, but he wondered if there might be someone else whose musical talent or knowledge he was ignorant of, who should figure into the equation. He had prayed about the matter, but no other names had presented themselves.

Linda had a new baby, but he rather expected that her husband could care for the baby along with their other three children for an hour each week while choir practice was held. When to hold it—that was another question. Probably right after the three-hour block, he surmised. It was hard to get people there early, especially with children to get ready—and doubly hard to get them to come back later, after they had already gone home, especially with the distances some of the members traveled. He shook his head. There was no easy solution. People were often tired and ready to head home and eat after the meeting block, and children would be restless. Still, the stake presidency wanted a choir, and the bishop agreed that one would add a spiritual tone and interest to their sacrament meetings, and would have the additional benefit of involving more people in the meetings—therefore, a choir they would have! He hoped.

He declined to go for tacos with Trish and the youngsters, made himself a sandwich, and enjoyed the unaccustomed quiet in the house to read a bit in the scriptures and to meditate and pray. There hardly ever seemed to be a surplus of time for those activities. He even recorded a few lines in his much-neglected journal, chagrined to see that the last entry was dated several months earlier. Before he left, he vacuumed the upstairs carpets and cleaned the children's bathroom as a surprise for Trish, then hurried out to his truck to pick up Sam Wright for the drive to the Birdwhistle homestead.

On the seat was a folded piece of paper. He picked it up. It was the note that Buddy Osborne's "Deddy" had left for him the night before. It read:

"Buddy—can't have you this wkd. Have to drive to Biloxi to pick up a part for my shovel, or it'd be clear to next week before they'd get it to me. Can't afford to miss work for that.

Tried to call your mother but you know she wont anser my calls, she's so sweet that way, so sorry I couldn't get word to you. See you probably next wkd. Dad."

The bishop groaned. "Ah, Gerald—why couldn't you have taken the boy with you, for once? He'd have enjoyed the trip, and maybe even felt wanted and cared for! And didn't you know your ex-wife was going out of town, too? Maybe not. Sounds like there isn't much communication, there. But even if you didn't know, what was Buddy supposed to do, once she dropped him off—hike all those miles back out to her trailer, late at night? It's a lot to expect."

He started the truck, sticking the paper in his pocket. If he felt injured and neglected on Buddy's behalf, how must Buddy himself feel? How could people have children and treat them like something to be shoved aside and dumped off? He'd never understand.

The drive up into the hills with Sam Wright restored his mood. Sam was good company with his jovial, down-home way of talking and his unfailing faith in his fellowman, despite that man's (or woman's) foibles. They were laughing heartily by the time they left the main highway for the network of roads that climbed past farms and orchards and an old mine entrance, up into the forested hills that, more than anything, announced the presence of mountains somewhere not too far away. They passed a small trickle of a waterfall just beside the road, its flow diverted into a culvert that ran under the road to continue as a miniature stream on the other side. There was a lot of water in this part of the state, not far from the great Tennessee River, and it lent beauty and diversity to the landscape.

The Birdwhistle land lay in a shallow valley between forested hillsides. The area reminded him of Shepherd's Pass, his ancestors' homestead, which was somewhat south of this, and a little more populated, but which had the same serene sense of peace.

"We're just about there," said Sam. "Right around this next bend, then look left."

The bishop whistled softly. For the first time, he understood the appeal the place had for Ernie and Nettie Birdwhistle—sufficient appeal to keep them isolated from near neighbors, let alone from town, school, and church. It was an idyllic layout, something out of a Grandma Moses painting, or a children's picture book farm. The two-story log farmhouse with its two chimneys was impressive, and perfect for its setting, as were the huge barn and other outbuildings. Horses grazed in a pasture that still showed patches of green, and smaller animals and children dotted the landscape, either romping or trotting purposefully on some errand. The bishop almost expected the girls to be wearing sunbonnets and long dresses, but jeans and long-sleeved shirts seemed to be the preferred style.

"Now, id'n that somethin'?" asked Sam Wright.

"It sure is," agreed the bishop.

"I tell you what, the wife and I figured the Birdwhistles had ten young'uns just to pervide company for 'em. There sure ain't nobody else around."

"And company for each other," his companion agreed. "They'd need some variety in their choice of playmates, with no friends around."

"Uh-huh, they would, 'ceptin' of course Lehi and Limhi."

"Of course." The bishop grinned. "But even they feud, sometimes. Hey, Sam—how does Ernie strike you, as a father?"

"Pretty amazin', I reckon, just to keep track of his young'uns' names. Basically, I think he's a tenderhearted kinda guy. Mama's the one to look out for."

"I wondered, because when I called, Ernie said he'd just been 'flogging a lad.'"

Sam chuckled. "He would put it that way. I reckon he fancies hisself a sort of Dan'l Boone type. Fact is, I think he claims to be a descendant of Dan'l. Reckon maybe it's gone to his head a tad. But no, I reckon the floggin' weren't much to worry about. 'Lessen, of course, he let hisself slip and chastise too harsh and angry. Reckon about any dad could do that on occasion. Kids can get to you."

"That's true. Well, let's kind of count noses, and make sure everybody's okay."

He pulled his truck down the drive and parked beside the family's two vans. He couldn't help comparing the openness of the farm, and the friendly, bouncing approach of children and dogs, to the controlled, fenced property of Ralph and Linda Jernigan. How much difference might it have made, he wondered, if the Jernigans had had other children in addition to Jodie Lee? Not that they still wouldn't have deeply grieved her loss, but maybe if they'd had others to see to and live for, it might have helped stave off the paranoia.

"Hey, y'all," greeted a young boy with a grin as big as his ears.

"Hey, your ownself, Matt," Brother Wright replied. "How ya doin'?"

"Good," the boy replied. "Y'all come on in. Ruth, go get Daddy and Mama."

Ruth, a girl just slightly taller than Matt who was balancing a toddler on her hip, gave him an exasperated look. "You go, Matt—I've got Emma. I'll take 'em inside and see to 'em. That's my job."

"Aw," objected Matt, but it was with a degree of good humor that he ran off toward the barn.

The visitors followed Ruth and Emma up the steps to the wide porch and in the front door of the log dwelling. The bishop wasn't sure what he had expected to see inside, but he was pleasantly surprised. The rustic look was carried on in the decor, but not overwhelmingly. There were braided rugs on the polished floor of the living room, and several comfortable sofas were grouped around a large fireplace. Bright pillows in varying colors picked up the colors of the rugs, and several good framed prints hung on the walls. Plants thrived on a low table before the window, and the fireplace was flanked by two burgeoning bookcases. The bishop noted religious titles, how-to books, novels, children's books, and school texts on varying subjects. The atmosphere of the room reminded him of the much smaller but similarly decorated living room of his fifth-grade teacher, Mrs. Martha Ruckman. He liked them both, very much.

"Y'all sit down, and I'll get you some lemonade," Ruth directed, setting down her small sister, who stood for a moment with her fist against her mouth, gazing at the two visitors, then turned to toddle after her sibling.

The two men occupied ends of a soft couch.

Sam Wright sighed. "Feels a lot like a nap waiting to happen, dud'n it?" he said with a smile.

The bishop nodded. Across the hall from this large room was a dining room, furnished with a long, picnic-style table and a hutch filled with dishes and glassware. A checkered runner was centered on the table, and an arrangement of Indian corn and colorful gourds ran the length of it. Trish would approve. She loved seasonal decorations.

Nettie Birdwhistle entered, followed closely by her husband, Ernie. Nettie smoothed back her hair with a self-conscious smile, and her hand, when the bishop shook it, felt still damp from being washed. Ernie's hands were damp as well, but he dried them on the sides of his overalls.

"Sorry to interrupt your Saturday chores, folks," Bishop Shepherd began. "Saturday's just about the only day Brother Wright and I can get together to visit folks, so we appreciate your willingness to have us. We won't stay long, I promise. Beautiful place you've got here."

"Glad you like it. We don't get much company, so it's a pleasure to have you come," replied Nettie. "Matthew, go round everybody up, tell them we've got company."

"'S'Ma'am," Matthew said in a resigned voice. Ruth, standing in the archway to the dining room, with Emma again in her arms, gave him a triumphant look.

Bit of a power struggle there, thought the bishop with some amusement.

"We're out a little too far for most folks to trouble to come," Ernie was saying. "I expect y'all know we stay after meetings so's our home teachers and Nettie's visiting teachers can see us. We don't hold 'em to coming all the way up here to see us, 'lessen' they want to."

"It's a real nice drive, though," Brother Wright said. "Wouldn't hurt 'em, once in a while, to get out of town and appreciate God's creations."

"Not to mention appreciating what you folks have made of this place," added the bishop. "It's like a picture book farm."

"Well, there's plenty to keep us all occupied, all the time," Nettie said. "We feel like the children need to be busy, so we've got the fields and the kitchen garden, and the animals, both livestock and pets, and then I expect you know we do home schooling and daily devotionals—plus we have crafts and music and books and games, and they can play ball out back—there's a field that's pretty good for softball, and we've strung up a net for volleyball or badminton. There's plenty of work in the summer and fall, weeding and hoeing and cutting wood, helping with cooking and canning and baking and cleaning. Nobody's ever bored, I daresay."

"If they were, they wouldn't admit it to you, Mama," said Ernie with a smile. "They know better!"

"Idle hands make mischief," she returned pleasantly. "Whatever our young'uns end up doing in their lives, they'll know how to work."

"That's important," agreed the bishop. "And it sounds as if they have opportunities to play, as well."

"Play is a kind of work for children," Nettie said. "You know what I mean? You watch little kids playing, and you see them copying the things they've seen grownups do—taking care of babies, pretending to cook or cut wood or drive cars—they're just practicing."

"That's true, isn't it?" the bishop mused. He remembered little Andrea Padgett, and the report he'd received from her daycare provider that she mimicked hitting and verbally abusing the other children when they played house. Poor little Andi, thinking that was normal grown-up behavior, and worthy of emulating.

One by one, the Birdwhistle children joined the group,

always coming forward to say hello and shake hands with the visitors. Ruth came back with a tray of lemonade, in tall glasses for the grownups, and paper cups for the children, who held theirs very carefully, obviously trained not to spill in the living room. The bishop carefully examined the boys, trying to discover which "lad" had been "flogged." He finally decided it must be sixteen-year-old Moroni, only because the young man was not as jovial as he usually appeared to be. Pratt, age eighteen, was open and friendly, typical of a Birdwhistle, and Lehi and Limhi seemed as giggly and mischievous as ever. He doubted it had been their greeter, Matthew, and the only other boys were little Joseph, around five, and Kimball, who seemed just older than baby Emma. Kimball, for some reason, came and stood at the bishop's end of the sofa, shyly edging closer and closer. Finally, the bishop patted his knee and held out his hands, and Kimball readily climbed onto his lap, smiling shyly.

The bishop was impressed, during the course of the conversation, that the children participated so eagerly and openly, and seemed perfectly at home conversing with adults. It was a rare enough thing among the families he had visited, in which the children usually hung back or answered questions in monosyllables. Something good was obviously going on with the care and training of the Birdwhistle children. The older ones spoke of their hobbies, their favorite subjects to study, their plans for the future, including missions and college, while the younger ones prattled about their pets or their tree house or their favorite food. Pratt mentioned that the one thing he wanted the most was a computer, which he felt they all ought to know how to use before they tackled college.

"Only thing is," he said with a grin, "that's the one thing Mama can't teach us, because she's never used one, either."

"You know who taught me?" asked the bishop. "Buddy Osborne, in our ward."

"Buddy?" asked Rebecca in surprise. "He's in my Sunday School class, and he never says a word."

"I know. He's quiet, but he knows a lot about computers. Plus, he's a terrific artist. You should see his work. It's amazing."

"I like to draw," volunteered Naomi, who was eleven. "I drew a picture of Mary and Joseph and baby Jesus once and sent it to the *Friend* Magazine, and they put it in. They made it just tiny, but it was there."

"That's great—I'd like to see that," the bishop said, and the little girl set off at a run to bring it to him.

"Don't run in the house," chorused her sister, Sariah, who was nearly thirteen, and Limhi, one of the twins.

Ernie Birdwhistle chuckled. "We teach 'em correct principles," he began, and Sam Wright finished for him: "And they govern themselves."

"That really does work, doesn't it?" agreed the bishop.

Ernie nodded. "Works 'specially well when the older ones set the example," he said, and the bishop saw Moroni duck his head. "Makes it tough on ever'body when they don't."

A-ha, I was right, the bishop thought. Naomi returned with the well-worn magazine and showed him her picture. It did show talent—not as startling as Buddy's, but definite talent. The bishop praised it, and Naomi glowed.

When the lemonade was gone, the Birdwhistles—all of them—took their visitors on a tour of the house and grounds, proudly explaining and showing their handiwork, inside and out. The little ones ran in circles around them, pausing to demonstrate the tire swing or to play with a litter of half-grown pups. A large sandbox was full of pails and shovels and toy road-graders. The vegetable gardens were extensive, well laid-out and organized. Pratt was sent to fetch a sack of potatoes to send home with each of the visitors, and Sariah to bring two loaves of pumpkin bread from the freezer, as well.

"You folks are amazingly self-sufficient," the bishop complimented the parents.

"This far out, reckon you have to be," agreed Brother Wright.

Ernie Birdwhistle smiled serenely. "Well, nobody's ever really self-sufficient," he said softly. "We all need the Lord, every day. But we're grateful to have this land and these young'uns. Without the land and all it produces, it'd be tough to raise a ten kids. Without the kids to help take care of the land and the animals, it'd be tough to produce as much as we do. I've hired some help, from time to time, but we're gettin' to where we can do it ourselves. We're blessed, brethren. We're happy here, and the kids are healthy."

"You'll miss Pratt, when he goes on his mission." Bishop Shepherd observed.

"We will that," the boy's father agreed. "But not enough to keep him home. We're grateful he knows his duty and is anxious to do it. Onliest thing I worry about is how much he'll miss home."

The bishop nodded. He would miss this place, if it were his home, he knew that.

At his own home, Trish, Muzzie, and all the children had returned, and the children were playing board games in the family room while Muzzie helped Trish with dinner.

"Well, hello, ladies. How are things?" he asked, trying to read the expression on either face. Trish's lips were pressed together as if she were angry or determined, and Muzzie's eyes were red and swollen again. Her chin trembled as she tried to direct a greeting to him, and he wondered why he had ever found her so intimidating.

"That good, huh?" he said dryly, and parked himself at the kitchen table. "Want to tell me?"

Trish turned from the stove. "You were absolutely right, Jimmy. Dugie had got to the school first and convinced the headmaster that he had to withdraw Brad from school because of a family crisis. He hinted at a death in the family, though the headmaster said he didn't come right out and say so. Muzzie's lawyer called and set the man straight, and he's very sorry and apologetic—but Brad's gone, with Dugie."

"And who knows what lies he's told Bradley!" Muzzie added. "Poor kid, what must he think is going on?" The tears began to form again, and she reached for a tissue from the box on the table.

"Wow—so what's the next step?"

Trish spoke. "The lawyer contacted the police and explained the whole thing. They're looking for Dugie and Brad, to talk to them, but they can't just take Brad away, since Dugie's his father and legal guardian, at this point. Anyway, they haven't come home, so apparently Dugie's on the run with him."

"I feel so awful," Muzzie grieved. "This is all my fault."

"It is not," Trish told her. "It's Dugie's fault; he's the one misbehaving, here."

"But why didn't I think? Why didn't I realize that's what he would do? I was so stupid!"

"Because you're too decent and nice to think the way he does," Trish said loyally.

Chloe sidled into the room, her eyes huge and frightened at her mother's tears. "Mommy? Why'd Daddy take Brad away from school? I thought he was s'posed to stay there till Thanksgiving vacation."

"He is, honey, but Daddy wanted Brad with him, since I have you girls with me," Muzzie said, trying to swallow back her tears. "We'll find him, don't worry."

"Well, then me and Marie can't go to school, either, 'cause Daddy might come get us."

"We'll talk about it later, okay? I'm not going to let Daddy take you away. I'll warn everybody at your school not to release you to him."

"But what if he comes when we're on the playground, and brings his gun, and makes us crawl through the hole in the fence, and—"

"I said, that's all for now, Chloe," Muzzie said sharply. Chloe bent her head and retreated to the family room. "Sorry," Muzzie said shakily. "But that girl has an imagination that won't quit, and I'm afraid she'll worry herself into a panic state. I'm about there, myself."

"It'll be okay, Muz," Trish said, giving her friend a hug. "There'll be some rough times ahead, but eventually things will work out. You'll see. Just try to have faith."

"You guys had better have faith for me," she replied. "I'm not sure I remember what that feels like—if I ever knew."

CHAPTER SIXTEEN

"MY ROOF'S SAFE SHELTER OVERHEAD"

Chloe and Marie accompanied Trish and the children and Buddy Osborne to sacrament meeting on Sunday morning. The bishop was glad to see that Buddy consented to sit with Jamie instead of by himself in the overflow area as he usually did. Chloe and Marie sat on the other side of Trish, between Tiffani and Mallory. Muzzie had declined their invitation, being in no mood to pay attention to a religious service or to be seen with her tear-swollen eyes. He hoped she would benefit from a few hours' privacy and the chance to reflect on her situation, which, admittedly, was a difficult one and fraught with many dangers. He and Trish had prayed for her, including the petition that she, herself, would be led to pray.

He watched as Lisa Lou Pope, sitting with her family, turned to beckon to a young man who accompanied the two full-time missionaries into the meeting. He—and they—came to sit by Lisa Lou, who snuggled up to the young man and held his hand. *Aha!* thought the bishop. *This must be Billy what's-his-name, that*

she talked about wanting to convert at Tiff's birthday dinner. It might
actually work—if he doesn't get discouraged about the Church when
her affections move on!

He was pleased to see Elaine Forelaw and her children come
in, and the Jernigans. Scott Lanier slipped into a seat by the
Jernigans and shook hands with Ralph. The bishop breathed a
prayer that all of them would be strengthened and comforted by
their attendance.

It was his turn to conduct the meeting, and as he and his
counselors had decided, he issued an open invitation to all
interested persons to attend an organizational meeting in the
chapel for a ward choir, directly after the third hour.

"President Walker has directed that all the wards in our
stake form a choir," he told them. "And some from each ward
choir will be asked to participate in a stake choir for stake conference in February. If you enjoy singing, playing the piano or
organ, or directing music, we ask you to come and participate.
We're excited about this, brothers and sisters, and feel it'll add a
new dimension of spirituality to our meetings. Thank you."

The speakers for the sacrament meeting service included a
youth speaker, Ricky Smedley, and the Winslow family—
Harville, LaThea, and would-be missionary son, VerDan. Ricky
spoke well but briefly about the First Vision, and then VerDan
proceeded to the pulpit. He looked well-dressed and well-
groomed, but he seemed distinctly uncomfortable before the
congregation. He adjusted and readjusted the position of the
microphone, smiled, shifted from foot to foot, and finally
spoke.

"So, okay—I'm VerDan Winslow. Well, I guess you know
that, cuz you've got programs, and you heard the bishop's

announcement. I've been away at the University of Utah, so I
don't know too many of you, but I sure see some people I'd like
to know better!" He smiled in the direction of Lisa Lou Pope
and two older Laurels who sat behind her. The Laurels looked
at each other and smothered giggles. "Yeah, so anyway, the
bishop asked me to talk about somebody from Church history,
and I picked Brigham Young. You all know who he was—they
named a university after him out in Provo, Utah, and his
descendant, Steve Young, played on their football team before
he went on to make it big in the NFL. Personally, I think
he'd've done better to've played at the U, but what the heck, I
guess it's cool to go to the school named for your great-grandpa,
or whatever. Anyway, Brigham Young was famous for having a
bunch of wives. I don't know exactly how many he had, but I
don't s'pose he ever got lonesome! He was also famous for lead-
ing the pioneers across the plains to Utah, and for saying, 'This
is the place,' which isn't really what he said. He really said,
'This is the right place,' and I guess that makes some kind of difference, at least to the folks who lead those Church tour groups
and stuff. Salt Lake City is kinda cool, but there's not a whole
lot to do there except ski in the winter and go to movies and
clubs, if you like a social life. Back in Brigham's day, I guess they
had square dances and put on plays with no swear words in
them. Today, that'd be called censorship, and somebody would
complain about it, but back then it was just how Brother
Brigham wanted it, and he was like the head honcho of everything—president and prophet of the Church, governor of the
territory, and on every board of directors there ever was. He
even started banks and department stores. So, he was a cool guy,

and had a lot of friends, and some enemies, too—but he was a smart old dude and knew how to get around people, so he usually got his way, and got things done. It was cool that he was strong enough to keep everybody in line and move 'em away from their nice houses in Nauvoo out into the desert. I s'pose God raised him up special to do that, 'cause it would've taken somebody strong to head up the Church in those times. So, um—that's my talk, name of Jesus Christ, amen."

The bishop scanned the congregation for reactions. T-Rex was leaning back in the corner of a pew, grinning. *No, Thomas, don't choose him for a hero,* he thought, and then decided that after Fairhaven High's defeat in their last home game, it was good that T-Rex was even here, grinning about anything. He knew the loss had been hard on the boy. Lisa Lou glanced at the girls behind her, who were apparently both scandalized and delighted at the irreverent tone of the talk. Trish frowned slightly, and Brother Warshaw frowned mightily. Most people looked noncommittal, but he caught a few exchanged glances that weren't hard to interpret—especially the one that passed between the two missionaries.

This boy, a missionary for the Lord? The bishop just wasn't sure he felt ready to unleash an Elder VerDan Winslow on the world. The jury was still out. LaThea stood and allowed what appeared to be a mink-trimmed jacket to drop from her shoulders to the seat she vacated to approach the pulpit.

"Brothers and Sisters, I'm just so delighted that we have the opportunity to speak and let you get to know our family better! VerDan is our youngest, and he'll soon be entering the mission field, following the examples of his older siblings. Our eldest, Martin, is named for the Martins of the Martin Handcart

Company, and I'm sure you all know that story. Marty served in Argentina, and was assistant to the president his last few months. Then our daughter, Laurel Anne, served in Vermont, near the birthplace of the Prophet Joseph Smith, and, incidentally, the birthplace of our own ancestor Richard Harbury, who joined the Church and came to Nauvoo, and later served a mission to England, leaving his wife and seven little ones to fend for themselves in the middle of a bleak winter, sustaining them only with his prayers from afar. Richard is only one of a whole bevy of pioneer ancestors we're blessed to call our very own, so you can see that VerDan comes from spiritually rich stock. I'm sure he'll be as excellent a missionary as his brother and sister were, and all who served before him, from our family.

"I've chosen to tell you of one of our dear pioneer ancestors as the subject of my talk today, since he was a close associate of Joseph Smith, Brigham Young, John Taylor, and all the other early Church leaders."

Bishop Shepherd watched a polite glaze begin to form on the eyes of the congregation as LaThea regaled the heroics and spiritual contributions of her ancestor, which admittedly were impressive. He couldn't say exactly where or why her remarks began to pall, but by the time she ended, he was relieved—for himself as well as those who faced the stand. A couple of older brethren were openmouthed—not in awe, however, but in restful slumber.

Brother Harville Winslow came to the microphone with only five or six minutes left, so his talk had to be cut rather drastically, but even so, it was by far the best of the day. Harville spoke of the early missionary efforts of the Church—the sacrifices, the difficulties, and the great successes and harvest of souls, especially in the British Isles, and how the influx of Saints from that area, Scandinavia, and other parts of Europe bolstered and renewed the faith and vigor of the Saints who had given so much to establish the Church in the American West. His talk was well-researched and without the—*dared he call it pomp?* the bishop wondered—that had characterized LaThea's offering. The congregation sang, "Come, Come Ye Saints" with more gusto than usual, which the bishop hoped indicated good expectations ahead for the choir.

After the prayer, he thanked Ricky Smedley and the Winslow family for their participation and made his way slowly from the stand, being stopped by several people with greetings, questions, tithing envelopes, and such. A little knot of people behind the back row of seats caught his attention. VerDan Winslow was holding court, surrounded by a group of girls that seemed to include every young woman in the ward. Tiffani was among them, smiling shyly at the handsome prospective missionary. "No, Lord," he prayed under his breath. "Not my Tiffani!"

As people were leaving the Relief Society and priesthood meetings, he stood by the door closest to his office and greeted all he could. Sister Forelaw collected her brood from Primary and shook his hand as they passed by. Suddenly, she pulled her youngest back and paused to lean in close to the bishop and whisper, "Guess what, Bishop? My Book of Mormon went missin', and where do you think I found it?"

He shook his head, and bent to hear her answer.

"In Sarge's truck! I never said a word about it, didn't let on I knew it was gone, let alone where, but I was so shocked I like to've died! Sarge hatn't ever wanted me to talk religion to him, said it was a person's private business what they believed, so I've gone along with that. I'm dyin' to know if he's readin' it, but I cain't ask." Her eyes sparkled.

"Probably best not to," the bishop agreed, his smile as big as his delight in the news. "We'll just keep talking about the gospel and the scriptures when I visit, and hope he listens."

"Oh, I think we can be pretty sure he's doin' that. What he might be thinkin' on the subject's a whole 'nother matter, but I sure hope it's good."

"Come on, Mama," urged little red-haired Katie. "I'm plumb starvin'."

"Hey, Katie, we don't want anybody starving around here! Hang on a sec." The bishop hurried to his desk drawer and pulled out several small packages of crackers with peanut but-ter that he kept on hand for days that were too busy to get home for a meal. "Is it okay, Sister Forelaw, if we stave off starvation with these?"

She smiled. "Sure, but watch what kind of trend you're startin'. Young'uns are like kittens—they don't forget who feeds 'em."

The bishop shrugged. "If I feed 'em crackers, maybe they'll let me feed 'em truth when I visit. I haven't forgotten that I'm bringing you kids a story, next time," he reminded them.

"Me, neither," said Carter. "Thanks, uh—mister."

"Just call him 'Bishop,'" their mother instructed, and the other two complied, adding their thanks. He was glad, at the moment, that there weren't other little ones in the hallway. His supply of crackers was limited.

Y

After Sunday dinner, there was a chance for the adults to relax in the living room of the bishop's home and visit. Muzzie's tears seemed to have abated, at least for the moment, and she told them how pleased she was with the response of the particular female attorney someone had recommended to her.

"I'll tell you what," she said, "she just jumped in with both feet and went to work, even if it was a weekend. It makes me feel better just knowing that she's on my side. She's dealt with some pretty tough situations before, sounds like, and she's a great advocate for kids and against pornography and such. She made me even more sure that I'm doing the right thing. And listen—she knows of a furnished condo I can probably rent for a reasonable price, so please don't think we're planning to camp on your doorstep for the duration! Y'all are so sweet to let us be here, though. I don't honestly know where we'd have gone. A motel or such would be the first place Dugie would look."

Trish spoke. "You're all welcome, Muzzie—you know that—for as long as you need to stay."

"Well, I surely am grateful for that. But here we are, right at the same time you have that poor little boy to take in, too. Not that he seems to be much trouble, though. He's sure quiet."

The bishop nodded. "I suspect Buddy's made a career of being as quiet and unobtrusive as possible. I get the feeling he's not completely welcome at either parent's home."

"That's so sad. And how's he going to feel, going back to that, after seeing what it's like here with you guys?" Muzzie wondered. "Because I hope y'all know there is a definite feeling in your home and family, that's different from any other home I've been in. I'm not sure what it is, whether it's because y'all love each other, or because you pray and believe God hears you, or what—but it's way different from the feeling we've had in our house, especially lately. In fact, I'd like to bottle it and take it with us." She laughed sadly.

"Don't have to bottle it," the bishop told her. "You can create it, yourself, bit by bit, same as we have. It does come with love and prayer and trying to do what's right, like you just said. And much as I hate the notion of separation and divorce, I do feel that by getting your kids away from Dugie's negative influence, you're taking a giant step in the right direction. You just pray for wisdom and guidance, for understanding, for your son's safe return to you or to his school, and for the Lord's will to be done concerning your husband." He couldn't believe he was counseling Muzzie Evans Winston this way, as if she were one of his ward members. And he didn't even feel nervous—just confident and sure that the counsel he heard falling from his lips was actually coming through him more than from him. "The Lord loves you, Muzzie, and he's aware of your situation, and all of your children. He stands ready to help you through this difficult time. Just turn to Him in confidence, and talk to Him as you would to a beloved father, in the name of the Savior—and then pause to listen for answers. I can assure you they'll come."

Across the room, Trish watched him, wide-eyed. Muzzie listened carefully, biting her lip against the tears that threatened to return.

"You really think He'd listen to my prayers? After all the years when I've gone along with Dugie, even though I hated it, and knew better, deep inside?"

He nodded. "I know He'll listen. In fact, I think He'll rejoice if you turn to Him.

"Look, we've all done things we regret. That's why Jesus suffered and died for us, so He could pay the price for the things we've done wrong. We can be forgiven for them as we repent and turn away from them, and ask for forgiveness and healing in our lives. It's more than just a pretty thought—it's real, and it really does work. I can assure you of that. I've seen it work—and I've felt it work. I can tell that you have a high degree of spiritual sensitivity, Muzzie, or you wouldn't feel so bad about what Dugie wanted you to do, and neither would you be able to sense the good feeling you find here. We call it the Spirit, by the way, meaning the Holy Ghost, who'll come and dwell with us as long as we're in harmony with Him. If we were to start to quarrel and fight, or deliberately do things we knew were wrong, the Spirit would leave us, because He can't be in a contentious place—it's contrary to His nature. But I believe that's really what you feel, right now."

Muzzie gazed at him as if mesmerized. "Do you know that you've taught me more about God in these few minutes than I think I ever knew?" she asked softly. "Here you've got me convinced that He's real, and alive and interested in me and my children—that He actually knows us and our problems, and cares! See, I've always wished it was like that, but I suspected God was so grand and far away that I could never approach Him and expect to be noticed. You know—like all mysterious and incomprehensible, and just sort of vapory intelligence or thought. I mean, I know we're taught to pray, 'Our Father, which art in heaven,' but I thought that was just an expression, because He apparently created the world, and all that's on it, including us. But I get the feeling y'all are talking about some-body a whole lot more personal than that."

"We are," Trish agreed. "We believe God is our Father, in a very real sense. He loves us just like you love your kids, only more perfectly and completely—and He wants us to turn to Him just like you'd like to hear from Brad while he's away at school, for example. He wants us to express our feelings and our needs, our joys and sorrows. Not because He doesn't already know, but because it helps us to grow and feel His love for us when we pray and keep in touch. Plus, it allows Him to bless us even more. It's pretty exciting, when you think about it."

"I'm going to try it, you guys, I really am. I've always thought, like, I should pray, I reckon, but what's the use? I mean, who am I, that God should listen? But maybe He does."

The bishop smiled. "We guarantee it," he said. "And if it seems awkward at first, don't worry. Just keep trying, and keep it simple. Thank Him for whatever blessings you feel you have, and ask Him for whatever you need—remembering that His will is ultimately in our best interests, so sometimes, like any good parent, He has to say 'no'—and then close in the name of Jesus Christ. It's very, very easy, and there's no need for fancy wording or repetition. Just a sincere, simple expression. I recommend it."

"So do I," said Trish. "It's the one thing that can help you get through times like this. In fact, I think it'll be even more support and help to you than your good attorney, necessary though she is."

"Wow," said Muzzie reflectively, gazing unseeingly at the flo-ral arrangement on the low table before her. "I'm sure glad I had nowhere else to turn this weekend."

"So are we," Trish said warmly.

"I'll say," agreed her husband, surprised that he really did mean it.

Y

"Jim," Trish said, later that evening when they were getting ready for bed, "you talked to Muzzie this afternoon almost like you were giving her a blessing."

He turned to look at her. "You know what, babe? I think the Lord was giving her a blessing—maybe not formally, with oil and all—but a blessing, nonetheless. I could tell because I could feel the words coming through me. So—it wasn't me talking. It was something more, and I'm grateful."

"Me, too. It was—kind of an electric moment, if you know what I mean. The hairs on my arms sort of stood up, like when you hear a really powerful testimony and the Spirit bears witness that it's true. And I think the Spirit bore witness to Muzzie."

He nodded. "I do, too. And the thing is, I think she was ready to hear it. Maybe all this misery has softened her heart and prepared the ground for the seeds of truth, you know? Now, I hope she really will pray. It'd help her, so much."

"I think she will. And see, you said it yourself—she has some spiritual sensitivity. She's way more than just a fun, flirtatious social butterfly! I've always known that."

He smiled. "Reckon you have, else you wouldn't have stayed friends, all these years. Have to confess, it's more than I knew, until the Spirit showed me. You know she's always intimidated me, from the time when we were very young."

Trish smiled. "I know—but now you're not fourteen,

anymore. We're all adults, and you've seen a totally different side to Muz."

"Yep. And I like it better than the other side."

"And she's seen a way different side to you, than just Mr. Grocer and Trish's hubby. And maybe a little different side to me, too. And a new perspective on the gospel."

"The Lord works in mysterious ways," he said softly. "This weekend sure has turned out different than I expected."

"Me, too," she agreed, sitting down beside him. "Better."

"Better? Even with four extra people as unexpected guests?"

"Yep. Even. Or because of."

He nuzzled her ear and kissed her cheek. "I'm proud of you, Trish. You rose to the challenge, and I know it wasn't easy."

"Piece of cake. Of course, who knows—I may fall apart tomorrow, or whenever they all leave. No promises."

Lying in bed that night, the bishop had a hard time turning down the volume on his thoughts. He thought of Buddy, when he had driven the boy the several miles back out to his mother's mobile home park. Buddy had hardly spoken, all the way, but when he'd gotten out of the car, he'd leaned back in to get his duffel bag and said, "Thanks, Bishop. Um—yer kids are real lucky. 'Bye."

He wondered what, if anything, he might do to make Buddy feel a little luckier, too. He also called up the image of Tiffani's face, smiling up at VerDan Winslow. He sincerely hoped she had gone unnoticed by the good-looking young man who seemed to have such a casual attitude about almost everything. He could see why LaThea wanted this son safely out in the mission field, but he wondered what kind of havoc the boy might wreak in that setting. He didn't think he wanted to find out. He especially didn't think he wanted to be responsible for sending him out, unless he could discover a different side of VerDan than he'd seen to this point.

Melody Padgett appeared next on his mental screen, anxious and nervous over the upcoming hearing about Andrea being returned to her. He could visualize, all too well, the arguments that some involved might put forth, saying that her not having managed to keep Andi from witnessing Jack's abuse to Melody was a form of neglect, if not a sort of abuse in itself.

Finally, his thoughts rolled him out of bed, and he tiptoed through the darkened house and down the stairs to his rolltop desk in the corner of the dining room. He had prayed before going to bed, both alone and with Trish, but evidently it hadn't been enough. He knelt at his desk chair and poured out his heart in behalf of all who troubled his mind. He prayed for Muzzie and all three of her children, especially her absent son— for Dugie, to be prevented from causing further harm to any of them, and to come to a realization of the destructive path on which he had set his feet. He pled for Melody, that she might be reunited with her little daughter—for Jack, that he might be able to make the changes necessary for them to be a family again. He remembered Buddy, and prayed that both parents might appreciate the boy and give him the love he needed and deserved. He prayed for the Winslows—Harville and LaThea that they might understand the needs of their son, and VerDan himself, that he might be strong enough to be honest with himself and with the bishop.

He mentioned the need for a ward choir, and the fact that only four people had attended its organizational meeting—

Trish, Tiffani, Claire Patrenko, and Sister Margaret Tullis, the ward organist. Thinking of Tiffani, as well as Lisa Lou Pope and the other young women of the ward, he prayed that they would be chaste and careful in their associations. He prayed for the Rexfords, that their needs might be met, spiritually and temporally. He rejoiced in the anticipation of the Wheelers, waiting for their little baby to be born to the birth mother who had chosen them to adopt it, and prayed that all might be well with mother and child. He remembered all who were ill or afflicted, including Elder Rand Rivenbark, Brother Bob Dolan, whose leukemia still appeared to be in remission, and the little Parsons baby, Alyssa, who had been born profoundly deaf. He prayed for the Jernigans, and for the ward's elderly, including Sister Buzbee, Brother and Sister Mobley, and Sister Hilda Bainbridge. Then his thoughts and prayers turned to Scott and Marybeth Lanier. He prayed, as he did every day, for Scott to be comforted and granted wisdom in his ordeal, and he prayed that Marybeth's eyes might be opened to the realities of spiritual things. Finally, exhausted but relieved, he returned to his bed, where he fell into the deep and restful sleep that comes to those who have done all they possibly can in any given day.

CHAPTER SEVENTEEN

"FOR 'TIS HIGH TO BE A JUDGE"

On Tuesday evening, Sister Linda DeNeuve brought to the clerks' office a tray of country ham, whipped potatoes with red-eye gravy, and home-bottled green beans. There were flaky, hot biscuits on the side, and a jug of lemonade.

"Dear Sister, you're bound to ruin us," complained Sam Wright, as he accepted the tray with a smile. "Purely bound to spoil us rotten, and then how'll we get our work done? We'll just be lazin' around here like a bunch of corn-fed hogs. No offense to present company," he added, to the plate of thick ham slices.

Sister DeNeuve smiled back, unperturbed. "Y'all work awfully hard for us. You deserve a good meal. Besides, I didn't make dessert, so I'm not spoiling you too badly. Now, don't worry about the tray—I'll pick it up Sunday."

"We'll put it right here, under the counter," the bishop told her. "And, since you're here, would you mind visiting with me for just a few minutes?"

She looked surprised. "All right," she agreed, and followed him into his office.

"Sister DeNeuve, you've had just a few months' rest—if you can call it that, having a baby and all that goes with it—since you were released as Relief Society president, and I was wondering if you might be ready to consider a new calling. I understand you're presently serving as a visiting teaching coordinator, is that right?"

"I am, and that's not too demanding, most months. Sometimes I need to go fill in when someone isn't going to get visited, but usually the sisters on my route are pretty faithful to go. What did you have in mind?"

"We're looking for a director for our ward choir."

She looked surprised. "Well, I've been Primary chorister, and Relief Society chorister, and I love music, but I've never really directed a choir. I'm told I have a pretty good ear, but you need to know, I surely haven't had any experience directing a full choir, with men and women."

The bishop nodded. "I'm not real sure anybody in the ward has had that kind of experience. I just can't remember when we've ever had a full-fledged choir. I mean, once in a while we've had the Relief Society sisters sing, or the children, or special numbers by a duet or a trio—but President Walker has directed that each ward develop a choir that performs about once a month in sacrament meeting. He suggested a Christmas program, and he wants us to contribute several singers to the stake choir for February conference."

She nodded. "I heard about that on Sunday, and I wondered who'd be directing. Oh, boy! I surely didn't think it might be me. Who's the accompanist?"

"We've got Claire Patrenko on the piano, and of course

Sister Tullis on organ. You could use both, or trade around, according to what you think sounds best with each hymn. And I think hymns are what President Walker wants us to work on, rather than a lot of fancy pieces that'd be beyond our capabilities, for now. We're thinking just one hour of practice a week, right after church on Sundays."

"How many people showed up last Sunday?"

The bishop made a little face. "Four," he admitted. "The two accompanists, and my wife and daughter."

"Ah! Then we've got our work cut out for us, recruiting, haven't we!"

He really liked the way she said 'we.' It gave him confidence that maybe he'd be able to follow through on his instructions from President Walker. It was always a little unnerving when one's ability to live up to a leader's expectations was dependent on the cooperation of others.

"Then you'll accept?" he asked eagerly.

"Sure," she replied with a smile. "I don't guarantee the quality of the results, but I'm willing to try to lead if we can get some people to sing."

"Sounds like a deal, to me. The Lord bless you, Sister," he added. "And thanks for the great meal, too!"

He had conducted two youth interviews and had a little break before meeting with Scott Lanier. The phone rang in the clerks' office just as he wandered in to refill his lemonade cup and see if there was a biscuit left over. Dan McMillan answered the phone, consulted the evening's schedule, then turned to the bishop.

"Bishop, have you got time to visit with Barker Reams for a few minutes? Says he can be here in five."

The bishop's eyebrows rose in surprise. "Why, sure," he agreed. "Tell him to come on over."

He went back into his office, pondering what might bring Barker voluntarily out to see him. Barker was not a member of the Church, but he allowed his wife, Ida Lou, to participate and to serve as Relief Society president, where the bishop considered that she was doing a bang-up job. He hoped Barker didn't feel she was being overworked or taking too much time away from home.

Barker arrived, looking nervous, clad in a clean white shirt and new-looking jeans. He was what the bishop's father would have called a portly man, a bit hefty through the upper body as some men tended to get, with age.

"Good evening to you, Barker! How are you?" the bishop greeted, shaking hands warmly. "Come and sit down. What can I do for you?"

Barker ducked his head and scratched the back of his neck. "Ain't rightly for me, that I'm here. I've come about my wife. That is, I need to ask you a couple of questions, kind of private-like, iffen you don't mind." He flicked a glance toward the clerks' office door.

"Not at all." The bishop closed both doors before sitting down.

"See, hit's about these here temples you folks have got. Ida Lou, she talks about 'em like they was a piece of heaven or somethin'—but I need to know what, for sure, goes on inside. Is that somethin' you can tell me?"

The bishop was surprised, to say the least, but he welcomed the opportunity, and sent up a quick prayer for guidance.

"I'll do my best. I reckon you already know that temples are different from meetinghouses like this one, where we worship on Sundays. Temples are built for a special purpose, which is to be a sacred place, as close to heaven as we know how to make it, where certain eternal ordinances are performed. We do some of these ordinances for living people, and also in behalf of those who have passed on, who didn't have the chance to do them for themselves while here on earth. For example, couples can be married in the temple, not just till death parts them, but forever, if they'll remain faithful. Baptisms are performed for deceased people by living people, in their name—and we believe that the deceased have the opportunity to accept or reject the work done for them. So a temple is a place of Christian service—doing things for folks who can't do for themselves, without any thought of thanks or of favors returned. We make covenants with the Lord in the temple, promising that we'll keep His commandments and devote our lives to His service. In turn, the Lord gives us wonderful promises and blessings which will mostly be realized in the hereafter, if we've kept our part of the bargain."

Barker frowned, but nodded, trying to take in what he was hearing.

"One other thing we do in the temples is what we call sealings. For example, a couple who had been married civilly might go and have their marriage sealed for time and all eternity—just as if they were getting married for the first time, like a young couple. Then their children are brought in, all dressed in white, and they all kneel around an altar and the children are made theirs forever, so that their family becomes an eternal unit."

Barker nodded. "Our son Billy and his wife done that, so I

know about that part. And I know about the—um—the clothes items."

The bishop smiled. "The temple garment. Right."

"Okay, so—reckon what I want to know is, iffen I was to let Ida Lou go through, what would change, in our lives?"

The bishop's heart leapt up. He knew how dearly Ida Lou desired the blessings of the temple.

"Nothing would change much, Barker. Ida Lou would wear the garment, of course, and we would hope you'd be respectful toward that. But she'd still be your same dear wife, only happier than ever. Ida Lou's already as committed to the Lord and to serving her fellowman as anyone who's been endowed in the temple. But you'd be doing her a wonderful service, to allow her to go, with your blessing. I don't believe you'd be sorry, in any way."

"You likely know how she takes a car full of older ladies down to the temple in Birmingham once a month. Then, they go in and do their thing, and Ida Lou just waits in the car, and does her crocheting and stuff, then brings 'em home. Now, she ain't complained, never said a word against me regardin' that. But of late, I've felt right bad about it. It's just that I don't want to stand in her way, you understand?"

"I understand," the bishop said softly.

"I mean, she's already there—she might as well go inside with them other ladies. It's only fittin', her bein' the president and all."

"I agree."

"So, I figger—whatever I need to do to let her go, I'll do it."

"Thank you, Barker. You're a good man. I can see why Ida Lou's so devoted to you."

"Aw, I ain't nothin'. I got me too many faults and

weaknesses. But like I say, she's a good woman, and I don't want to hold her back none."

"Then you just go home and surprise her with the news. And she is a good woman. She's doing a great job with the sisters. They all love her."

"Reckon they should! She sure goes out of her way for 'em. Like that little old lady up on the farm? One she took the sweet potater pie to? Land, that thing was nasty—the pie, I mean—plumb bitter with nutmeg, but that old soul shore did enjoy it! And as if the pie weren't enough, Ida Lou had sat down and made that lady a dress just like the one of her own that the woman had admired! Worked on it all night, didn't get her a wink of sleep. I tell you, she's somethin'!" It was the most the bishop had ever heard Barker Reams say.

"Something special," he agreed. "And so are you, Barker. Thank you, so much. The Lord bless you."

Barker shrugged, and turned his head away in embarrassment. "Least I can do," he said.

He shook hands again and left, and the bishop knelt to offer a prayer of thanks.

The next evening at dinner, Trish said, "I had a call from Meredith, today."

"That right? How's she doing?" asked her husband, with interest.

Trish smiled with satisfaction. "Sick as a dog."

"That's great!"

"Mommy!" Mallory scolded. "That's not nice, for you and Daddy to be glad Aunt Merrie's sick. Is it, Jamie?"

Jamie looked confused. "I don't get it," he said. "What's goin' on?"

Trish smiled at her two youngest.

"I'll bet I get it," Tiffani said, cocking her head to one side. "Aunt Merrie's preggers, isn't she!"

Trish looked at her. "Where'd you get that term?"

"It's British. But am I right?"

"You're right. Aunt Merrie's expecting a baby."

"I knew it. That's so cool!" Tiffani said.

"A baby?" Mallory said in wonder. "For reals?"

"So we get a new cousin!" Jamie put in. "I sure hope it's a boy. We've only got one boy cousin, and I never get to see him."

"Well, Tim lives in Oregon, and that's a long way off," Trish reminded him. "You do have two boy cousins on your dad's side, but they're pretty much all grown up, aren't they?"

"Oh, yeah—Raden and Jerry. Yeah, they're like—what? Eighteen? Nineteen?"

Raden and Jerry were the two sons of the bishop's next older sister, Ann Marie Futrell. Ann Marie and her family lived near Baton Rouge, Louisiana, and the Alabama contingent didn't see them very often.

The bishop thought for a moment. "Let's see, Raden's a senior this year, so he probably is eighteen by now, and Jerry's about twenty. He joined the Navy, remember?"

"Oh, yeah—that's right. I wish he'd come see us, and wear his uniform. That'd be way cool. And Tiff could show him around, and everybody'd think she had a date with a sailor!"

Tiffani ignored her brother's teasing. "So, Mom, when's Aunt Merrie's baby due?"

"Not for a long time. About next May—just before school's out."

"How come it takes so long to grow a baby?" asked Mallory.

Her mother smiled fondly. "Got to have time to grow all the things inside the baby, like its bones and heart and tummy, and to get its eyes and skin all finished, and its little tiny fingernails and toenails—and nine months is just right to get all that done, so the baby can live outside the mother and be healthy."

"Well, why don't we grow another one? I think a baby sister would be fun."

"Nuh-uh," objected Jamie. "A brother, if anything! There's too many girls around here already. Even the cat's a girl."

"We'd like another baby, too," Trish said, smiling at them. "But it probably won't happen. We had a hard time getting the three of you here."

"How come?" asked Tiffani.

"I have some problems getting pregnant," her mother replied. "I'll explain it to you, sometime." She winked covertly at her elder daughter, who then understood that Mallory—and perhaps Jamie too—was too young to hear the details.

"Samantha's a girl—when's she gonna have a baby kitty?" Mallory pursued.

"Bite your pretty little tongue," admonished her father, reaching to tweak her nose. "If there's anything we don't need, it's more little Samanthas running around the place. Besides, she's still too young." He thought a minute, and frowned in his wife's direction. "Isn't she?"

Trish returned his look, her eyebrows raised. "I'll call the vet," she promised.

The bishop enjoyed the mealtime conversation with his family—the first private one they'd had for several days. Muzzie and her girls had gone with the lawyer to look at the condominium they'd been promised and to have dinner with her as well. Dugie and his son had not yet been heard from, according to the local police, who were on the alert to watch for them, regarding Dugie as a potential problem.

He watched Trish fondly as she brought in brownies for dessert. There were a couple of things he wanted badly to tell her—about Barker Reams's generous offer to let Ida Lou go to the temple, and about the imminence of the birth of the baby for the Wheelers—things that would make her happy to know, but he was learning the bishop's need for privacy and confidentiality regarding the members' lives. Other people might speculate, gossip, or just spread good news—but he had to be very careful. He hadn't spoken to Trish about Marybeth Lanier's request to have her name removed from membership in the Church, either—nor would he, unless she brought up the subject, even though he knew she was already aware of the situation. It was not that he didn't trust Trish—he did. But he had been counseled to be very circumspect, and to let people's news be their own to announce, if and when they chose. Besides, there was nothing Trish could do, except worry, about such things. It wasn't fair to burden her.

He could, however, ask for general opinions. "So, what'd you think of the talk by Brother VerDan Winslow on Sunday?" he asked.

Trish gave him a look which he knew could be properly interpreted as, "Oh, brother!" or "Give me a break," but Tiffani brightened.

"He is so cute! Really hot. Don't you think so, Mom?"

"Mm-hmm. Almost as hot as he thinks he is," said Trish dryly.

"Mom! What—you think he's stuck-up?"

"I get the impression he's rather full of himself," her mother replied.

"What does that mean?" Tiffani pursued.

"Means I think his whole approach to his talk was designed to get the attention of all you girls, and not in the best possible way, either. He bordered on being disrespectful to President Brigham Young, just for the shock effect. It seemed to work, too—the way all of you were crowded around him. I don't think he'll make a very good missionary, either. He'd be trying to convert all the girls to *him,* and forget about the Lord, or the gospel."

The bishop couldn't help a small chuckle. "Why don't you go ahead and tell us how you really feel, honey?" he teased.

"Well, I think y'all are awful," Tiffani objected. "We were just trying to welcome him into the ward. And he is cute. So what if he doesn't give the best talks?"

"He's very nice-looking," agreed Trish, emphasizing the "looking." "And I hope you'll stay as far away from him as possible."

"Mom! Shouldn't you and Dad be nice to him, and try to get him to do better, if you think he's so bad? I mean, Dad's the bishop, and—"

"Sugar, I'm speaking only for myself in this matter," Trish assured her. "As the bishop, of course your dad has to deal with him as he sees fit, and as the Lord directs him to, but as for me, as a mom, that young man scares the daylights out of me, and I think all you girls ought to be very, very careful of him."

Tiffani frowned doubtfully at her mother. "You think he's a player?"

"Big time. I could be wrong, of course. But those are the vibes he gives off."

Amen, thought the bishop. *So glad you said it, Trish, because I shouldn't—at least, not yet.*

He dressed with care on Friday morning, choosing a conservative tie and trying to look as knowledgeable and responsible and clergy-like as possible. He attempted to plan what he might say, if given the opportunity to support Melody in her plea to have Andrea returned to her custody, but he gave up and decided to let the Lord give him words in the moment they might be needed.

A small crowd of people milled around the marble hall outside Judge Williams's chambers. He recognized some of them—Sister Hallmark from LDS Social Services, and Mrs. Parkman, Melody's caseworker, who had taken exception to his referring to the removal of Andrea from her home in the early morning hours as "snatching." He would try to be more careful in his terminology today, if the opportunity arose. His opinion of the act, however, had not changed.

He nodded to Sister Hallmark and then saw Melody, who had been standing behind her. Melody spotted him at about the same time, and hurried over to greet him.

"Bishop, I'm glad you're here," she said, her voice low and tense. "Thanks so much. I'm so nervous, I could die."

She did, indeed, look tense. Already slender, she appeared to have lost weight over the last few weeks, and her tan had begun to fade, so that there was even more contrast between her complexion and her dark hair.

"I'm kinda nervous, too," he responded. "Let's step around this corner for a minute, shall we, and have a word of prayer?"

They moved into a window alcove, out of the sight of others on the mezzanine, and bowed their heads.

"Heavenly Father," he prayed softly, "Thou knowest the importance of this hearing today. We pray Thee to bless us, especially Melody, with a calm spirit and a knowledge of Thy love for her and her little daughter. Thou knowest, too, how greatly we desire Andrea to be returned to her home, and we beseech Thee, if it is Thy will and in her best interest, that she be allowed to do so. We, and others, have fasted and dedicated our fast to this purpose, and pray that it may be effective. Now, we thank Thee for this opportunity, in the name of Jesus Christ, amen."

Melody drew a long, shaky breath and let it out again. "I think that helps," she said. "I know I need to appear to be calm and competent. Sister Hallmark told me that, because Mrs. Parkman keeps worrying that I'm too emotional to be a good single parent to Andi."

"I know," he said, steering her back toward the group. "I think it's a little unrealistic to expect you not to be emotional, under the circumstances, but let's both do our best to keep our cool, and allow the Lord to do His work here."

"I like that thought. That He's here—in charge."

"So do I."

The hearing finally convened in the judge's chambers, which gave it an aura of privacy and informality that may have been misleading, the bishop thought. It wasn't too evident, for the first forty-five minutes or so of the proceedings, that the Lord had anything to do with the matter. In spite of the coziness of the room, with its fireplace, several wingback chairs, bookcases and long, red-draped windows, Judge Teresa Williams's demeanor was anything but cozy. A small, squat woman whose sour expression suggested too many encounters with the dishonest and unsavory, she sat behind her mahogany desk with her hands folded, and listened impassively to the testimony of the experts. She heard Mrs. Parkman's doubts about Melody's emotional state, the policeman's uncertainty regarding Jack Padgett's chances of being sufficiently rehabilitated to return to the family—even if Melody decided that she wanted him to—and the list of complaints against Jack, evidences of things that had happened in the home which little Andrea, age six, had witnessed and internalized to the point that she acted them out with her young peers at the daycare center. The judge asked occasional searching questions, made notes, and gave no sign of how her opinion was being formed. Bishop Shepherd found himself wanting very badly for Jack Padgett to be able to prove the policeman wrong and to move ahead full-steam with his rehabilitation.

"Mrs. Padgett, I'd like to hear from you, at this point," Judge Williams finally invited.

"Yes, your Honor," Melody responded, her voice low but not shaking. The bishop sent up one more petition in her behalf.

"It would appear that one of the chief concerns here is the fact that you allowed your young daughter to witness your husband's verbal and physical abuse of you on numerous occasions. Would you comment, please?"

"It's true, your Honor. There were times when I wasn't able to prevent her seeing or hearing what went on, especially when my husband would suddenly erupt in anger over something I hadn't anticipated. Other times, when I thought he might likely become upset, I did arrange for Andrea to stay longer at the babysitter's, and we would go pick her up after Jack had settled down. Sometimes when he would come after me, I would head away from her room, or wherever she was at the time, in hopes that she wouldn't be aware of what was going on. But frequently she would hear our voices and come to see what was wrong."

"Was he ever physically or verbally abusive to her?"

"No, ma'am. I did fear that it might escalate to that, but thankfully, it never did. The closest he came was punishing me for not teaching or controlling her better, when she'd made some mess or done something he didn't like. He did—does— really care about Andrea."

"Do you think he cares about you?"

Melody looked at her hands, clenched before her. "I—don't know, your Honor."

"How have things been for you, since Jack and Andrea were both removed from your home?"

Melody looked back at the judge. "Very lonely," she said. "More peaceful, of course, without the fear of Jack's outbursts, but very lonely without my daughter. Way too quiet and empty. And I've been so worried about Andrea—what she might be thinking, whether she's well and happy, or missing us."

"Do you actually think she's missed her father?"

Melody looked steadily at the judge, who leaned forward and peered at her as if she couldn't quite make out Melody's features. "Yes, your Honor, I'm sure she misses her daddy. Jack isn't all bad, and Andrea loves him—the good part of him."

"And do you love Jack, Melody? The good part of him?"

"Honestly, I'm still trying to work that out in my own mind and heart. Lately I've been very angry with him for all he put us through—but I know, in my mind, that I was to blame, as well. For letting him do it, for so long. For putting up with it."

"Why did you put up with it?"

Melody's lips held the ghost of a smile. "I'm still learning about that, too," she admitted.

"I guess I bought into the idea that it was all my fault, that if I could just be better—do better—not make him angry, that things wouldn't be that way. If I could just anticipate what might set him off, and not let it happen, we'd be happier. Now I know that I was fooling myself. The problem was mostly within Jack, and not so much to do with me or with Andi, and anything we did or didn't do. I just—I enabled him to be abusive, by blaming myself. I'm not entirely sure how I ever got roped into doing that." She paused for a moment, then continued. "You see, the thing is, I wanted—I really wanted our family to stay together. What's happened—all of us apart, Andi not with either of us—that was like my worst nightmare. And yet I helped to make it happen. And for that, I'm very, very sorry."

"Would you rather that things had gone on as they were?"

"No. No, ma'am."

"Would you say you're depressed, Mrs. Padgett?"

Melody considered this. "Not depressed so that I need medication," she said. "But am I sad, because of how things are? Yes, ma'am—um, your Honor—I'm sad without my little girl. It's like my reason for doing things has disappeared. There's not much color in my life these days. I just go through the motions, but it's not fun to make dinner just for me, and Halloween was miserable. I kept wondering if Andi had a costume, and if she got any treats. I don't even like to think about Christmas. But, no, I'm not what you'd call clinically depressed. I'm just missing her. And my counseling sessions help, because I can explain all my feelings to my counselor, and she understands."

"That would be Mrs. Hallmark?"

"Yes, ma'am."

"Is Mrs. Hallmark here?"

"Yes, your Honor." Sister Hallmark stood.

"You may sit down, Mrs. Padgett. Mrs. Hallmark, would you characterize Mrs. Padgett as a good mother?"

"Mrs. Padgett desires above all else to be a good mother, your Honor, and she's making admirable progress in learning to stand up for herself and for her child. In my opinion, she already was an excellent mother, but laboring under very difficult circumstances, and adapting her responses the best she could at the time to keep her family intact and continue to mother her child. Now, she's learning healthier responses, and I feel that she and Andrea would do well together."

"Without Mr. Padgett, you mean?"

"For the time being, at least. I don't believe there's any question, is there, of reintroducing him into the family setting anytime soon?"

"Hell, no," growled the policeman from his corner, and Mrs. Parkman shook her head.

"That'll do," reprimanded the judge calmly, with a glance in their direction, and they murmured their apologies. "And thank you, Mrs. Hallmark. Mrs. Padgett, I'm interested in learning what made you change your thinking about your husband's behavior, and your part in enabling it. Did your thinking just begin to change on the morning when Jack and Andrea were removed from the home?"

Melody stood again, and slowly shook her head. "No, your Honor. My thinking had already begun to change, but I hadn't acted on it. I wish I had."

"Well, when did it begin to change, and why?"

"It was because of my bishop—my church leader. He sensed that something was wrong, that Jack was being abusive, and he asked us about it, on several occasions—especially me. I always denied it, because I guess that was how I felt I could keep our family together, and I didn't want Jack to think I was telling on him. I could only imagine how mean and angry Jack would be if I did that. But Bishop Shepherd didn't buy my denials, and gradually, what he said kind of wore me down, and I found myself almost admitting to him that he was right. I began to see that I didn't really deserve the way I was being treated, and that there might be some way to change things for all of us, and get Jack the help he needed. I was actually contemplating asking for help when everything blew up."

"I see. And is your—bishop—here today?"

"I am, your Honor. James Shepherd," the bishop said, rising to his feet. Melody sank back down.

"So you—sensed—that there was abuse going on in the Padgett home?"

This was dangerous ground. "I suspected, yes. But Melody always denied it, and even begged me not to talk to Jack about it. But eventually I confronted him, and told him what I suspected. He tried to downplay it, but didn't really deny it. He finally confessed to me that he didn't know any other way to deal with his frustrations, and I told him that either he would voluntarily get help, which I could help him initiate, or that I would have to intervene and contact the authorities."

She looked at him coolly. "Perhaps you should have intervened sooner."

"Perhaps so," he agreed. "But I feel it's always better if a person recognizes his need for help and asks for it. That's what I was trying to get Jack and Melody both to do."

"What's your opinion on whether Melody should regain custody of her daughter?"

"Your honor, one of my most deeply cherished beliefs is in the validity and integrity of the family, as the most basic unit of society and of my religion. Anytime we can arrange for a family to remain as intact as possible and work out their problems together, I'm all for it. Melody's a good mother, and she's in the process of becoming an even better one. She's great with kids—I've seen her in action, working with them at church, and I believe she and Andrea are devoted to each other. I don't believe Jack's ready to return to them, but I sincerely hope that one day he and their relationships will be healed to the point that he can do so, if that's what Melody decides she wants. In the meantime, my most sincere recommendation would be to allow Melody to regain custody of Andrea."

"I didn't ask you for your recommendation, Mr. Bishop—er, Shepherd, excuse me, I merely asked for your opinion."

"I'm sorry, your Honor. In any case, they're one and the same."

The judge glanced toward her bailiff. "Is the child here?"

"Yes, your Honor."

"Will you have her brought in, please?"

The bishop saw Melody stiffen. *Calm, Melody, calm,* he thought, wishing he were capable of thought-transference.

Andrea came into the room through a side door, her eyes wide at the assemblage of solemn adults. She held her arms folded, as if she were in Primary. The bishop put a smile on his face, in case she glanced his way. Melody gave a small gasp, and her eyes began to fill. Andrea found her mother, and took a small step forward, then paused.

"Mommy?" she said in a small voice. "Mommy, are you okay? I've been lost. You and Daddy forgot to come get me. I thought you didn't like me anymore."

"Oh, honey," Melody whispered. "I'm so glad to see you. I love you so much! Can I . . ."

She appealed to Judge Williams. "Can I hug her?"

"Well, I think you'd better," the judge said, with a tight little smile.

Melody held out her arms, and Andrea went into them, but her eyes were still big with apprehension and confusion, and glanced from face to face even as she returned her mother's embrace. She finally saw the bishop, and he winked at her. She waggled the fingers of one hand uncertainly. After she had examined each face in the room, she looked up at Melody.

"Daddy isn't here?" she questioned, and Melody shook her head. "No, honey. Just Mommy."

"Oh. Okay. Can we go home, just you and me?"

Melody's chin wobbled. "I hope so, sweetheart."

"Would you like that, Andrea?" asked Judge Williams. "Do you want to go home with just your Mommy, even if Daddy isn't there?"

Andrea nodded. "I thought my mommy was dead, 'cause her and Daddy didn't come get me. I thought it was my fault 'cause I was bad," she said, twisting her face to look up at her mother. "Was I bad, Mommy? Is that why you didn't come?"

"No, no, never, honey. It was never your fault, not at all." Melody buried her face in her child's curls.

See? See? the bishop cried silently, to the powers that had taken and detained and sheltered the little girl for these long months. Hadn't they explained things to her? Surely they had, but it must be that she had to make sense of things in her own way. If Mommy and Daddy hadn't come to get her, it must be that they'd forgotten her, or died, or that she'd been so bad they didn't want her anymore. Her six-year-old's reasoning broke his heart.

The judge was speaking, issuing her decision that the custody of Andrea Padgett was to be immediately turned over to her mother, Mrs. Melody Padgett, and that both, together and separately, were to continue to undergo counseling and therapy until such time as the acting agencies and the courts were satisfied that they were sufficiently whole to be released. Andrea, who had started attending first grade, was to continue in the elementary school nearest her home. Jack Padgett was to continue, for at least another six months, to be under a restraining order to stay beyond a three-mile radius of the family home and the school at all times, which distance was sufficient to allow him to access his business on Melville Street. If he should accidentally come across his family, he was not to talk to them, nor they to him—and he was to immediately distance himself from them for the prescribed three miles. They were to do the same, and neither party was to seek the other out, nor make phone calls to one another, nor in any way violate the restraining order. Jack also remained under court orders to continue to attend therapy and counseling sessions as presently set up.

Melody rocked Andrea back and forth, tears of happiness blending with her smiles as she thanked the judge. The bishop thought it was probably the first real smile he had ever seen from Melody. He also thought he detected a certain moisture in the eyes of Judge Teresa Williams as she dismissed the hearing and turned aside.

CHAPTER EIGHTEEN

"THE SPIRIT'S DIVINEST TUITION"

Saturday morning, while Trish and the children were helping Muzzie and her girls get settled in their rented condo,
Bishop Shepherd sat at his dining room desk attempting
to write the required letters to and about Marybeth Lanier. He
had prayed for words, but so far they hadn't appeared on the
paper. Marybeth had taken exception to being addressed as
"Sister," so he had begun by writing, "Dear Mrs. Lanier," but for
some reason, that troubled him, and he crossed it out and wrote
"Mrs. Marybeth Lanier" on the first line, and under that, "Dear
Marybeth." That seemed better—friendlier—although the feelings he was experiencing at the moment were less than friendly.
He was upset with Marybeth, yes, even a bit angry with her, for
her stubborn refusal to try again to find out the truth of the
gospel of Christ, for her cavalier attitude toward the tender feelings of her husband and family and the covenants they had
made, and for her light dismissal of the beliefs he, himself,
cherished and tried to abide by.

He threw down his pen and headed for his truck. It was time

for a drive to Shepherd's Pass, the homestead his forebears had settled, and a place his heart turned to in times of stress and struggle. He kept the radio off as he drove, trying to allow his mind to relax and be open to promptings of the Spirit. The day was cool and windy, and it felt good to be out in it. His favorite tunnel of trees, instead of shading the road as they did in summer, now cast moving shadows of nearly bare limbs across the pavement. Fields had been harvested and plowed under, animals were kept closer to barns, and the land waited for winter.

He stopped at the farmhouse, the home of his cousin Spurling Deal, to let the family know he was about, so that no one would think he was trespassing.

"Well, hey, Jim," greeted Spurling's wife, Kaylene. "To what do we owe the honor?"

"Hey, Kaylene. No honor, I'm afraid. Just another of my hiking trips around the property, if y'all don't mind."

"No problem. I'll just call Spur and let him know you're here."

She extracted a cell phone from her apron pocket and did so.

"He says maybe you'll run into him. He's cuttin' brush up by the falls."

"Good, maybe I will, then. You know, I'm going to have to get me one of those phones, much as I hate to think of not being able to get away from some calls."

"Well, they've been a blessin' for us. Like now, I can get ahold of Spur anytime I need to. Wisht we'd've had 'em years ago."

"Reckon I'll have to move on into this century, pretty soon. I've even been learning to use a computer. So—how's everybody up here?"

Her smile was cheerful. "Oh, we're same as. Can't complain, except that we seem to get older, ever' birthday. How's your family?"

"Great, thanks. Can't complain, either—except that the kids seem to get older, every birthday!" He grinned. "Reckon it's planned that way, but I'd sure like to keep 'em young, and they're rarin' to grow up fast as possible. My Tiffani's sixteen, now—kind of a scary age."

"Oh, mercy. No more peace in the valley for y'all! I remember when Davey turned sixteen, I near thought I'd die of worry every time he took the truck anywheres. He'd peel outa here and kick up enough dust to bury us all! I'd keep the radio goin' the whole blessed time he was gone, just listenin' for news of accidents. Is your girl drivin', yet?"

"She's working on it. I don't look forward to her first solo drives."

"First hundred, is more like it. Well, you enjoy your hike, Jim, and give my love to Trish and the young'uns."

"Will do. Thanks, Kaylene."

He tramped along the edge of the fields where they bordered the woods until he found his favorite sitting rock, where he perched with his knees drawn up and his head on his folded arms. He listened to the wind in the trees, the gentle clacking of the branches and rustling of brown leaves, the occasional buzz of an insect, or cry of a bird, and allowed the stress and frustration to seep out of him.

"You see, Father," he prayed, "I think I feel partly defensive on my own behalf, partly on Brother Scott Lanier's behalf, and partly in Thy behalf, that this sister makes light of Thy revealed truth and the gospel of Thy Son. Now, I know Thou art able to fight Thine own battles, and I know Thou art aware of Sister

Lanier's state of mind and whatever the causes and reasons may be for the decision she's made. Wilt Thou please bless me to know how to deal with her according to Thy will, and forgive me for the upset feelings I have toward her, and for anything, no matter how small, that I may ever have done to help to bring about her loss of faith. Please bless me with Thy love, Father, and grant me a portion of the pure love of Christ, that I may learn to have charity toward Marybeth and toward all my fellow beings. I'm so very human, with so many obvious weaknesses, and I pray Thee to make up the difference, so that those I'm called to serve may be served in a way pleasing to Thee."

He sat and thought and listened for a while, prayed some more, then stood and stretched and walked into the wooded area, his shoes making a satisfying crunch in the fallen leaves and twigs. He heard the sound of sawing and chopping and followed it until he came upon his cousin of some degree or other, he wasn't exactly sure what, Spurling Deal. Spur was several years older than he—of a generation about halfway between his and his father's, and while they weren't exactly intimate friends, they'd always been cordial, and the farmer seemed to understand the grocer's occasional need to walk these lands and get away from the pressures of life in town.

"Hey, Spur," he called, and his cousin put down his saw and held out a hand to shake.

"Hey there, your ownself," Spur answered. "How in the world are you?"

"I'm good," the bishop replied. "Or at least, I'm trying to be. Thanks for letting me come up here and tramp around. It does my soul good, somehow."

"Know what you mean," the older man agreed. "There's somethin' about bein' out in God's green earth that heals a body, and helps him think clear. Reckon that's one reason I was set on raisin' my family up here, so the kids could grow up feelin' that." He lifted his cap and scratched the back of his head. "I'm not one hundred percent sure it worked on all of 'em, but I do think the distance from town held down the problems just a little, and workin' the earth is kinda like helpin' the Lord out, if you catch my meanin'. It puts things into perspective, and it gives you faith to see how regular the sun comes up ever' mornin' and the crops ever' spring."

"Exactly. Perspective. I think that's what I come up here looking for," the bishop agreed. "What you doing today—cleaning out some undergrowth?"

"Yessir, I don't like this area to get too wild and overgrown. Too many critters take up habitation here if it does—some that harm the crops. Even at that, we get a passel of deer and coon and rabbits and skunk and possum. If I made it too friendly for 'em, we'd never harvest a leaf of anything. Plus, when it's dried out, there's a fire danger from lightnin' strikes. So how's the store-keepin' business?"

"It's not bad. We won't become millionaires as independent grocers, but it's a living, and I enjoy most things about it. We're always real happy to get fresh produce from you folks. It sells out fast."

"Uh-huh, that's good. Reckon if it was me, I'd be worried that the big superstore chains'd force me out of business."

"They sure do provide some stiff competition, and we can't beat 'em in a lot of ways," the bishop admitted. "I don't know, for certain, whether there'll be a business to pass on to my Jamie when he's grown—and of course, that's assuming he's interested, which I reckon I shouldn't assume." He looked out over the fields. It was a concern he had—not a major worry, but a concern.

"Wal, yeah—iffen he's interested. See, I thought my David would take over the farm, here, but no—he's gone off to Huntsville and become an accountant. It's Harvey that loves the place, and when he was a young'un I couldn't hardly get him to turn a hand to do anything around the fields or the animals, neither one. Now I depend on him, and he's stepped up to the plate like a trooper. So, go figger."

"So far, Jamie's most interested in the space program, but who knows how things might change by the time he's grown."

Spurling wiped his hands on his jeans and picked up his saw again. "Whoo-ee! This old world's changin' so fast, I cringe to think how things might be by then. Y'all keepin' up with this terror business?"

"Oh, sure we are. Can't avoid it, even if we wanted to. It's a wake-up call, for certain."

"Kaylene and me, we figger folks better turn to the Lord, and stop tryin' to outdo one another in sin and greed."

"Spurling, I totally agree. Listen, I won't keep you from your work, but thanks again for letting me hike around up here."

"You're fam'ly," Spurling said, his tanned face creasing into its well-established pattern of wrinkles and laughlines. "Come anytime. Bring your young'uns next time, hear?"

"Thanks. I'll do that."

The bishop continued his hike to the falls that Kaylene had mentioned, where he spent some time watching the trickle of water that fell little more than a yard into a mossy pool that fed a minuscule stream meandering down through a meadowland. In the spring there was much more volume and rush to the water, but just now the small-scale trickle was pleasing to the eye and ear and spirit. This spot had been a place of prayer for him a number of times, and it was so, again, on this occasion. He enjoyed attending the temple in Birmingham, and was grateful to have such a blessed place relatively close to his home, but somehow, this little glade felt, to him, almost as hallowed as that sacred edifice.

When he returned home that afternoon, he still didn't know how to word his letter to Marybeth Lanier, but he was calm, and no longer angry—and for that, he was grateful.

"Hey, Bish-upp!" It was the unmistakable voice of T-Rex in the church parking lot, and the way the young man emphasized the second syllable made the bishop smile. Obviously, the lesson on speaking respectfully to and of priesthood leaders and others had taken, and T-Rex was letting him know it. He grinned and joined him on the way into the building.

"Hey, Thomas! How's it going?"

"Aw, Bishop, I'm pretty bummed about the season bein' over, and we didn't get to the finals. That sucks. Uh—pardon the expression."

"I know it does. Well, if it's any comfort, you did your part—you were unstoppable! Hey, that reminds me, Thomas, I've got something for you, and I think it'll blow you away. I'll bring it over to your house, first chance I get."

"Aw, Bishop, you shouldn't have! I don't really need a new motorcycle."

"Yeah, right. I'm not convinced you need the one you've got! Now, an old truck to work on and race—that's the ticket."

"Is that what you did, back when?"

"It sure is. And I still get this nostalgic, yearning feeling whenever I see an old truck of that vintage, or whenever I see something on TV about the Nascar truck series. Takes me right back to those glorious Saturday mornings with all the dust and the roaring engines and speed and cheering."

"Yeah, that'd be cool, all right! I didn't know you were into racing and stuff."

"Oh, yeah. Every now and then I get mesmerized, standing in front of the television watching a race, when I only meant to walk through the room on my way somewhere else. Then my wife notices, and waves her hand in front of me, like, 'why are you standing there with that look on your face? I thought you were going to wash the car.' See, my wife's wonderful, and I'm grateful I married her, but she just doesn't get this fascination I have for trucks and cars chasing each other round and round in circles."

"Don't reckon most girls—or ladies—would. Lots of women do go to races, though."

The bishop sighed. "Not mine. Jamie likes it, though. He's a kid after my own heart. So anyway, Thomas, I'll bring that little gift around, soon."

"Great. Thanks, Bishop!"

"Oh, Thomas—are you folks going to be around for Thanksgiving, or are you heading off to be with family or something?"

"Reckon we'll be around. Mama says we're keepin' it simple this year. Just chicken and dressing and football on TV."

"Okay, then I'll catch up to you sometime during the holiday."

After teaching his priests that day, the bishop followed VerDan Winslow down the hall toward the back door of the building, waiting while the boy chatted with several young people, then placed a hand on his shoulder and asked for a few moments of his time. He had studied VerDan during sacrament meeting, and it had become clear in his mind what he must do. VerDan followed him to his office.

"Brother Winslow, I've been giving the matter of your mission some serious and prayerful consideration, and I have a proposal for you."

VerDan combed his hand through his hair. "I'll bet you didn't like my talk last week very much, did you, Bishop? My mom got all over me about it, but I was just trying to add a little humor, that's all. I'm sorry if it didn't come across okay."

The bishop shook his head. "Actually, I wasn't going to mention your talk. I'm pleased with you for making the effort, and I've never objected to a little humor, as long as it's in good taste. You were a little hard on Brother Brigham, true, but that's not what I called you in here for."

"Oh. Okay. What's the proposal?"

"Well, I strongly feel that in order to be prepared to represent the Lord Jesus Christ and His restored Church to the people of the world, prospective missionaries need to develop a sure and certain testimony of their own regarding His divinity and atonement, and regarding the truthfulness of the Book of Mormon and the mission of the Prophet Joseph Smith. I'm going to speak very plainly, VerDan. So far, what I've heard from you with regard to testimony has been kind of half-hearted and wishy-washy, and frankly, we don't need half-hearted, wishy-washy missionaries, we need strong, clean, righteous, and committed young people to go out and sound a warning to the world. You remember the scripture about the trumpet giving an uncertain sound?"

VerDan frowned. "Uh—I don't know. Where is that?"

The bishop pushed his Bible across the desk to the young man. "First Corinthians, chapter fourteen, verse eight."

He watched as VerDan paged through the volume, obviously at a loss to find First Corinthians.

"It's in the New Testament," he prompted.

"Oh. Sure." It was still apparent that he was confused, but the bishop watched patiently until he found the reference.

"Want to read that for us?" he asked.

"Okay. 'For if the trumpet give an uncertain sound, who shall prepare himself to the battle?' Is that all?"

"That's it. What d'you think that might mean, VerDan?"

"Um—I guess it's something about going to war, and somebody blowing a trumpet, getting ready for a battle, but . . ."

"Okay, good. Now how does that relate to being a good missionary?"

VerDan set the scriptures back on the desk. "Well, I know the angel Moroni on top of the temple blows a trumpet, I guess to wake up the world to hear the gospel. Is that what you mean?"

"Close. See, our missionaries are like Moroni, bringing the restored, everlasting gospel to people. They don't literally blow trumpets, of course, but they do sound a warning and try to get people's attention so they'll listen to the message of the restoration and the good news of the gospel. Now, if a missionary's trumpet—his voice, or testimony—is uncertain-sounding, if he isn't sure of what he's teaching, how is that going to give people confidence in his message? You wouldn't want a group of soldiers saying, 'Uh, was that the battle call? I thought maybe I heard it, but I'm not sure, so I'll just sleep a while longer, until I know for certain.' Then, all of a sudden, 'uh, oh! Here's the enemy upon us!' Do you hear what I'm saying, VerDan?"

"Yes sir, I suppose I do. I need to get a stronger testimony before I go out, is that it?"

"Exactly, so that you'll be confident and excited to be there, and committed to what a mission is all about. And, see—this scripture applies to me, too. What if I'm the trumpeter, but I give you an uncertain call to the battle for men's souls? What if I say, 'Well, VerDan, you're a nice guy, and personable and well-groomed, and I'm sure you'll make a fine missionary even if you don't know the scriptures or teach with much power and conviction—at least, people will like you, so it's probably okay if you go out and try to serve.' Then the burden would be upon me, for your success or failure—and frankly, I'm not ready to take that on myself. So what I'm counseling you is to go home and study the gospel and the scriptures like you've never studied them before. Pray as you've never prayed before, for knowledge and wisdom and testimony of what you study. Pray for forgiveness of any sins you might have committed. Keep the commandments to the best of your ability. Don't worry about dating, right now. Work until you have a testimony that shines bright as day and you're excited about the idea of going out and sharing it with others. Then come back and see me, and we'll talk about a mission."

"I see. Wow. Um—about how long do you think it'll take me to get ready?"

"That's entirely up to you and the Lord. I just know it's been made clear to me that you're not ready, now."

"Oh, man, my mom's going to be—hey, Bishop, could you talk to her for me? I just don't think I can go home and face her and tell her this. I mean, she wants me out in the mission field like, yesterday!"

The bishop smiled. "Your mother is a fine and a formidable woman, and I understand exactly what you're saying. You just tell her the bishop thinks you need to prepare some more before you go out, and refer her to me for the rest. Okay? Now, let me tell you about a couple of guys who are serving from our ward at the present time."

He described Elders Donnie Smedley and Rand Rivenbark, and read aloud his last two letters from them. He then gave VerDan a list of scriptures he had hastily compiled during the Sunday School hour and told him to start by studying those. VerDan rose, his expression more sober than the bishop had ever seen it, shook hands and departed. The bishop leaned back in his chair and closed his eyes, feeling as though the weight of the world had just been lifted from his shoulders.

He strolled toward the chapel to see how choir practice was going. Trish and Tiffani sat on one side of the choir section, with Rosetta McIntyre, apparently an alto, on the other. Claire Patrenko was at the piano, and Sister Tullis at the organ. Jamie slouched on the front pew of the congregational seating, looking bored and mutinous, with Mallory beside him on her knees, using the pew for a table while she colored a picture from

Primary. Linda DeNeuve stood before her choir of three with her arms folded, as they talked in low voices.

"Is this the choir, for today?" the bishop asked, trying to keep his voice cheerful.

Linda turned and smiled. "Afraid this is it, Bishop. What do you suggest we do?"

"Looks like I'm going to have to issue a few calls," he replied. "I was reluctant to do it, because it seems to me a choir should be a volunteer organization based on interest and musical ability—but obviously our members just aren't used to thinking in those terms." He thought for a minute, then added, "in the meantime, let's sing!"

"All three of us?" Trish asked wryly.

"All five of us," he replied. "Come on, James, we're needed up here!"

Jamie looked alarmed. "Who, me? I can't sing!"

"Yes, you can, better than I," returned his dad, motioning him forward with his arm.

Jamie dragged himself up to a seat beside his mother, who leaned down and whispered, "You can just sing the melody, along with Tiff and me."

"What part do you sing, Bishop?" inquired Linda hopefully.

"I'd probably be a bass if I knew how to carry a part, but I don't. Why don't we just all sing the melody, for now? What hymns have you selected, to start with?"

"Seeing as it's November, I thought we might start with 'Prayer of Thanksgiving,' number ninety-three."

"Excellent! Let's do it. With the support of both piano and organ to—er—drown us out, we should sound pretty good, don't you think?"

Amid the chuckles, Linda took her place and raised her

small white baton. The bishop thought she looked properly competent, and as she directed their song, he was confirmed in his impression. Linda DeNeuve knew her stuff! They sang enthusiastically, they learned something about breathing and phrasing, and when the rehearsal was over, they had a plan to sing the next Sunday and to have the congregation join in on the third verse. The bishop drove his family home feeling much more cheerful about several things than he had when the Sabbath began.

"So you got Muzzie settled okay, did you?" he asked, as he and Trish, dressed snugly in matching sweatshirts, took their customary Sunday evening stroll around their neighborhood.

"Yes, but—it's just so sad, Jim. I mean, I know the condo's just temporary, and it's not too bad, not a dump or anything, but it's just so—generic. It has three bedrooms, and they set one up for Bradley, in the hope that they'll be able to have him join them, but I just don't know—it's so bizarre—what's Dugie thinking, to take Brad and run? Where could they be?"

"Yeah, makes you wonder if he grabbed the boy because he genuinely wanted him, or just to get back at Muzzie for taking the girls and splitting. I sure feel bad for Muzzie and the girls— and the boy, too. Who knows what kind of stuff his dad is feeding him—literally and psychologically."

"Right. I am encouraged, though, by Muzzie's new interest in praying and trying to establish a relationship with the Lord. She's always just been a sort of brand-X Christian, if you know what I mean. She believes in Jesus, but doesn't really know much about Him, or about the scriptures. If nothing else, maybe this miserable experience will help her to discover His love for her—and eventually, maybe she'll even want to know more about what we believe. She's sure impressed by you. Said she had no idea you were so spiritually insightful."

"Did you explain how it's not me, but the Spirit working through me, that she felt?"

"Tried, but she still thinks you're wonderful. Of course, I had to agree with her, there."

He smiled and squeezed her hand. "Well, sure," he teased, and then sobered, thinking of the many ways in which he knew he was much less than wonderful. The letter to Marybeth was still on his mind, and he dreaded the confrontation he knew was coming with Sister LaThea Winslow over VerDan's lack of preparation. He had prayed to know how to find a balance between making clear VerDan's needs and deficiencies without insulting his mother and her desire for her son to serve a mission as soon as possible. Sometimes being a bishop was a lot like walking a tightrope, he reflected. His balance bar was the Lord, his safety net his counselors and clerks—or was it vice versa? In any case, there was no way he could make it safely to the other side of this experience without any of them.

The concepts for the letter came to him in the early hours of Monday morning, and he rose before daylight and padded down to his desk in his robe and slippers.

"Dear Marybeth," he wrote.

It is with great regret that I acknowledge your request to have your name removed from the

membership rolls of The Church of Jesus Christ
of Latter-day Saints. I had hoped never to have to
comply with such a request during my term as
bishop. I would much prefer to be welcoming you
into the fellowship of the Saints and the household
of God. However, I respect, and so does the Church,
your God-given right to make your own choices and
decisions in matters of faith and religion.

You should know, however, that taking this step
will cancel all the covenants and ordinances into
which you have entered—baptism, confirmation,
the gift of the Holy Ghost, and all your temple
blessings, including your endowment and temple
sealing. The consequences are that you will have
no claim on your family, nor they on you, in the
eternities, nor will you be able to attain the Celestial
Kingdom of the Father and enjoy the great blessings
that had been in reserve for you if you had remained
true and faithful to your covenants.

I am aware that in your present frame of mind,
these things seem of no consequence, but I urge you
to contemplate the reality and finality of these
decisions and the great loss that will come to you
and to your family as a result of your decision.

If you still feel determined to leave the Church
and relinquish all your above-named blessings, you
will need to write a letter to me, officially making
your request. If that is your intent, I will fill out the
necessary paperwork and forward the documents,
along with your record of membership to our stake
president. There follows a thirty-day waiting period to

allow you time to reconsider your decision, and if, at the end of that time, you still are determined to have your name removed, your request will be honored.

After that, you will no longer be able to participate in any Church ordinances or partake of any of the blessings and privileges of membership, such as attending the temple, praying or speaking in meetings, partaking of the sacrament, holding Church positions, and so forth. You will still be welcome, of course, to attend any regular Church meetings to which the public is invited.

If you in fact pursue this course and your name is removed from the membership rolls of the Church, and should you ultimately desire to rejoin the Church, it will be necessary for you to be rebaptized, following a thorough worthiness interview.

Marybeth, as your friend and bishop, I must encourage you once again to consider well the step you are taking, and the effects it will have on you and your loved ones and all who know and care for you. I still feel that you can learn to know the truthfulness of the restored gospel of Christ through sincere study and prayer. My prayer is that you will make the effort to learn of these things, and I assure you of my willingness to help you in any way you feel I can.

Sincerely,
Bishop James D. Shepherd

He read over the letter, then laboriously typed a clean copy and folded it into an envelope. This task attended to, he put his head down on his arms and gave himself up to the sorrow of the moment. *Why, Father?* he prayed silently. *Why can't she see the truth, the worth of all Thou hast provided? Why is this necessary?*

Just before he roused himself to go upstairs and dress for the day, the answer came, gentle but unmistakable: "Suffer it to be so now, for the sake of Marybeth's soul." He sat up then, thrills of recognition coursing through him.

"Thy will be done," he whispered.

CHAPTER NINETEEN

"OF MERCIES AND OF MIRACLES"

On his way to the store that Monday morning, Bishop Shepherd detoured by the residence of Scott and Marybeth Lanier to give her the letter. Their one-story home was constructed of old brick in pastel shades with white wrought-iron railings and columns. The early morning sun sent long shadows of tree trunks across the spacious lawn. He rang the doorbell, surprised at the calm he felt.

Scott answered the door. "Oh—good morning, Bishop," he said. "Please, come on in."

"Good morning, Scott. I have a letter for Marybeth. Does she happen to be up and about at this hour?"

"Actually, she's out jogging. Can I give it to her?"

"Sure. And let me give you a heads-up regarding the fact that she'll need to write a letter making her request and detailing her reasons for it, however she chooses to do so, and give that to me. I've told her that in here and also tried to explain the consequences of her choice." He gazed at the polished parquet floor for a moment, then looked up and continued. "I'll tell you something interesting, Scott—this whole thing makes me real sad, but the Lord's made it known to me that, for some reason, this is what's in Marybeth's best interest, right now. That's of some comfort to me, and I hope it can be to you, too."

Scott frowned. "I wonder—how can that be? I mean, it seems so wrong, so senseless . . ."

"Believe me, Scott, I understand you. Those have been my exact feelings. But early this morning, I was blessed to know just that much—not why, or what'll happen down the road—but just that for now, this is what needs to happen, for the sake of her soul."

"Well, thanks for sharing that insight with me. I'll let it soak in and try to comprehend what it might mean. I remember reading that in cases of excommunication, it's actually kinder to the person to remove their Church membership and its obligations than to allow them to continue to sin as members, but I don't exactly see that applying here."

The bishop shook his head. "We know so little of what goes on in another's heart and mind," he said. "Generally, only what they allow us to know. I surely can't claim to understand Marybeth's thinking right now, but it may be that she'll have to lose her membership and her temple blessings before she can realize that they're meaningful and valuable to her. Ultimately, this may be a learning experience for her that she needs."

Scott blinked. "It's certainly a tough learning experience for me," he said. "I sure hope I wasn't the one who needed it to happen, in order to grow spiritually!" He attempted a wobbly smile. "I'm pretty sure I didn't volunteer for this in the premortal life. If I did, somebody should have yanked on my robe and told me to sit down."

"I hear you, Brother." The bishop glanced at a framed

photograph of the family on a small table in the foyer. "How's John doing?"

"He's finally figured out that his mother is serious about this, and he's pretty upset. He and his wife, Meg, are fasting and praying for her."

"That can't hurt. You might share with him the insight I was given, in case it helps."

"I'll do that. Bishop, you're a rock—thanks so much for standing by me."

"Glad to do it. Have as good a day as you can, okay?"

About eleven-thirty, he heard himself being paged by Mary Lynn Connors, asking him to come to the office. He had been back in the storeroom, and hurried to his office on the northeast front corner of the market.

"Hey, Mary Lynn, what's—oh, I see! How are you, Jack?"

Jack Padgett stood by Mary Lynn's desk, shifting uneasily from foot to foot. He shook the bishop's outstretched hand. "I'm in town checking on my store here, and figured it was my turn to treat you to lunch," he said. "Unless, of course, you've got other plans."

"Nothing I'd like better. Let me just wash my hands and grab my jacket, and we'll run out and try to beat the rush."

In the restroom, he took a moment for a quick prayer of guidance, then hurried back to Jack. "You pick the place," the bishop told him. "Whatever sounds good. I'm not particular."

They drove in Jack's SUV to a home-style cafe on the far south end of town.

"Gotta stay as far from the house and Andi's school as

possible, you know," he remarked dryly. "Guess you're aware of the new situation."

"I am," the bishop agreed. "I was at the hearing. I'm glad Andi's back with Melody. But I know it must be hard on you, not to be able to see them."

Jack didn't reply, but concentrated on the menu. "Meatloaf," he told the server when she appeared. "Mashed potatoes, corn, and a cola."

The bishop ordered smothered pork chops with rice and a green salad. Just water," he told her when asked about a beverage. Trish would be proud of him. When the server left, Jack turned to the side, leaned back, and stretched his legs out on the seat of the booth.

"So, how does Andi look? She okay?" he asked.

"She looks great. She was really glad to see her mom, and she asked if you were there, too."

"Did she? Little pun'kin'." Jack allowed a pleased grin to touch his lips for a second. "You know, it's kinda ironic the way things work out, sometimes."

"How's that?"

"I used to be so dang sure that if I gave Melody half a chance, she'd take Andi and leave me. Now she's got the opportunity, and she can't leave the area, by decree of law."

The bishop shrugged. "You know, I never got the impression that Melody wanted to run off with Andrea," he said. "She's never said a word to me that indicated that."

"Oh, don't you worry. She thought of it, plenty of times."

When you were hitting her and pushing her around? the bishop asked silently. Aloud, he said, "I imagine lots of wives have a few times when the thought enters their minds. But from everything

Melody's said, it's seemed to me that one of her main goals was to keep the family together."

Jack gave one of his quick sideways glances. "That's been one of my goals, too. Guess I just didn't go about it the right way."

The bishop took a sip of his water and squeezed a spritz of lemon into it. "Well," he said mildly, "force and intimidation don't usually work real well with people. Especially in a family setting."

Jack ducked his head. "Worked for my old man," he said in a low voice.

Their food arrived, served family style so that each could try some of every dish if they wanted. The bishop picked up on Jack's last statement, knowing from the way it was delivered that it was important and true. Jack had a way of throwing away his most meaningful comments as if they were nothing.

"Have a pork chop, Jack," the bishop invited. "Two're plenty for me, and they smell real good. Tell me about the family you grew up in," he added. "How many kids were there?"

"Just me and my brother," Jack said. "Help yourself to meat-loaf, too. I get it every time I come here. It's not bad."

"Thanks. Were both folks at home while you were growing up?"

"Huh. Unfortunately."

"Which one would you have tossed out, if you could've?"

"My dad, no question. He was a hell-raiser, no doubt about it. Didn't give a hoot for either of us kids. Guess we weren't any great prize, for that matter—couple of little ruffians—but yeah, whenever he was gone, things were easier at home."

"How'd your mom deal with him?"

"They fought. He was a drinker, and liked to gamble. He'd

gamble on horse races, football games, whether a storm would hit when the weatherman said it would—anything to bet a buck. You can imagine, he lost way more than he ever won— and Mom'd get mad and yell at him for hours, till he'd either leave or knock her across the room." Jack was silent for a moment, eating, then stole a glance at his companion. "I know what you're thinking, and you're right. I learned it from him."

The bishop nodded. "It's pretty hard not to learn from what we see, every day of our lives." Inwardly, he gave thanks for the peace-loving, kindly man his father had been. "Were you close to your mother, then?"

Jack didn't answer immediately. Instead, he raised a hand to signal their server and asked for a refill on his drink. Then he glanced away out the window to the parking lot. "Couldn't trust her," he muttered. "Have some of these potatoes, will you? They really pile 'em on."

Aha, thought the bishop. *Another throwaway line.* He worked on his lunch for a few minutes, then after the refill had arrived, he ventured another question.

"So your mother wasn't trustworthy, either?"

Jack frowned. Finally he shook his head. "Hm-mm," he agreed.

"This is hard to talk about," the bishop observed in a quiet voice. It wasn't a question.

"Well, you know—all these blasted counselors and thera-pists, they keep picking and picking at old sores, trying to get 'em to drain all the infection out so they can heal. Guess I see the reasoning, but it hurts like hell, Bishop, I gotta tell you that."

"I'll just bet it does. I'm sorry, my friend. You don't have to tell me anything you don't want to. I'm just interested, because I care about you and Melody and Andi."

Jack took a long drink of his soda. "Mel used to try to get me to tell her about my family. I didn't want to. I mean, I'd left all that behind when I turned eighteen. I figured there wasn't anything the Marines could throw at me that I hadn't already been through. So no point in dredging it all up again, was there? It's not exactly a pretty family history to put in an album."

"I understand. But did you really leave it all behind?"

"You a therapist, too, Bishop? You're starting to sound like one."

"No, no. Sorry. It just occurred to me that sometimes when we try to stuff hurtful things out of sight and out of mind, without really coming to terms with them, they sort of come out sideways, when we least expect it."

"Yeah. Yeah, I'm beginning to see that." He picked at his potatoes. "Hell, I'll tell you about dear old Mom, if you wanta know. She never stood up for us, me and Dan. We were named Jack and Daniel, get it? For the old man's favorite beverage. Anyway, she'd let Dad beat us up, even when she knew we hadn't done whatever it was he was beating us for. And she'd tell on us, things we'd done, so that he'd come after us. It was like—how she pleased him."

"I imagine she was afraid of him."

"Oh, yeah. We all were. He was dangerous. But, man— don't you see? She sacrificed us! Even when we were little kids. We couldn't tell her anything, 'cause she'd run to him and blab. We learned early on that she couldn't be trusted. So that's my sweet, sainted mother, for you. Now you know."

"So, did you and Dan turn to each other for companionship, and to keep each other's secrets?"

"For a while. But then he turned into as big a snitch as Mom. See, Dad always tried to turn us against each other, so we'd tattle. He'd go easier on one of us if we were the first to let him know something bad the other one had done. So I guess I shouldn't blame Dan too much. There was a lot of pressure on both of us. But, nah—we haven't been close, for years."

"I can see why. And now your folks are gone?"

"Yep, both of 'em. Guess I shouldn't let 'em bug me anymore, since they aren't even on the face of the earth, should I?"

"Well, easier said than done, I expect, when things were so . . ." He couldn't think of a word.

"'Dysfunctional,'" Jack supplied in a mocking tone. "That's the current catchphrase for hell on earth. That's what the therapists call it." He signaled for the server again, and ordered apple pie for both of them.

"Cheese or ice cream?" he asked.

"Oh, um—cheese, thanks," the bishop said, not at all certain that his appetite was up to the challenge. It didn't do his digestion any good to mix food with feelings such as this meeting had engendered. He kept wanting to hug the little kid Jack had been, and set him on his knee. He wished it were possible.

"What's on the menu tonight, brethren?" the bishop joked as he entered the clerks' office on Tuesday evening.

"You mean by way of dinner, or appointments?" asked Sam Wright with a grin. "Sister Arnaud's bringing us over a pot of her gumbo. Then I hear Sister Winslow wants a few minutes of your time."

The bishop winced. "I expect she'll want to feed me a little humble pie, or a piece of crow with sour grapes on the side, but I'm not biting. I'm afraid she's not going to be real happy with me for a while."

"That's all right," said Robert Patrenko, patting his shoulder. "A bishop's gotta do what a bishop's gotta do."

"Reckon that's so. Who else is on the schedule?"

Dan McMillan showed him a list. "Looks like you have an interview with Rosalin Rivenbark, who's turning twelve next Saturday, then LaThea, then a few minutes with Sister Reams, and finally, Brother and Sister Parsons would like a word with you."

"Great. And what have we found out about anyone who needs food, or a place to eat on Thanksgiving?"

Brother Patrenko answered. "Nobody's admitting to needing anything, but I wonder about a few families. Of course there's the Rexfords, and the Mobleys, although I expect Junious and Nita will be going to their son's place. Dolans insist they're doing fine, even though he's still only able to work part time. Hilda Bainbridge is invited over to eat with the Reams. I suppose Melody Padgett will be okay, now that Andrea's home."

"Melody and Andrea are invited to our house," the bishop said. "But I'm wondering about Buddy Osborne. Reckon it'll depend on which parent he's with for this holiday. I think I'll call him, just to be sure."

"What about Jack Padgett?" asked Sam. "Reckon he's likely to be the loneliest of anybody, this holiday season."

"Don't worry about Jack," the bishop replied. "I happen to know that the Smedleys have invited him over—and they're far enough south that he won't violate the court order by going there. Brother Smedley, you know, was Jack's home teacher."

"Is Jack attending church anywhere?" asked Robert.

"I know he's been to the Anniston Ward a couple of times."

"How's he doing, anyway?"

"You know," the bishop said thoughtfully, "I believe I can see the beginnings of a change in Jack—just a little softening up. But he has a long way to go—a lot to overcome."

The interview with Rosalin Rivenbark was first, so that she could get to her Beehive activity. She was a pretty little girl with brunette coloring and hazel eyes that were reminiscent of her big brother's, and a sweetness of spirit that further endeared the Rivenbark family to the bishop. He wanted to get to know them better. He congratulated Rosalin on completing her requirements for graduation from Primary and asked her to recite some of the Articles of Faith. As he suspected she would, she quoted them flawlessly. He also encouraged her to pay particular attention to the Young Women values and her Personal Progress program before sending her off to her first Mutual meeting.

Shortly after she left, LaThea Winslow breezed in through the open door.

"Evening, Bishop. Are you ready to see me?" she asked, standing behind one of his guest chairs and gripping its back.

A good question, he thought. "Of course, Sister Winslow, how are you?" he asked cordially.

"I'm well, thank you, and I have two items to run by you," she said. He thought her voice was a little cool, like the brisk autumn winds outside. "First of all, the plans are firmed up for our Family Festival of Booths on the thirtieth. Flyers have gone out to families suggesting what kinds of materials they might use to build their booths in the cultural hall. Have you received yours? You should have."

"Um—probably Trish has. I haven't seen it, yet."

"Well, everything seems to be shaping up on schedule. For the dinner, we're having apricot chicken, apple-stuffed acorn squash, broccoli salad with seeds and raisins, and for dessert, carrot-zucchini cake or candied apples for the children, which is a traditional treat for this festival. The idea is to use a lot of harvest foods. Brother Warshaw is going to talk about the meaning of the festival, and the children will play traditional games."

"LaThea, bless your heart, you go to so much trouble for these occasions—"

"It's my calling, and I enjoy it. We should have held this one earlier in the fall, for it to be more authentic, but of course there was Halloween last month and the special nine-eleven project the month before. Anyway, I just wanted you to know that things are coming along."

"Thanks. It's great to know that I can depend on you."

"Of course you can. Now, Bishop, if only I could depend on you not to throw up roadblocks in front of my son, who needs to be out serving the Lord on his mission! I thought I had made it clear that we wanted VerDan to go out as quickly as possible, while he has the Spirit of missionary work. I'm afraid if he waits, he'll lose that burning desire. Don't you see? And yet, he tells me you think he needs more time to prepare."

The bishop folded his hands on top of the desk. "Dear Sister, please sit down."

LaThea drew in her breath sharply, but she sat.

"I would like nothing better than to be able to expedite

VerDan's mission call, but the Spirit won't allow that to happen," he said carefully.

"What can you possibly mean?"

"I don't mean to be unkind, but the fact is, VerDan isn't ready, and we wouldn't be doing him any favor by sending him out into the mission field with great haste. He needs to have a stronger testimony of the Lord and His gospel and the Book of Mormon than he presently has. He could really use a lot more knowledge of all the scriptures, and I'm not totally convinced that he's ready to put the world behind him for two years and go out and serve with commitment and honor."

"No, no, Bishop! You don't understand VerDan. He's just shy about speaking his deepest feelings in front of others. He's not a bad boy, and I'm certain he has a testimony! All my children do."

"I'm not saying that VerDan's a bad person. Certainly he's a personable young man, and he has, I'm sure, many fine qualities. It may be that he truly does have the foundation of a testimony. Obviously your other children served with distinction, and I hope that, with adequate preparation, VerDan will do the same. I had a good visit with him, and he knows exactly what he needs to do. Now, it's up to him."

"But, Bishop, you know how intensely they study the scriptures in the MTC, and he could be brushing up while he's waiting for his call. He's bright, and he could catch up! No. Wait— I know what it is. It was that talk he gave, wasn't it? I *told* him—"

"No, ma'am, it wasn't his talk. It isn't anything he's said, in particular. It's more what the Spirit has said, and it constrains me from recommending VerDan for a mission until I see some real changes, and the Spirit approves it."

Her face crumpled, and he was afraid she'd begin to cry. "Isn't it possible—isn't it *ever* possible—that what you think is the Spirit is really something else? Couldn't you be wrong?"

"You know, I'm sure I'm often wrong. And it's true there are times when I feel a prompting and wonder if it came from the Holy Ghost or just from somewhere inside me. But not this time. This was sufficiently strong that I know, as things stand, it would be displeasing to the Lord and not in VerDan's best interest to send him on a mission. I'm awfully sorry—I'd like to accommodate you folks—but I can't do it."

LaThea stared at her hands, twisting her diamond around on her finger, trying to regain control of her face and feelings. "Harville told me I ought not to beg, but I just had to try," she said in a small voice.

"I understand your desire to see your son serve the Lord," he replied gently.

"If he doesn't go now, I'm afraid he won't go, at all."

"Why is that?"

"Because—because there's a young woman who's after him, and she's the type who'll stop at nothing to get him. This is a window of opportunity for him to escape her, but sooner or later she'll find out he's here, and then I'm afraid it'll be too late. She'll persuade him to marry her."

"Well—how does VerDan feel about her? He told me he didn't have a special girlfriend."

"He doesn't! There's nothing special about her, and she's the one who insists they're going together. VerDan's just too sweet and kind for his own good. He doesn't know how to say no to her."

"So that's why he dropped out of school so suddenly and

came home? Not to serve a mission, but to get away from a pesky girl?"

LaThea's voice grew small again. "I was the one who suggested a mission, and he agreed, right away. He could see it was the only thing to do."

"What do you know about his relationship with this girl? Have they been intimate?"

"Certainly not! My children would never . . ."

The bishop shook his head. "Now, we're not talking about your children, in the plural. And I'm in no way implying that your teachings on morality have been less that excellent. I'm just asking what you know about VerDan and this particular young woman."

LaThea shook her bent head. "I honestly don't know. VerDan says not, but I have to wonder, because of the way he's talked about her in the past. And she's been downright shameless in her chasing of him. It's been going on for a year or more."

"So you wanted to send him quickly away on a mission, so that he could escape her—uh—overtures, even though you weren't entirely sure he was worthy?"

LaThea broke down into sobs, her words gushing out along with the tears. "I'm so sorry, Bishop! I was just trying to protect my boy. Harville told me not to push things, but I just felt I had to."

"I understand your position, Sister Winslow. And I hope now you understand mine."

"I do," she said humbly. "I know you're right. I've made a fool of myself, haven't I? I'm so sorry. And I'm so embarrassed. Nothing like this has ever happened in my family."

He pushed a box of tissues across the desk to her. "There's

no need for you to be embarrassed, LaThea. This conversation will stay just between us. No one else needs to know about it."

She looked up from behind her tissue. "Oh, Bishop—are you sure? No one?"

"No one at all," he assured her. "I'll need to talk further with VerDan, but no one else will need to know about that, either. This is a confidential matter between VerDan, me, and the Lord."

She nodded, and a fresh flood of tears began to fall. He felt these were cleansing tears, rather than those of rage or frustration.

He was drained by the interview with LaThea, and welcomed Sister Ida Lou Reams in with pleasure, knowing that this meeting, at least, would be a happy one.

"Bishop, reckon you already know what I'm gonna say," she began, her kind face a study in joy mixed with something else he couldn't quite define.

"Barker had something to say to you, I believe?" he said, returning her smile. "Something you've been hoping to hear, for a long time?"

"Oh, I'll say! He carried me down to Birmingham, to the temple grounds, and he parked and said, 'Now, Ida Lou, I brung you here to tell you that the next time you come down here, you can go in. I've made up my mind not to hold you back no longer.' Bishop, I tell you, I just sat and bawled like a baby! But then I up and says, 'No, Barker, I don't want to go in without you. The temple's a place for families to get sealed for eternity, and what would I do in there, without you?' I purely couldn't believe I heard myself asayin' that, but I did."

"Really! What'd Barker say to that?"

"Well, he got all solemn, and stared out the car window 'thout saying nothing for the longest time, and finally he says, 'Ida Lou, you know it ain't likely I'd ever qualify to go in there, and you know why. And you know it ain't 'cause I don't care for you and the family. Now I want you to go in there and do what-ever there is that you can do, 'thout me, and get you a head start. You deserve it, and it's my gift to you.' Well, then I couldn't hardly do nothin' but agree, could I? So I said I would. Will you and your sweet wife go with me, Bishop, my first time?"

"Wild horses couldn't keep us away," he told her. "And I'm certain I speak for Trish as well."

"And I thought I'd ask the other Relief Society ladies who work with me, and the ladies I take down there ever' month—Hildy, and Nita, and Sister Strickland—oh, and I'm gonna call my boy Billy's wife, and see if there's a chance they can drive up. I'll let you know when, all right? I'm just so thrilled I feel like a bride, or somethin'! I only wisht I was, with my Barker agoin', too."

The bishop nodded. "Just let Barker see how much joy it brings you, and how appreciative you are to him. Remember, we believe in miracles!"

"Well, I know I do! Speaking of such, you might be surprised to hear who's taking Thanksgiving dinner with us."

"Who's that?"

"Sister Hazel Buzbee."

"No way! She told me she never goes anywhere, not even to the doctor."

"Well, I don't know why it was, but I felt to invite her, and

I think she was surprised as anybody when she said she would. It's maybe because I told her Hildy was comin', an' she wants to see her, again. I'm going to get ever'thing done as early as possible, then late Thursday mornin', me and Barker'll drive up and fetch her down."

"That is truly amazing, Ida Lou. Thank you for being such a friend to her! And I heard about the dress you made her, too."

"Oh, that weren't nothin'. I was glad to."

Another miracle came in, carried in the arms of her father, Joe Parsons, who was grinning from ear to ear. Little Alyssa Parsons, with her dark, curly hair and rosy cheeks, was a picture to behold. Her mother, Lori, sat down in one of the chairs, while Joe stood beside her, bouncing the baby in his arms. Lori seemed about to bubble over with something.

"It's great to see you folks, and your beautiful little girl," the bishop said. "What can I do for you, this evening?"

"Bishop, do you believe in miracles?" asked Lori.

"I surely do—in fact, I was just saying so not ten minutes ago! Have you got one to tell me about?"

Lori's eyes brimmed. It was obviously a night for women to cry in his office—but for good reason, so far—and this looked to be for a good reason, as well. "You know that Alyssa was born profoundly deaf. You know that we've been planning on getting her a cochlear implant, right?"

"Right," he agreed. "Have you been approved for one, already?"

Lori glanced up at Joe. "We don't think we're going to need one," she said. "The last couple of weeks, Alyssa's been unusually fussy, and I just blamed it on teething, but the other day, our dog barked suddenly, right behind her, and she jumped, and started to cry! At first, I didn't take it in—then gradually, I realized that she had heard the dog! His bark had startled her. She'd never shown any sign, before, of hearing him barking—or anything else. I told Joe, and he said that it was likely a coincidence, or that maybe she felt the vibrations of the bark, or something. So we did an experiment. We went outside, and I stood with Alyssa by the front of the car, and Joe honked the horn. She jumped again, and started to cry, just like before!"

"You're kidding!" The bishop's pulse began to increase. "She actually heard?"

"Well, we took her right to the doctor the next day, and he told us to calm down, that it was virtually impossible that she had heard anything, but we insisted that they test her again. And, Bishop, we were right! She does have some hearing! Just in one ear, but it's pretty good! Can you believe it?"

"Oh, that's such good news—I'm so grateful! Lord be praised, for this great blessing! And it truly is a miracle, isn't it?"

"Well, the doctor called it one, and you know doctors don't throw that word around very often," said Joe Parsons. "He wants to do a study on her, see if he can figure it out. We were all prepared to go for the implant, saving up for it, and we already started learning how to sign. We weren't bitter about Alyssa's problem, or anything, and we surely weren't expecting this! But we're very thankful."

"I just can't stop smiling," Lori added. "Now I give thanks when she's fussy, or can't seem to sleep, because I realize she's getting used to having sound in her life, and it's all new and scary. You know, I've always sung to her when I've held her close to me, thinking that maybe the vibrations of my voice would soothe her even if she couldn't hear it—but now I'm so humbled by the fact that she hears, that I just cry when I try to sing, even though I'm smiling!"

"I don't think I'll be able to stop smiling for a while, either," Bishop Shepherd told them. "Isn't it great to know the Lord knows each of us, and our needs?" He didn't say so, but the thought flitted through his mind why the Lord would choose to heal some but not others. He thought of Rand Rivenbark and of other good people he knew who struggled with physical or mental problems. None of that diminished his joy for Alyssa and her parents, it was just a part of this mortal puzzle he hadn't yet been able to solve.

To her beaming parents, he said, "I'm thrilled for you. What a blessing!"

Joe said, "We can't explain it, but we've wondered if there isn't some reason why Alyssa has been healed. Maybe, as it says in the Bible, that the works of God might be made manifest in her."

Lori quickly added, "We've also thought that maybe her own mission in life might require her to have at least some ability to hear. But whatever the reason, we're just rejoicing over it—and we wanted you to know, too."

"I rejoice with you, and so will the whole ward," he assured them, and went to give them each a hug. "We are truly blessed."

CHAPTER TWENTY

"PRAISE GOD, FROM WHOM ALL BLESSINGS FLOW"

On Wednesday morning, since Jamie was out of school for the Thanksgiving holiday, the bishop took him along to Shepherd's Quality Food Mart, where together they packed a box of food—turkey, stuffing mix, cranberries, various fruits and vegetables and rolls, and drove to the Rexford home.

Tom Rexford answered the door, a quizzical frown on his face. "Hey, Bishop—what's goin' on? Y'all makin' deliveries these days, down at Shepherd's?"

"Sometimes we do just exactly that," the bishop agreed, with a smile. "Now, I know nobody ordered these things, but I figure they'll go to good use. I'd hate to have them lying around the store over Thanksgiving, going to waste. Are Lula and Thomas here?"

"Now, Bishop, we don't take charity, I thought I'd made that clear. Lula! Bishop's here. And get the boy."

"My word, Bishop, what's all this?" Lula asked, gazing at the box. "We don't need anything, honest!"

"I was coming over here anyway, to talk to Thomas and give him something, and I saw this fresh turkey, here—never been frozen—I've got several left that nobody's claimed, and I thought I'd just bring it along and see if you knew what to do with it. Reckon I ordered a few too many, this season. Other stuff is just to go with, you know. It's not much, really. I mostly came to give Thomas a little remembrance."

"Well, that's mighty nice of you. Tommy! Bishop's here, T-Rex!" called Lula, and eventually the young man emerged from his room, sleepy-eyed, pulling a sweatshirt on above pajama bottoms.

"Hey, Bishop! I was just takin' advantage of a day off from school to sleep in."

"Tiffani's doing the same thing," the bishop said. "Good chance for it. But Jamie and I are early birds, so we're up and about, bothering people."

"Sit down, ya'll," Lula instructed, doing so, herself. Her husband subsided into an easy chair, still frowning at the box of food in the center of the floor.

"Thomas, when I saw this, I just knew I had to give it to you, and your folks," the bishop said, extracting from the side of the box a wrapped rectangle and handing it to T-Rex. "At first, I was just going to make you a copy and keep the original, but I decided you deserved the original, so I made a copy for myself. It's by Buddy Osborne."

"Buddy?" T-Rex questioned, pulling the framed drawing from its wrapping. "Oh, my gosh! You tellin' me little ol' Buddy Osborne done this?" He gazed in awe at the charcoal sketch, which was even more impressive framed than it had been just torn from the sketch pad. "That is so dang cool! I cain't believe it."

His parents both went to peer over his shoulder.

"Oh, my land!" Lula exclaimed. "We're gonna have to hang that right in here, by your other pictures. This is that little Osborne boy in the ward, Bishop? Gerald Osborne's boy?"

"That's right. Buddy's real quiet and shy, so hardly anybody even knows he has this gift, but he's been going with Jamie and me to Thomas's home games, and he's loved it—I think he really looks up to Thomas. He gave it to me for taking him with us, but I knew Thomas would want to have it, too."

"I sure do! That little dude—I sure didn't know he could do this. Man! I gotta talk to him."

"He's real cool," Jamie offered. "He's good at video games, too."

"I hatn't seen Gerald Osborne in a coon's age," remarked Tom Rexford. "He used to come to church when he was a teenager, but I thought he'd fell off the face of the earth, or somethin'."

"No, he still lives here in town. He and Twyla divorced when Buddy was just little, and they share custody, so he goes back and forth between them."

"You remember Twyla Hotchkiss, don't you, Tom?" asked Lula. "Her and her mama joined the Church when Twyla was about fourteen, and then later they fell away, and her mama moved down to Birmingham. I don't know where Twyla is."

"She's living in a mobile home park just off Two-seventy-eight."

"She don't never come out anymore, does she?"

"Haven't seen her in church since I can remember," replied the bishop. "She and Gerald both allow Buddy to come, but I don't think they give him much encouragement."

"Well, he's sure a talented boy," said Lula, taking the

drawing of her son to admire it again. "Hope he'll keep workin' on it, and make something of himself."

"I hope so, too," agreed the bishop, although he privately thought that Buddy was already quite something. "Listen, folks, y'all have a nice Thanksgiving, all right? We'd better head, James."

T-Rex and Lula shook hands with both of them, which made Jamie grin in pleased embarrassment, and Tom followed them out onto the porch.

"Now, Bishop, I don't want to seem ungrateful, and I won't make you take the food back, since Lula and the boy've already seen it, but I still gotta say, I don't hold with takin' charity, and we're gettin' by okay. So no more, all right?"

Jamie ran out and hopped into the truck, but the bishop paused, one foot on a step, and looked up at Tom. "You know, Tom, I totally appreciate your independence and self-reliance, and I understand your feelings. But you and I both know that things have been pretty tough for your family, lately, and this is just a little personal gift from me to you, as a friend. This wasn't bought with Church funds. But even if it had been, would that be so bad? I know that the Lord inspired the welfare program that we have in the Church, and it's a program of helping each other in times of need. There are times when we help others, and times when we accept help. If nobody accepted, how could anybody give?"

Tom looked down. "I know. Reckon I'm just too proud. Don't mean to be, but that's how I was brought up—you don't be beholden to nobody. Even if you starve, you do it with pride."

The bishop smiled. "Yep, I'm familiar with that attitude. But you might want to look up what the Lord had to say about pride," he suggested softly. "It's not always a good thing. Sometimes it means something other than dignity. Sometimes being proud's the opposite of being humble, and the Lord wants us to learn to be humble. Check it out, Tom. We'll talk about it again, sometime. In the meantime, now, don't choke on that turkey—enjoy it!"

Tom grinned reluctantly. "Don't reckon I'll choke. Thanks, Bishop. And for the pitcher, too."

The bishop called Buddy Osborne, and found him at his father's house. He invited both of them over for Thanksgiving dinner the next day.

"Thanksgiving dinner? I dunno. Let me ask Deddy."

He could hear bits of the conversation going on in the background, including Buddy's voice saying, "She's a real good cook. Better'n any ol' cafe!"

Buddy came back on the line. "Deddy says we've got plans for dinner, but thanks anyway," he reported. "It's real nice of y'all to ask."

"Well, if you guys change your minds, dinner's at two," he replied. "Jamie'll be disappointed if you don't come. He and I were hoping to get some more guys on board. It's another of those times when the girls are outnumbering us. Oh, say, Buddy—I made a copy of your drawing of T-Rex for myself, and gave him the original. You should have seen how tickled he was! You'll be hearing from him, I'm sure. He and his folks were all amazed at how good it was."

"You—did? They were?"

"No kidding, they were delighted. His mom said she's going

to hang it in their living room. I put it in a frame, and it looks great."

"Wow. I hatn't never seen any of my stuff in a frame. That's cool. Thanks, Bishop."

"Mine's framed, too, and I've got it on top of my desk at home, where I can see it while I work on church stuff. Thanks again, Buddy. That was a great gift."

He had no sooner put the receiver down than the phone rang.

"Bishop Shepherd?" came a woman's voice. "This is Candace Kingsley, with LDS Family Services."

The bishop thought rapidly. Kingsley, Kingsley. Not Hallmark, who was Melody's therapist. The lady from Atlanta. "Oh, yes, Sister Kingsley. What can I do for you?"

"Well, I have good news for you, if you have the same for me! The baby boy chosen for Don and Connie Wheeler has been born, and everything seems fine with him. I'm just calling to check one last time about the worthiness of the Wheelers, before I let them know."

"Ah." He smiled. "I'm happy to report that the Wheelers are still one of the finest young couples I know, and I can't think of a better way for them to spend Thanksgiving than by becoming parents!"

"They're still worthy temple recommend holders, active and faithful in the Church?"

"That they are, with absolutely no reservations."

"Thank you, Bishop. I expect you'll be hearing from them, before long."

"Thank you. And let me just say, this makes my day, as well!"

"And mine," she agreed, a smile in her voice.

He bowed his head for a moment's prayer of fervent thanks, and went to find Trish, wondering how he was going to keep from bursting with this good news.

She looked at him, and a smile spread over her flushed face as she took a pie from the oven. "Jim, I overheard your part of that last conversation, when I was coming into the dining room. I backed out, but I couldn't help it. That is so exciting!"

He hugged her exuberantly. "Isn't it? I sure have learned to appreciate good news in the last few months, and this is the best kind! Hey, lady—what kind of pie are you making?"

She looked at him strangely. "Pumpkin, of course. And Dutch apple. What I always make for Thanksgiving."

"Well, you're going to make a sweet potato one, aren't you? With lots of nutmeg?"

She grabbed a dish towel from the handle of the oven and flicked it in his direction.

"Git!" she ordered, and laughing, he "got."

He went back to the store for the afternoon, helping out with the checking and stocking as needed for the last-minute Thanksgiving shoppers. After several hours, he took a short break, sprawling wearily in his father's old chair in the office.

"Hey, Jim," Mary Lynn said, "that was him the other day, wadn' it?"

"Him?" he asked, trying to follow.

"The wife-beater. That guy who came to take you to lunch."

"Oh. Well—I shouldn't say so, I reckon, but you're pretty perceptive. It was."

"Thought so. How're they all doin'?"

He nodded. "Not bad. Little girl's back with her mother, the dad has to stay away for the foreseeable future. They're all in therapy."

"Does it help, you reckon? All that therapy stuff?"

"I think it can. Especially if it's done by somebody with a faith-based take on things, and sound understanding of people."

"Huh. Hope so."

"Hey, Mary Lynn, what are you doing for Thanksgiving?"

"Me? I'm goin' up to Mama's. All of us that can, will be there."

"Good, good."

"Y'all havin' a tableful?"

He nodded. "Looks like it, all right." He added them up on his fingers—five in his own family, Hestelle Pierce from next door, Muzzie and her two girls, Melody and Andrea Padgett—eleven. And if Gerald and Buddy Osborne should change their minds, there would be thirteen. It was a goodly company, if a bit overbalanced on the female side.

"So, Jim?" Mary Lynn was twisting her long hair, frowning at him speculatively.

"Yes, ma'am?"

"Have you give that man one of them blessings you was tellin' me about?"

He sat up straight. "No," he said slowly. "I haven't."

"Well—has anybody?"

"Not that I know of—and I think I'd probably know." He gazed beyond Mary Lynn at the bulletin board with its copies of ads and notices, not seeing them, but examining instead his relationship with Jack Padgett. Jack, he felt sure, would never ask for a blessing. Were they to a comfortable enough point in their relationship that he, as Jack's bishop, could bring himself to offer? Certainly, Jack needed all the aid and comfort he could get, and he was making an effort to keep in touch, and to coop-erate with the Social Services therapist assigned to him. His records were still in the Fairhaven Ward, so Jack was still offi-cially under the bishop's jurisdiction. Melody had been the recipient of two blessings during this painful time, but he hadn't thought of offering a blessing to Jack—probably, he thought, due to the man's attitude of defiant belligerence. But lately, as he had told his counselors, there had been signs of softening. Maybe . . .

"Uh, Jim?"

"M-hmm?"

"You did say them blessin's was for more than just bein' sick physically, didn't you?"

He nodded.

"So that's why I figgered maybe it'd help him. But you'd know best about that."

"Mary Lynn, you're an amazing woman. I'm ashamed to admit I hadn't even thought of giving Jack a blessing. Now, thanks to you, I am thinking about it."

Mary Lynn ducked her head in pleased embarrassment. "Well, you know. Whatever."

The house was redolent of wonderful smells—roasted turkey, onion and sage, hot rolls—and the tables were set. Had been, in fact, since the previous afternoon. Muzzie and Melody were in the kitchen with Trish, one stirring gravy, one whipping potatoes, and the other filling pitchers with ice and water as the bishop picked his way through from the family room to answer the doorbell.

"Welcome, Miz Hestelle, and a happy Thanksgiving to you," he greeted, as their neighbor stepped inside, carrying a large jelled salad.

"And the same to you, Mr. Shepherd," she replied. "Y'all are so nice to ask me over! I'd thought I was goin' to my sister's in Tennessee, you know, but then she broke her hip, and she'll have to be in rehab for several weeks. I tell you the truth, my own hip's been achin' ever since I heard about hers! What do you make of that?"

"You must have a sympathetic connection with your sister, Miz Hestelle, is all I can figure," he told her kindly. "May I take that salad for you? Come on into the kitchen—that's where the ladies are hanging out—just lazing around, you know, with nothing to do."

She laughed merrily. "My nose is a-tellin' me just how lazy they've been, indeed. Oh, land—ever'thin's so festive and pretty!"

"Well, Trish says Thanksgiving's about her favorite holiday, 'cause there's no candy attached to it, and no gifts to buy."

"That's true. Most ever' holiday means cookin' for the womenfolk, though, isn't that right, Miz Shepherd?" she added as she saw Trish.

"Hey there, Miz Hestelle, it's so good to have you! Thanks so much for that yummy-looking salad. Let me take that, Jim. I'll put it in the fridge till we're ready to serve, which should be in about five minutes. Oh, there goes the phone. Jim, honey, would you get that? It's probably for you, anyway."

Jim-honey went to the phone on his desk in the corner of the dining room. He answered, and a boy's timid voice said, "Mr. Shepherd?"

"Yes?"

"Um—this is Brad Winston. I was wondering if maybe your wife might know where my mom is?"

"Bradley!" he almost shouted. "*I* know where your mom is! She's right here. Hang on!"

He ran for the kitchen. "Muzzie! Come quick, Brad's on the phone!"

Muzzie almost dropped a bowl of potatoes. Trish saved them, and Muzzie made a beeline for the phone on the kitchen wall. The talk in the kitchen fell silent, as all watched Muzzie's reaction. Hestelle, of course, knew nothing of the import, nor did Melody, but both sensed the drama of the moment, and were still.

"Brad! Is that really you? Where are you? Where's your dad? Really?" Her voice squealed, and she turned to nod a tearful smile in Trish's direction. "Honey, leave right now. You remember where Shepherds live? Good. Don't worry about your clothes or anything. We'll get them, later. Just leave, and ride over here. But come down Hickory Street, not Main, in case he wakes up and goes looking for you. And listen, Brad—I'm coming to meet you, in the—uh—?" She sent an imploring look toward the bishop.

"In the Shepherds' white truck," he supplied. "I'll drive you."

Muzzie repeated that to her son, then hung up and looked around her, as if dazed. "He's at home—he's safe! He says Dugie's asleep, snoring and drunk. Gotta go—tell you later," she finished excitedly, and ran for the truck. The bishop, fishing in his pocket for his keys, was right behind her.

"Oh, Jim—what if Dugie wakes up and follows him! Hurry, Bradley, hurry—and be quiet. Oh, I hope he's all right. Where have they been, all this time?"

The bishop smiled at her. "You're about to find out," he told her. He steered the truck down the nearly deserted Hickory Street, driving as fast as he dared, keeping his eyes open for a boy on a bicycle. Finally they spotted him, pedaling furiously, glancing behind him as if being chased by the devil. The bishop slowed and made a U-turn, stopping at the side of the street. Muzzie was out of the truck before it stopped rolling, waving her arm, tears flowing as she rushed to hug her boy. The bishop grabbed the bike and lifted it into the bed of the pickup, and held the door open for mother and son. They scrambled in, and he made even better time getting back to the house, where he stashed the bike safely in a backyard shed. He didn't hear much of their whispered, tearful conversation except Brad's pained comment that "Dad's different than he used to be—I hate the way he is, now."

In the house, Chloe and Marie had joined the celebration, hugging their brother and jumping up and down at the same time while Muzzie laughed and cried.

"Oh, you guys!" she exclaimed, reaching out to squeeze Trish's hand. "Prayer really does work! I've been praying as hard as I could that Brad could somehow get away from his dad, and here he is!" She hugged her son's blond head to her, kissing the top of it, until Bradley finally objected.

"Hey, I'm getting pulled apart," he said, laughing too, and squirming away from his adoring sisters. "It's okay, though. I've kinda missed being mauled."

Dinner was put on hold for a few minutes, to give the Winston family time to reunite and settle down a bit, and for Muzzie to have her most urgent questions answered. Trish explained to Hestelle and Melody the basic facts of the situation behind the reunion, and Melody's eyes filled with sympathetic tears.

"I'm so happy for her," she said softly. "I know just how she feels." She glanced at her little Andrea, playing dolls with Mallory in a corner of the family room, both so absorbed they were unaware of the excitement in the next room.

"Set another place at the children's table," Trish instructed Tiffani, smiling. "I think we'll let you and Muzzie preside there, because it doesn't look like she's going to let Brad get beyond arm's reach for days—and I don't blame her."

"Cool," Jamie remarked. "Finally we got another guy!"

A sentiment from the Bible sprang into the bishop's mind: "This my son was lost, and is found." He retreated into the living room for a minute's private meditation. It was their family's custom, during the Thanksgiving meal, to go around the table, with each diner identifying something for which he was most grateful. What, this year, could he possibly single out? His personal world had expanded to many times its original size since last Thanksgiving. Now he held dear to his heart people who, this time last year, had been casual friends, mere acquaintances, or even strangers. Now he rejoiced over a baby born to be adopted and another baby miraculously receiving a gift of partial hearing. Now his heart yearned over two fine young missionaries who were determined to serve the Lord at all costs. Now he worried over a shy, sad boy whose antagonistic parents didn't realize the treasure they shared. Two women, his wife's sister and friend, who once had intimidated him, now had turned to him for counsel and had become his friends.

Since last year, his country had been attacked, and his freedoms, having been jeopardized, were sweeter than he had ever supposed them to be. Now his prayers were deeper and more meaningful than they had ever before been—and the answers more readily recognizable. His wife and children now seemed even more precious, since he had witnessed firsthand the sorrows and divisions that existed among some families. There were many things to rejoice over—one of them having just taken place before his eyes—but also many problems yet unsolved, many sorrows not yet assuaged. Maybe—just maybe—the thing for which he felt the most gratitude this year was the simple fact that he was involved, that he had the opportunity to try to help.

"I thank Thee, Father," he whispered, "for all thy tender mercies and miracles to thy children in the Fairhaven Ward. Bless us all, this day, with gratitude and joy and peace."